Praise for
THE MONKEY'S RAINCOAT

"With his first novel, Robert Crais places himself among the best writers in the field. His plot is tight and believable, the dialogue crisp and trenchant, the characters fresh and memorable. . . . The overriding sense of empathy and understanding makes the book much more than the usual exercise in style and grit. For my money, Elvis Cole and Pike are already the best partnership in detective fiction. I hope they're back for more, and soon."

—Stephen Greenleaf

"When I put *The Monkey's Raincoat* down, I believed in Elvis Cole, a tough and sentimental pro. Along the way, I laughed at Elvis' reports on L.A.'s own particular lunacy and felt the danger of his quest. Best of all, Crais creates characters you care about. Come back, Elvis Cole!"

—Ben Schutz

The Monkey's Raincoat is terrific! Not only is it a dynamite plot with more twists and turns than a corkscrew, but the characters are absolutely sensational. I read every page with a smile on my face. Never was I more sorry to see a story end. *The Monkey's Raincoat* is a sheer delight from beginning to end."

—Stan Lee, Marvel Productions

The Monkey's Raincoat is a witty, fast-paced entertainment. Robert Crais is a welcome addition to the mystery fold.

—Roger L. Simon

Bantam Books offers the finest in classic and modern American murder mysteries. Ask your bookseller for the books you have missed.

Stuart Palmer

The Penguin Pool Murder
The Puzzle of the Happy Hooligan
The Puzzle of the Red Stallion
The Puzzle of the Silver Persian

Craig Rice

Having Wonderful Crime
My Kingdom for a Hearse
The Lucky Stiff

Rex Stout

And Four to Go
Bad for Business
Death of a Dude
Death Times Three
Double for Death
Fer-de-Lance
The Final Deduction
Gambit
The League of Frightened Men
Not Quite Dead Enough
Plot It Yourself
The Rubber Band
Some Buried Caesar
The Sound of Murder
Too Many Clients

Victoria Silver

Death of a Harvard Freshman
Death of a Radcliffe Roommate

William Kienzle

The Rosary Murders

Joseph Louis

Madelaine

M.J. Adamson

Not Till a Hot January
A February Face

Richard Fliegel

The Next to Die

Max Allan Collins

The Dark City

James Dana Haynes

Bishop's Gambit, Declined

Barbara Paul

The Fourth Wall
Kill Fee
The Renewable Virgin

Benjamin Schutz

All the Old Bargains
Embrace the Wolf

S.F.X. Dean

Death and the Mad Heroine

Ross MacDonald

Blue City
The Blue Hammer

Robert Goldsborough

Murder in E Minor
Death on Deadline

Sue Grafton

"A" Is for Alibi
"B" Is for Burglar
"C" Is for Corpse

Max Byrd

California Thriller
Finders Weepers
Fly Away, Jill

R.D. Brown

Hazzard

A.E. Maxwell

Just Another Day in Paradise

Robert Crais

The Monkey's Raincoat

Rob Kantner

The Back-Door Man
The Harder They Hit

Joseph Telushkin

The Unorthodox Murder of Rabbi Wahl

Richard Hilary

Snake in the Grasses

Walter Dillon

Deadly Intrusion

The Monkey's Raincoat

*

Robert Crais

BANTAM BOOKS
TORONTO · NEW YORK · LONDON · SYDNEY · AUCKLAND

THE MONKEY'S RAINCOAT
A Bantam Book / August 1987

Grateful acknowledgment is made for permission to reprint the
excerpt from *On Love and Barley: Haiku of Basho*, translated by
Lucien Stryk, Viking Penguin Inc., 1985.

ISBN 0-553-26336-6

Published simultaneously in the United States and Canada

PRINTED IN THE UNITED STATES OF AMERICA

O   9 8 7 6 5 4 3 2 1

*For Pat, who met Joe Fike and
decided to hang around.*

That ain't tactics, baby. That's
just the beast in me.
> —Elvis Presley,
> *Jailhouse Rock*
> (the movie)

Winter downpour—
even the monkey
needs a raincoat.
> —Basho

1

"I'm sorry, Mr. Cole, this has nothing to do with you. Please excuse me." Ellen Lang stood up out of the director's chair across from my desk. I'd had it and its mate fitted in a nice pastel burgundy a year ago. The leather was broken in and soft and did not crack when she stood. "We shouldn't have come here, Janet," she said. "I feel awkward."

Janet Simon said, "For Christ's sake, Ellen, sit down."

Ellen sat.

Janet Simon said, "Talk to him, Ellen. Eric says he's very good at this sort of thing. He can help."

Speak, Ellen. And I rearranged two of the Jiminy Cricket figurines on my desk and wondered who the hell Eric was.

Ellen Lang adjusted her glasses, clutched her hands, and faded back into the director's chair. She looked small, even though she wasn't. Some people are like that. Janet Simon looked like a dancer who'd spent a lot of time at it. Lean and strong. Good bones. She wore tight beige cotton pants and a loose cotton shirt striped with shades of blue and pink and red. No panty line. I hoped she didn't think I was *déclassé* in my white Levi's and Hawaiian shirt. Maybe the shoulder holster made up for it.

Ellen Lang smiled at me, trying to feign comfort in an uncomfortable situation. She said, "Well, perhaps if you told me about yourself."

Janet Simon sighed, giving it the weight of the world. "Mr. Cole is a private detective. He detects for money. You give him some money and he'll find Mort. Then you can get Perry back and kiss off Mort and get your life together." She said it like she was talking to someone with brain damage. Great legs, though.

"Thanks, Mom," I said.

Janet Simon gave me a look, then turned away and stared at the Pinocchio clock. It's on the wall beside the door that leads to my partner's office, just above the little sign that says *The*

1

Elvis Cole Detective Agency. As the second hand sweeps around, Pinocchio's eyes move from side to side. Janet Simon had been glancing at it since they walked in. Probably thought it was peculiar.

Ellen fidgeted. "I was just curious, that's all. I'm sorry."

"You don't have to be sorry, Mrs. Lang," I said. "I'm thirty-five years old and I've been licensed as a private investigator for seven years. The state of California requires three thousand hours of experience before they'll give you the license. I spent that time with a man named George Feider. Mr. Feider was an investigator here in Los Angeles for almost forty years. Before that I was a security guard, and before that I spent some time in the Army. I'm five feet eleven and one-half inches tall, I weigh one hundred seventy-six pounds, and I'm licensed to carry a firearm. How's that?"

She blinked.

"Yeah, it impresses me, too," I said. "I don't take custody work. I might find your husband and your son but after that it's up to you. I don't steal children unless there's reason to believe the child is in danger."

Ellen Lang looked as if I'd kicked her. "Oh, no. No, no. Mort's a good man, Mr. Cole, please don't think he isn't." Janet Simon said something like *shumphf.* "You have to understand. He's been under enormous strain. He left ICM last year to start his own talent agency and things just haven't gone the way they should. He's had to worry about the house payments and the cars and schools. It's been terrible for him."

Janet Simon said, "Mort's an asshole." She was standing by the sliding glass doors that lead out to the little balcony. On a clear day I could go out there and see all the way down Santa Monica Boulevard to the water. The view had been the selling point. Janet Simon fit nicely with the view.

"I just want Perry home, that's all." Ellen Lang's eyes went from Janet Simon to me, sort of like the Pinocchio clock. "Mort will settle for McDonald's. He'll let Perry stay up all hours—"

I cleared my throat. "Mrs. Lang, I don't bill by the day. I charge a flat fee exclusive of expenses and I get it in advance. You're looking at about two grand here. Why don't you wait? Mort might call." McDonald's. Christ.

"Yes," Ellen Lang said. She looked relieved. "I'm sure you're right."

"Bullshit," Janet Simon said. She turned away from the balcony to sit in the other director's chair. "That's not right and she knows it. Mort's been threatening to leave for almost a year. Mort treats her like a sop. He runs around." Ellen Lang made a little gurgling noise. "He's even hit her twice that I know of. Now he's taken their son and disappeared. She wants her son back. That's all she wants. It's very important to her."

Ellen Lang's eyes widened but didn't seem to be looking at anything. "Ms. Simon," I said evenly, "as much as I'd like to lick chocolate syrup off your body, I want you to shut up."

Ellen Lang said, "Oh, my." Janet Simon stood up and then Ellen Lang stood up. Janet Simon put a hand on Ellen Lang's shoulder and shoved her back down. "Who do you think you're talking to?" she said.

"A woman who's very concerned with her friend's problem. But a woman who, right now, is acting like a royal pain in the ass. If the sexual nature of my comment surprised you it's only because I needed to be shocking to get your attention."

She chewed at the inside of her cheek, trying to decide about me, then nodded and took her seat.

"Also," I said, "I find you devastatingly attractive and it's been on my mind."

She leaned forward and said, "Eric told us you had a partner. Maybe we should speak with him."

Eric again. The Mystery Man. "Fine by me."

Janet Simon looked at the door beneath the Pinocchio clock. If she looked close enough she'd see the little ridge in the jamb from the time someone had forced the lock. Three coats of paint, and you could still see the crack. She didn't notice. "Is that his office?" she said.

"Unh-hunh."

"Well?"

"Well, what?"

"Aren't you going to introduce us?"

"Nope."

Janet Simon stood up, steamed over to the door, and went through. I smiled at Ellen Lang. Ellen Lang looked nervous but smiled back. After a while Janet Simon rejoined us.

"That's no office," she said. "There's no desk, no furniture, nothing. What kind of office is that?"

"Italian moderne?"

She cocked her head a little to the side. "Eric said you'd be like this."

Eric. "How do you know Eric?" I smiled. Mr. Sly. I have

quite a charming smile. Like Peter Pan. Innocent, but with a touch of the rake.

"We worked together when I was in the legal department at Universal."

That brought it back. Eric Filer. Three years ago.

"He said you found some film negatives for him. He said it wasn't easy. He recommends you highly."

"M'man Eric."

"He also said you were like this."

"Were you ever a dancer?" I said.

If she wanted to smile, she fought it. She took out a pack of Salem Lights, lit up in the office but stood in the balcony door, blowing smoke out over West Hollywood. I liked the way her neck looked when she lifted her chin to send out a plume of smoke. Some woman. I bet her mouth tasted like an ashtray.

"Listen, Mrs. Lang," I said, turning back to Ellen, "I don't know if Mort is going to call or not, or what you want, or what Mort wants. A couple hundred women have sat where you're sitting, and usually their husbands call. But not always. You're going to have to decide which way you want to jump."

Ellen Lang nodded. Pinocchio's eyes shifted back and forth a few times. Janet Simon smoked. After a while Ellen Lang took two photographs out of her purse and put them carefully on the desk. "On Friday Mort always picks up Perry from school. Perry goes to Oakhurst and the girls go to Westridge. That's Cindy and Carrie. Fridays, Perry gets out two hours earlier. Only this past Friday they never came home. I tried all weekend to find Mort. I phoned Oakhurst Monday but Perry wasn't there, and I phoned again this morning and he still wasn't there. They've been gone for four days."

I looked at the pictures. Mort was four or five years older than me, balding on top with a round face, thin lifeless hair, and skinny arms. He was wearing a tee shirt that said *U.S.S. Bluegill, Maui, Hawaii.* He had the sort of eyes that had just been looking somewhere else. On the back of the picture someone had written *Morton Lang, age 39, 5' 10", 145 lbs, brown hair and brown eyes, no visible scars or tattoos, mole on right forearm.* The writing was even and firm, all of the letters identical in size.

"I wrote that," Ellen said. God bless television.

The other picture was a wallet-size school photo of a little boy who looked like a smaller, less-worn version of Mort.

Perry Lang, age 9, 4' 8", 64 pounds, brown hair and brown eyes, no visible scars or tattoos or moles.

I put the pictures on the desk, then opened my right top desk drawer and took out a Bic pen and a blank yellow legal pad. I had to move my gun to get the pad. The gun was a Dan Wesson .38 Special with the 4-inch barrel, a gift from George Feider the day I got my license. It was a good gun. I closed the drawer, put the pad beside the pictures and the Bic on the pad.

"Okay," I said. "Did Mort leave a note?"

"No."

"Why would Mort take your son but not your two girls?"

"I don't know."

"Was Perry Mort's favorite?"

"That would be Carrie, our youngest daughter. I asked her if Mort said anything about this to her, thinking he might have, but she said no."

I nodded and wrote *Carrie* on the pad.

"Your husband make any large withdrawals recently?"

Ellen Lang said, "I'm not very good with figures. Mort handles all our business affairs." She said it apologetically.

"How about work? Someone there who might know what was on your husband's mind?"

Ellen Lang looked at the floor. "Well, he's not part of an office anymore, like I said. He worked out of the house, and he didn't really talk . . ." She trailed off and turned red, her lips a tight purple knot.

I tapped the Bic against the pad, which wasn't exactly brimming with information.

I looked at Janet Simon. She had a tight, sexy grin on her face. Or maybe it was a sneer. "I wouldn't think of interfering," she said.

"Maybe if I said please."

Janet Simon took a final pull on her cigarette, tossed it out over the railing, and came back inside. "Tell him about the girlfriend, Ellen."

Ellen Lang's voice was so soft I could barely hear her. "He has a girlfriend. She lives at the Piedmont Arms off Barrington in Brentwood."

"Her name is Kimberly Marsh," Janet Simon said. "She's one of his clients. 412 Gorham, just above San Vicente. Apartment 4, on the ground, in the back. An actress." She took two rolodex cards from her purse and flipped them down on the desk next to the photographs. The top one had **KIMBERLY MARSH** typed on it along with the address and a phone number.

"We followed him." Ellen Lang said it the way you say something that embarrasses you.

I looked at Janet Simon. "And I'll bet you drove."

She looked back. "And I got out of the car and I checked the apartment number and I matched it to a name on the mailbox." Some woman, all right.

"Okay," I said. "What about friends?"

Neither of us bothered to look at Ellen Lang. "Mort was trying to get a film project off the ground with a producer named Garrett Rice. That's his name and number on the second card. It was one of those deals where you do a lot of talking about firming up Redford with a commitment from Coppola so you can get the money from Arab investors. That kind of thing. They call it 'blue-sky.'"

I nodded. "How come you know more about her life than she does?"

Ellen Lang leaned forward out of the director's chair. It was the first time she'd shown any animation since they'd walked into my office twenty minutes ago. "Garrett is an old friend. We used to play bridge with Garrett and his wife Lila until they were divorced, oh, I guess it was five years ago. We used to play every week for almost a year. Mort was so happy to be back in contact with him. Garrett was Mort's best friend. I guess that's why he told me."

Janet Simon sighed the way you sigh when you've been holding your breath at a horror movie, and said, "Mort didn't believe in sharing his life. At least, not with his wife."

"Well, that was his way," Ellen Lang said. Her eyes were still wide. "Mort would just die if he knew about this, Mr. Cole. That's why I wouldn't go to the police, even though Janet said that's what I should do. I couldn't get my own husband in trouble with the police. He'd never forgive me. You can see that, can't you?"

Maybe it was my expression. Ellen Lang's face got dark, her chin trembled, and she said, "What's wrong with a woman caring how her husband feels?" I got the feeling she'd been saying it a lot lately.

"You'll take the job?" Janet Simon said.

"There's the matter of the fee."

Ellen looked away from me again. "I'm afraid I forgot my checkbook."

Janet said, "She's not used to this. Mort always paid for everything, so she didn't think to bring it."

I tapped the Bic against the pad.

"You can understand that, can't you?" Janet said.

I stood up. "Yep, I can understand that. Why don't I come by your house this afternoon, Mrs. Lang? You can give me the check and we can go through your husband's things."

"Why do you have to do that?"

"Clues, Mrs. Lang."

Janet Simon said, "You look like John Cassavetes twenty years ago."

"Who do I look like now?"

Janet Simon smiled grimly and stood up. Ellen Lang stood up, too, and this time Janet Simon didn't push her back down. They left.

I wrote *old friends* on the pad, drew a box around it, then tore off the sheet and threw it away.

Some notes.

2

I went out on the balcony and watched the street. After a few minutes they pulled out from beneath the building in a sky-blue Mustang convertible. Janet Simon was driving. It was the GT handling package. Great maneuverability. Tight in the curves. Without sacrificing a smooth ride.

I went back into my office, called the deli on the ground floor to order a pastrami on rye with Chinese hot mustard, and then I called Joe Pike.

A man's voice said, "Gun shop."

"Give me Joe."

The phone got put down on something hard. There were noises and words I couldn't understand, and then the phone got picked up again. "Pike."

"We just had another complaint about your office. Woman goes in there, comes out, says what kind of office is that, empty, no phone, no desk? What could I tell her?"

"Tell her she likes the office so much she can live there."

"It's a good thing we don't depend on you to sweet-talk the customers."

"I don't do this for the customers." Pike's voice was flat. No smile. No humor. Normal, for Pike.

"That's why I like to call," I said. "Always the pleasant word. Always the cheery hello."

Nothing came back over the line. After a while I said, "We added a new client today. Thought you'd like to know."

"Any heat?" Pike's only interest.

"We got through the interview with a minimum of gun-shots."

"You need me, you know where to find me."

He hung up. I shook my head. Some partner.

An entire afternoon ahead of me and nary a thing to do except drive out to Ellen Lang's and dig through six or seven months of phone bills, bank statements, and credit card receipts. Yuck. I decided to go see Kimberly Marsh. The Other Woman.

I slipped the Dan Wesson into my holster, put on the white cotton jacket, and picked up the sandwich on my way to the parking garage. I ate in the car driving up Fairfax, turning left at Sunset toward Brentwood. I've got a Jamaica-yellow 1966 Corvette convertible. It would have been easier to take Santa Monica, but with the top down Sunset was a nicer drive.

It was shaping up as another brutal Los Angeles winter, low seventies, scattered clouds, clearing. The sky was that deep blue we get just before or just after a rain. The white stucco houses along the ridges were sharp and brilliant in the sun. I passed the coed-specked running paths of UCLA, then wound my way past a house that may have been the one William Holden used to slip the repossessors in *Sunset Boulevard*. Old Spanish. Same cornices and pilasters. The ghosts of old Hollywood haunting the eaves. I've wondered about that house since I discovered it, just two days after I mustered out of the Army in 1972. I've wondered, but I've never wanted to know for sure. After the Army, magic was in short supply and when you found some, you held on tight. It wouldn't be the same if I knew the house belonged to some guy who made his millions inventing Fruit Loops.

A half mile past the San Diego Freeway I turned left on Barrington and dropped south toward San Vicente, then hung another left on Gorham. The Piedmont Arms is on the south side of the street in a stretch of apartment houses and condominiums. I drove past, turned around at a cross street, and parked. It looked like a nice place to live. An older woman with wispy white hair eased a Hughes Market cart off a curb and across a street. She smiled at a man and a woman in their twenties, the man with his shirt off, the woman in an airy Navajo top. L.A. winter. They smiled back. Two women in jogging suits were walking back toward Barrington, probably off to lunch at one of the little nouveaux restaurants on San Vicente. Hot duck salad with raspberry sauce. A sturdily built Chicano woman with a purse the size of a mobile home waited at a bus stop, squinting into the sun. Somewhere a screw gun started up, then cut short. There were gulls and a scent of the sea. Nice. Four cars in front of me, north side of the street, two guys sat in a dark blue '69 Nova with a bad rust spot on the left rear fender. Chicanos. The driver tried to scowl like

Charles Bronson as I cruised past. Maybe they were from the government.

The Piedmont is a clean, two-story, U-shaped stucco building with a garden entry at the front braced by stairs that go up to the second floor. Around each stair is a stand of bamboo and a couple of banana trees for that always-popular rain forest look. There are two rows of brass-burnished mailboxes in front of the bamboo, with a big open bin beneath them for magazines and packages and Pygmies with blowguns. Kimberly Marsh's drop was the fourth from the left on the top row. I could see eight or nine envelopes through the slot. In the bin there were three catalogs and a couple of those giveaway flyers that everyone gets. Lot of mail. Maybe four days' worth.

I walked through the little courtyard past some more banana trees. Apartment 4 was all the way back on the left. That Janet. I knocked, but there was no answer. I walked back up to apartment 1, where a little sign on the door said MANAGER. A fat man built like a pear came around the mailboxes, started up the stairs, and saw me. Jo-Jo isn't here," he said. "He's got the aerobics class on Tuesday."

"Jo-Jo the manager?"

He nodded. "He'll be back around five or six. But I can tell you, there aren't any vacancies."

"Maybe I could pitch a tent."

He thought about that. "Oh, that was a joke."

"You know Kimberly Marsh?" I said. "In number four."

He said, "Number four," and thought about it. "That the pretty blonde girl?"

"Yes."

He shrugged. "You see her around, that's all. I said hi once and she said hi back, that's all."

I took out the photograph of Mort. "You see this guy around with her?"

He squinted at me. "Mr. Suspicious I don't know who you are," he said.

"Johnny Staccato, Confidential Investigations."

He nodded and stared at the picture and rubbed his arm. "Well, I dunno," he said. "Gee." Gee.

I thanked him and walked around until I heard a door upstairs open and close. Then I walked back to number 4. I knocked again in case she had been in the shower, then took out two little tools I keep in my wallet and popped Kimberly Marsh's deadbolt lock. "Ms. Marsh?" Maybe she was taking a nap. Maybe she just hadn't wanted to answer the door. Maybe she was waiting behind it with an ice pick she had dipped in rat poison.

No answer.

I pushed open the door and went in.

There was a davenport against one wall with a wicker and glass coffee table in front of it and a matching Morris chair at the far end. From the doorway, I could see across the living room to the dining area and the kitchen. To the left was a short hall. Above the couch was a slickly framed poster of James Dean walking in the rain. He looked lonely.

A dozen brown daisies sat in a glass bowl on the coffee table. Propped against the bowl was a little lavender card. *For the girl who gives me life, all my love, Mort.* Papery petals had rained around the card.

On the end table there was a Panasonic phone-answering machine. I passed it, walked back to the kitchen, then glanced down the little hall to the bedroom before I went into the bath. No bodies. No messages scrawled in blood. No stopped-up toilet with red-tinted water. There were two towels on the bathroom floor as if someone had stepped out of the shower, toweled off, then dropped the towels. They were dry, at least two days old. There was a little chrome toothbrush holder with the stains those things get when you park a toothbrush in them, only there was no toothbrush. The medicine cabinet held all the stuff medicine cabinets hold, though maybe there were a couple of spaces where things had been but now weren't. I went back out into the living room and checked the message machine. The message counter said zero—no messages. I played it back anyway. The counter was right.

I went into the bedroom. The bed was made and neat. There was a little desk in the corner beneath the window, cluttered and messy with old copies of the *L.A. Times*, *Vogue*, I. Magnin shopping bags, and other junk. Halfway down a stack of trade papers and *Casting Calls* I found the kind of 8x10 black-and-white stills actors bring to readings. Most were head shots of a pretty blonde with clean healthy features. At the bottom of the 8x10 it said *Kimberly Marsh* in an elegant flowing script. On the back was stapled a Xeroxed copy of her acting credits, her training, and her physical description. She was 5′ 6″, 120 pounds, had honey hair and green eyes. She was 26 years old and wore a size 8. She could play tennis, enjoyed water sports, could ski, and ride both Western and English.

Her credits as an actress didn't amount to much. Mostly regional theater from Arizona. She claimed to have studied with Nina Foch. Farther down the stack I found some full body shots, one with Kimberly in a fur bikini doing her best to look like a Pictish warrior. She looked pretty good in that fur bikini. I thought of Ellen Lang invisible in my director's chair. Sit, Ellen. Speak. I put one of the head shots in my pocket.

I finished with the desk and moved to the closet. There were twelve shoe boxes stacked against the wall. I found a snapshot of a sleeping dog in one of them. There was a large empty space about the size of a suitcase on the right side of the closet shelf. Maybe Morton Lang had called and said, *I've finally had my fill of this invisible sexless drudge I'm married to so how's about you and me and Perry hit the beach in Hawaii?* And maybe Kimberly Marsh had said, *You bet, but I havta get back for this role I got on "One Life to Live,"* so she'd pulled down the suitcase and packed her toothbrush and enough clothes for a week and they had split. Sounded good to me. Ellen Lang wouldn't like it, but there you are.

I shut the closet and went through the dresser, starting with the top drawer and working down. In the third drawer from the top I found a small wooden box containing a plastic bag of marijuana, three joints, two well-used pipes, a small bong, a broken mirror, four empty glass vials, and a short candle. Well, well, well. There was a 9 × 12 envelope under the stash box, folded in half and held tight by a rubber band. There was a pack of photographs in it. The first picture featured a nude Kimberly seated on her davenport, stark white triangles offsetting a rich tan. Not all of the shots were raw. A couple showed her posing on the back of a Triumph motorcycle, a couple more had her at the beach with a big, well-muscled, sandy-haired kid who had probably played end for the University of Mars. Near the bottom of the pack I found Morton Lang. He was naked on the bed, grinning, propped up on one elbow. A well-tanned female leg reached in from the bottom of the picture to play toesies with his privates. Mort. You jerk. I tore the picture of Morton in two and put it in my pocket. I put the rest of the stuff back, closed the drawers, and made sure the apartment was the way I'd found it. Then I let myself out.

The pear-shaped man was standing by the mailboxes on a little plot of grass they have there, waiting for a rat-sized dog on a silver leash. The dog was straining so hard its back was bent double. It edged sideways as it strained. Awful, the things you see in my line of work. The pear-shaped man said, "You're not Johnny Staccato. That was an old TV series with John Cassavetes."

"Caught me," I said. "That's the trouble with trying to be smart, there's always someone smarter." The pear-shaped man nodded and looked superior. I gave him a card. "You see Ms. Marsh around, I'd appreciate a call."

The Mexicans in the Nova were still there, only now they were arguing. Charlie Bronson gestured angrily, then fired up their car and swung off down the street. Hot-blooded. The pear-shaped man put the card in his pants. "You aren't the only one looking for that woman," he said.

I looked at him. "No?"

"There was another man. I didn't speak to him, but I saw him knocking on number 4. A big man."

I gave him my All-Knowing Operative look. "Good-looking kid. Six-three. Sandy-haired. Could be a football player."

He looked at the dog. "No, this man was dark. Black hair. Bigger than that."

So much for the All-Knowing Operative. "When was this?"

"Last week. Thursday or Friday." He belched softly, said "That's a sweetie" to the dog, then eyed me again. "I think she had quite a few men friends."

I nodded.

The pear-shaped man *tsk*ed at the little dog and gently jerked the leash, as if that would be coaxing. The dog looked up with sad, protruding eyes. The pear-shaped man said, "I'd feed him dog meal, but he whines so much for chicken necks. That's all he'll eat. He loves the skin so."

I nodded again. "Same with people," I said. "You never like what's good for you."

3

I walked back along Gorham and down to San Vicente where I phoned Ellen Lang from a Shell station, and got no answer. I took out the rolodex cards Janet Simon had given me. There were two phone numbers typed on Garrett Rice's card, one with a Beverly Hills prefix, one from The Burbank Studios in beautiful downtown Burbank. It was almost four and traffic was starting to build, the sky already a pallid exhaust orange. Ugly. Bumper to bumper. Fifty-five delightful minutes later I was on another pay phone across from the Warner Brothers gate asking a secretary I knew for a walk-on pass. I would have phoned Garrett Rice directly, but people tend not to be in for private cops. Even when they brave the rush hour.

I jaywalked across Olive Street and gave the guard my name. He flipped through a little file where they keep the passes after the teletype prints them out and said, "Yes, sir."

I said, "I'm going to see Garrett Rice. Can you tell me where that is?"

"What's that name again?"

Usually, you tell these guys a name, they're spitting out directions before you finish saying it. This guy had to look in a little book. Maybe nobody ever asked for Garrett Rice. Maybe I was the first ever and would win some kind of prize. "Here we go," he said, and told me.

A lot of production companies share space at The Burbank Studios. Warner Brothers and Columbia are the big two. Aaron Spelling Productions rents space there. So do a couple zillion lesser companies. All tucked away in warm sand-colored buildings with red tile roofs and pseudo-adobe walls. Mature oaks fill the spaces between the buildings, making a nice shade. The quality of the space reflects your position within the industry.

Garrett Rice was beneath the water tower at the back of the lot. I missed the building twice until a cross-eyed kid on a bicycle pointed it out. It was a squat two-story brick box, six single offices on the bottom and six more on top, with a metal stair at either end. There were palm trees at either end, too, and more palms in a little plot right out front. The palms didn't look like they were doing too well. A backhoe and a bulldozer were parked beside the building, taking up most of a tiny parking lot. This probably wasn't where they put Paul Newman or David Lean. I looked at the names stenciled on the parking curbs. Second from the right was Garrett Rice. Room 217. The backhoe was in his spot.

I went up the stairs and found his office without having anybody point it out. The door was open. There was a little secretary's cubicle, but no secretary. A spine-rolled copy of *Black Belt* magazine was on the secretary's desk, open to an article about hand-to-hand combat in low-visibility situations. Some secretary.

Behind the secretary's space was another door. I opened it and there was Garrett Rice. He stood behind his desk with the phone pressed to his ear, bouncing from foot to foot like he had to go to the bathroom. There was a dying plant on the desk and another on the end table by a worn green couch. There was a can of Lysol air freshener on a file cabinet. The cap was off.

When he saw me, he pressed his hip against the desk, closing a drawer that had been open. He did this in what some might call an understated fashion, then murmured into the phone and hung up.

Rice was about six-one with thin bones and the crepey skin you get from too much sun lamp. There was a mouse under his left eye and another on the left side of his forehead. He had tried to cover them with Indian earth. He had beer wings and shouldn't have been wearing a form-fit shirt.

I handed him one of my cards. "Nice office," I said. "I'm trying to find Morton Lang. I'm told you and he were close and that maybe you can help me out."

He glanced at the card, then looked at me with wet, shining eyes. Nervous. "How'd you get in here?"

"My uncle owns the studio."

"Bullshit."

I gave him a shrug. "Mort's been missing since Friday. He took his boy with him and didn't leave word. His wife's worried. Since you and he were associates, it makes sense that he might've said something to you."

He licked his lips and I thought of Bambi's mother, the way her head jerked up at the first sound of the hunters. Only she was pleasant to look at. The longer I looked at Garrett Rice, the more I wanted to cover my face with a handkerchief and fog the air with the Lysol.

He read the card again and flexed it back and forth, thinking. Then he said, "Fuckin' asshole, Mort."

I nodded. "That's the one. When did you see him last?"

He glanced at the doorway behind me and spread his hands. "You shoulda called. I'm busy. I got calls."

"Consider it a favor to the Forces of Good."

"I got calls."

"So make'm. I've got time." I sat down on the couch between his briefcase and a large brown stain. The stain looked like Mickey Mouse run over by a Kenworth. It went well with the decor.

Garrett Rice hustled over and closed the case. Maybe he had the new Hot Property in there. Maybe Steven Spielberg had been calling him, begging to get a peek. Maybe I could sap Garrett Rice, make my getaway with the Hot Property, and sell it to George Lucas for a million bucks. I put my arm up on the back of the couch so the jacket would open and he could see the Dan Wesson. I waited.

He was breathing harder now, the way a fat man does after a flight of stairs. He looked at the door again. Maybe he was waiting for a pizza delivery. "I got calls," he said. "I dunno where Mort is. I haven't seen him for a week, maybe longer. What do I look like, his keeper?" He went back to his desk with the case.

I stared at him.

He fidgeted. "What?"

"Who beat you up, Garrett?"

He held the briefcase to his chest like a shield. "You'd better not fuck with me. I'm warning you."

"I don't want to fuck with you, Mr. Rice. I just want to ask you about Morton Lang."

He looked past me at the door again, only this time he said, "Well, thank Christ! Where the hell you been?"

The man in the doorway was a little taller than me and a lot wider, with the sort of squared-off shoulders boxers get. He wore a heavy Fu moustache, a little business under his lower lip, and a two-inch Afro that was thicker on top than on the sides. Not quite the Carl Lewis look. He was very, very black. He looked at me. He looked at Garrett Rice. "Nature call. You didn't want me to mess the floor, right?"

Rice said, "Throw this asshole outta here. C'mon."

The black guy looked back at me and sucked a tooth. "How 'bout that, Elvis? Think I oughta throw your ass outta here?"

I sucked a tooth back at him. "She-it," I said. "How's it goin,' Cleon?"

Garrett Rice looked from Cleon Tyner to me and back to Cleon. "What the hell is this? 'Cleon. Elvis. Howzitgoin?' Throw the sonofabitch out, goddamnit!"

Cleon said, "Unh-unh," and let himself down in the chair opposite Rice's desk. He wrapped one arm over the back of the chair so I could see his Smith. It was in a pretty, gray brushed-leather rig. Cleon was wearing dark blue designer jeans, a ruffled white tuxedo shirt, and a gray sharkskin jacket. The jacket was tight across his shoulders and biceps. "You're looking good," I said.

He tried to give me modest. "Cut down on the grits. Dropped a few pounds. Workin' out again. How's Joe?"

Garrett Rice said, "Hey, hey, this guy walks in here, he's got a gun. Look right there, under his goddamned arm. He starts pumpin' me, he won't leave when I ask, he could be anybody, goddamnit, and you're shootin' the shit with him. What in hell I hire you for?" His forehead was damp.

Cleon let out a long, deep breath and shifted forward in the chair. Rice jerked back an inch. Probably didn't even know he'd done it. Cleon's voice was polite. "I know this man, Mr. Rice. He won't take muscle work. If he *does* decide to move on you now, why, then I'll step in. That's what I take the money for. But if all he wants to do is ask you about something or other, then you talk to him. That's the smart thing." Cleon gave me the sleepy eyes. "That's all you wanna do, blood, is talk, am I right?"

"Sure."

Cleon looked back at Rice. "There. You see. Why make somethin' out of nothing?"

Garrett Rice chewed his lip. He said, "I don't know where Mort is, all right. I told you."

"You told me you saw him about a week ago. He say anything about leaving his wife?"

"Look, it was a party, see? A social situation. We were meeting with a potential backer about this project of mine. Mort had some bimbo with him. An actress. It was good times, that's all. Mort wouldn't've brought up any shit about his wife."

"Kimberly Marsh?"

"Yeah, I guess that was her name. The bitch was all over me. That's the way it is, see? These bimbos find out you're a producer, they're all over you." Talking about that brought him to life.

"Sounds rewarding."

He leered and made a pistol with his fingers and shot me. I considered returning the gesture with my .38. Cleon picked his thumb, ignoring us. I said, "Can you think of anyone else Mort might've talked to?"

"How the hell should I know?"

"You were friends."

"We had business."

"You played cards with them. Every week for almost a year."

"Hey, I'm everybody's friend. You want me to be your friend? I'll be your friend, too. I'll even play cards with you. I'll even *lose*, you want me to."

I looked at Cleon. He shrugged. "It's a gig, man."

"Not what you call your quality employment."

"Is it ever?"

I stood up. Cleon shifted, rolling the big shoulders. "Leaving," I said. Cleon nodded but stayed forward. Cleon knew the moves. I looked back at Garrett. "I like the bruises. They go with the liver spots."

"Some asshole thought I stole his script. That happens, this business."

"Must be some asshole, you hiring on Cleon."

"Man just dig quality, bro, that's all."

I nodded. Garrett Rice gnawed at his lip.

I said, "This has been disappointing, Garrett. I bucked rush hour for this."

"Tough."

I said, "I see Ellen Lang, I'll give her your best."

"Tell her Mort's an asshole."

"She might agree."

"She's an asshole, too. So are you."

I looked at Cleon. There was a little smile to his eye, but you'd never know it unless you knew him well.

I went out along the cement walk and down the metal stairs and took the long walk back to my car. I drove to Studio City to pick up eggplant parmesan and an antipasto from a place called Sonny's and a six-pack of Wheat beer from the liquor store next door. By the time I got out of Sonny's, the sky was a deep purple, coal red in the west behind black palm-tree cutouts. I drove south on Laurel Canyon, up the hill toward home.

I had very much wanted to turn up some good news for Ellen Lang. But good news, like magic, is sometimes in short supply.

4
_____

It was eight o'clock when I pulled into the carport. I put the eggplant in the microwave to reheat and ate the antipasto while I waited. Oily. Sonny's had gone downhill. The little metal hatch I'd built into the door off the kitchen clattered and the cat walked in. He's black and he walks with his head sort of cocked to the side because someone once shot him with a .22. I poured a little of the Wheat beer in a saucer and put out some cat food. He drank the beer first then ate the cat food then looked at me for more beer. He was purring. "Forget it," I said. The purring stopped and he walked away.

When the eggplant was ready I carried it and the beer and the cordless phone out onto the deck. The rich black of the canyon was dotted with jack-o'-lantern lit houses, orange and white and yellow and red in the night. Where the canyon flattened out into Hollywood and the basin beyond, the lights concentrated into thousands of blue-white diamonds spilled over the earth. I liked that.

I'm in a rustic A-frame on a little road off Woodrow Wilson Drive above Hollywood. The only other house is a cantilevered job to my east. A stuntman I know lives there with his girlfriend and their two little boys. Sometimes during the day they come out on their deck and we'll see each other and wave. The boys call my place the teepee house. I like that, too.

When I bought the house four years ago I tore off the deck railing and rebuilt it so the center section was detachable. I detached it now, and sat on the edge of the deck with my feet hanging down, eggplant in my lap, and nothing between me and Out There. The chill air felt good. After a while the cat came out and stared at me. "Okay," I said. I poured some more of the Wheat beer on the deck. He blinked, then lapped at it.

When the eggplant was gone I called the answering machine at my office. There were three messages from Ellen Lang and one from Janet Simon. Ellen Lang sounded scared in the first two and teary in the third. Janet Simon sounded like Janet

Simon. I called Ellen Lang. Janet Simon answered. It works like that sometimes.

"Mort came back and tore up the house. Could you come over here?"

"Is she okay?"

"He was gone when she got here. I made her call the police but now she's saying she won't let them in the house."

"Want me to pistol-whip her?"

"Don't you ever let up?"

Apparently not. It took me eighteen minutes to push the Corvette down the valley side of Laurel, up onto the freeway, and over to Encino. Ellen Lang lived in the flat part above Ventura Boulevard in what's called a sprawling California Tudor by realtors and Encino Baroque by people with taste. Janet Simon's pale blue Mustang was on the street in front of the house. I pulled into the drive behind a Subaru wagon, cut the engine, and went up to the door. It opened before I could knock. Ellen Lang was pinched and thin behind her glasses, more so than this morning. She said, "I called you. I called and called and you weren't there. I came to you so the police wouldn't get involved and now they are."

Janet said, "Oh, for God's sake, Ellen."

I had one of those dull aches you get behind the eyes when your beer drinking is interrupted.

Ellen Lang said, "Well, it's Mort's house, isn't it? He can do what he wants here, can't he? Can't we call the police back and tell them it was a mistake?"

I followed them like that into the living room.

Every large piece of furniture had been turned over and the bottom cloth ripped away. Books had been pulled off the shelves and cabinets thrown open. The back was off the television. A palm had been worked out of its heavy brass pot, scattering dirt over the beige carpet. The Zenith console stereo was turned on its face and about two hundred record albums spilled out on the floor. One of those large ceramic greyhounds you see in department stores was cracked open on the hearth, its head intact but lying on the carpet upside down. It looked asleep.

Some mistake.

"How long ago did you call?" I said to Ellen Lang.

Janet Simon answered. "About forty-five minutes. She told them it wasn't an emergency."

"If you had they'd have been here forty minutes ago. As it is, they've called it out to a radio car. They'll be here any time."

Ellen Lang crossed her arms in the keep-me-warm posture and began nibbling the side of her mouth. Every light in the house was on, as if Janet or Ellen had gone through, making a point of driving out as much darkness as possible. There was a little night-light behind a wingback chair beside the fireplace. Even it glowed.

"He leave a note?" I said.

She shook her head.

"Take any clothes for the boy?"

Shook her head again.

"Take anything else?"

She squinted and did something funny with her mouth, blowing air out the corners while keeping the lips together. "I checked my things. I checked the silver. The Neil Diamond records are still here. Mort loves Neil Diamond."

"This is A-plus help you're giving me, Mrs. Lang."

She looked at me like I was fading out and tough to see. "Mort isn't a thief. If he took anything of his, that isn't thievery, is it? He paid for it, didn't he? He paid for all this and that gives him some rights, doesn't it?" She said that to Janet Simon.

Janet Simon reached a cigarette out of a little blue purse, tamped it, fired up, and pulled enough smoke into her chest to fill the Goodyear blimp. "When are you going to wake up?" she said.

I left them to it and went down the hall. There was a door on the left, closed, with the sounds of running water. "That's the bathroom," Janet Simon called. "The girls are in there." The girls' bedroom was just past the bath but on the right. It was pink and white and had twin canopy beds and probably used to be quite nice. Now, the mattresses were half on and half off and one of the box springs had been turned upside down. There was a dresser and a chest, but all the drawers were out and the clothes were scattered on the floor. Bruce Springsteen was on the closet door, which spoke highly for at least one of the girls. Clothes hung neatly on the crossbar even though the closet floor had been trashed. Just outside the closet, there were two three-ring binders and two stacks of schoolbooks. The binders and the dust covers on the books were covered with doodles and designs and words. *Cindy loves Frank. B.T. + C.L. Robby Robby Robby, I want you for my hobby.*

BOOK YOU. I found a folded piece of three-hole paper in Cindy Lang's geography book with a message written on it in pencil. The message was ELAM FREID BITES THE BIG ONE!!!!! I wondered if Elam Freid knew that. I wondered how much he'd pay to find out.

I went to the boy's room next. It was smaller than the girls', with a single bed and a dresser and a big oak chest. The chest was turned over and the dresser was on its side and the mattress and box springs leaned drunkenly against the wall. I had wanted to go over the boy's room. I had wanted to read his diary and sift through his comics and peek under his mattress. I had wanted to go through the wads of paper in his trash and page through his notebooks and study the drawings that he made and pinned to the wall. A week before they left, maybe Mort had said something to the boy and the boy had left a clue. All of that was gone. There was only a big mess here that made me hope the boy wouldn't suddenly come through the front door, run back here, and see it.

The master bedroom was at the back of the house looking out on the pool through some nice French doors. It smelled of Anaïs Anaïs. I pulled the bolts at the top of each French door and ran my fingers along the stiles. They hadn't been jimmied. There was a kingsize platform bed, a dresser, a chest, and a desk, and all of it was torn up pretty much like the others. They had one of those sliding wall closets with the mirrored hanging doors. The left half was Ellen and the right Mort. Boxes and shoe bags and a Minolta camera case and a larger box that said Bekins had been tossed out to the center of the room. Mort had some nice pants and some nice shirts and half a dozen pair of Bally shoes. There was a tan Nino Cerruti shirt I liked a lot hanging beside three dark gray Sy Devore suit bags and two from Carroll's in Westwood. A lot of clothes to leave behind, but maybe Mort traveled light.

A collection of family pictures hung over the bed. The kids. Mort and the kids. Ellen. Mort and Ellen. Mort didn't seem to be playing favorites. The nicest had Mort in the pool with the younger girl on his shoulders and Perry and the older girl in his arms. Nothing looked wrong in those pictures. Mort didn't look crazy. Ellen didn't look small. Nothing ever looks wrong in the pictures. Everything always goes wrong when the camera's turned away.

The bathroom door was still closed, the water was still running, Janet Simon was still smoking, Ellen Lang was still standing with her arms crossed, cold. I went into the kitchen. Every cupboard had been emptied, every bag of sugar and rice and flour and box of cereal spilled. The grill had been pulled off the bottom of the refrigerator and the stove had been dragged away from the wall, scarring the vinyl with ragged furrows. I found a bottle of Extra Strength Bayer aspirin in a mound of Corn Chex, ate three, then went back out into the living room.

Janet Simon gave me frozen eyes. Ellen Lang watched the floor. I cleared my throat. "Someone was looking for something and someone knew where someone else might want to hide it," I said. "This was professional. Mort didn't do this. You're going to need the police." Stating the obvious is something I do well.

Ellen Lang said, "No." Softly.

Janet Simon crushed out her cigarette and said, "*Yes.*" Firmly.

I took a deep breath and smiled sweetly. "I'm going to check around outside," I said.

It was either that, or hit them with a chair.

5
___

I went out to the Corvette and got the big five-cell I keep in the trunk. I looked for jimmy marks on the front door lock stile and the doorjamb, but didn't find any. Three bay windows at the front of the house overlooked a flower bed with azaleas and snapdragons. The windows weren't jimmied and the flowers weren't trampled. I walked around the north side of the house and there were four more windows, two and a space and then two more, each still locked on the inside. I let myself through a wooden gate and walked the back of the house past a little beaded bathroom window to the pool. No openings punched in the wall, no sliding door off its track, no circular holes cut into glass. No one slugged me with a ball peen hammer and disappeared into the night.

I stopped by the pool and listened. Motor sounds from the freeway to the south. Water gurgling through pipes to the little bathroom. Somewhere a radio going, Tina Turner coughing out *What's Love Got to Do With It?*. Through the glass doors, I could see Ellen and Janet in the living room, Ellen with her arms squeezed across her chest, Janet making an explanatory gesture with her cigarette, Ellen shaking her head, Janet looking disgusted. I thought of great teams from the past: Burns and Allen, Bergen and McCarthy, Heckle and Jeckle. I took a deep breath, smelled jasmine, and kept going.

On the south side of the house it was the same thing. No footprints beneath the windows. No jimmy marks. No sign of forced entry. That meant a key or a lock pick. Maybe Mort had hired somebody to go in there and given them his key. But if so, what could he have wanted? Stock certificates? Negotiable bonds? Nudie shots he was scared Ellen would show their friends?

I went back out to the front just as a black and white pulled up. They pegged me with their spotlight and told me not to move.

"Should I grab sky?" I said.

The same voice came back, "Just stand there, shithead."
Service with a smile.

One of the cops came forward with his hand on his gun. The
other stayed behind the light. You can never see what they're
doing behind those lights, which is why they stay there. The
cop who came out was about my height but thicker in the butt
and legs. It didn't detract from his presence. His name tag
read SIMMS.

I spread my arms, careful not to point the five-cell in their
direction. "White pants and jacket. The latest in cat burglar
apparel."

Simms said, "Little man, I've cuffed'm that went out in red
tights. Let's see some ID."

"I'm Cole. I work for the owner. Private investigator. There's
a Dan Wesson .38 under my left arm."

He said okay, told me he was going to reach under and take
the gun, then did it. "Now the paper," he said.

I produced the PI license and the license to carry, and
watched him read them. "Elvis. This some kind of bullshit or
what?"

"After my mother."

He looked at me the way cops look at you when they're
thinking about trying you out, then gave me the benefit of the
doubt. "Guess you take some riding about that."

"My brother Edna had it worse."

He thought about it again, figured I wasn't worth the paperwork and handed back the gun. "Okay. We got a B&E call."
The other cop came around and joined us but left the spotlight
on. I clicked off the five-cell.

"They're inside," I said. "The client's name is Ellen Lang.
She owns the place. She came home and found it busted up.
Another woman is with her. I checked the windows and the
doors but it looks okay."

The new cop said, "You don't mind if we see for ourselves,
do you?"

I said, "This guy is good, Simms. He's a comer."

Simms put his hand on my arm and pointed me toward the
house. "Come on, let's you and me go see the ladies. Eddie,
take a walk around."

When we got into the living room I said, "Look what the cat
dragged in." Ellen Lang said, "Oh, Lord," and sat down as the
two girls walked in. The oldest was fourteen, the youngest
maybe eleven. The older one was tall and gawky and had a

couple of major league pimples forming up on her forehead. The younger one was slender and dark and looked a little bit like Ellen. They were carrying pink-and-white overnighters. The oldest had a pissed-off look on her face. "We're packed," she said. She ignored me and the cop.

"Oh, honey, that's not warm enough. Get a sweater."

The younger one stared at Simms, then at me. "Is he the detective?"

"Wanna see my sap?" I said.

Ellen Lang took off her glasses, rubbed at her eyes, put her glasses back on, and said, "Please, Mr. Cole."

The younger one said, "What's a sap?"

Simms ignored all that. "This place looks like hell."

The older one said, "It's not the arctic, Mother. We're only going to Janet's." Her face reeked of disapproval. Teenage girls reek of disapproval better than anyone I know.

"Oh, honey, please," Ellen Lang said. It wasn't nice to hear. It's never nice to hear an adult whine to a child. The older one closed her eyes, sighed dramatically, and said, "Come on." They went back down the hall and disappeared.

Simms said, "I'm Officer Simms. There's another officer outside checking the yard. What we're going to do is look around, then sit down with you and talk about it, okay?" He had a good style. Relaxed and easy.

Ellen Lang's "Yes" was very soft.

Eddie tapped at the glass doors that led off the dining room out to the pool and Simms went over. They mumbled together, then Simms said, "Poolhouse is inside out. I'll be right back," and went out to see. The jasmine floated in the open door.

I said, "You want the cops in on this or not? They're in now and it's smarter if they stay in."

She shook her head without looking at me.

Janet Simon said, "Oh, for God's sake, Ellen," for maybe the 400th time, and took a seat on the hearth.

I said, "It is my professional opinion that you allow the police to investigate. I checked Kimberly Marsh's apartment this afternoon. It looks like she went away for a few days. If she did, there's a good chance she went somewhere with Mort. If Mort's out of town, then he couldn't have done this. That means you had a stranger in your house. Even if Mort hired somebody, that's over the line and the cops should know."

Janet Simon said, "Wow. You work fast."

Ellen Lang went white when I mentioned Kimberly Marsh.

She tried to swallow, looked like she had a little trouble, then stood up and said, "I won't have the police after my husband. I won't do that to him. I don't want the police here. I don't want ABPs. I don't want Mort in any trouble."

"APB," I said. "All Points Bulletin. That went out with Al Capone."

"I don't want that, either."

My head throbbed. The muscles along my neck were tight. Pretty soon I'd have knots in the trapezius muscles and sour stomach. "Listen," I said. "It wasn't Mort."

Ellen Lang started to cry. No whimpering, no trembling chin. Just water spilling out her eyes. "Please do something," she said. She made no move to hide her face.

The cops came back and glanced into the kitchen. Eddie mumbled some more to Simms and headed out to the radio car. Simms stayed with us. "We're gonna get the detectives in on this," he said.

Ellen Lang folded up and sat down like she'd just been told the biopsy was positive. "Oh, God, I can't do anything right."

I watched her a moment, then took a long breath in through the nose, let it out, and said, "Simms?"

Simms' eyes flicked my way. Flat, bored eyes. Street-cop eyes.

I brought him aside. "She thinks it was her husband," I said. "It's a domestic beef. They're separated."

Simms said "Shit" under his breath and called out the front door for Eddie to wait. He stood in the living room, one thick hand on his gun butt and one on his nightstick, looking around the place like he was standing hip deep in dog shit. The older girl came back in, saw her mother crying, and looked disgusted. "Oh, for Christ's sake, Mother." She went back down the hall. Maybe she wanted to grow up to be Janet Simon.

Ellen Lang cried harder. I went over to her, put my hand on her shoulder, and said, "Stop that" into her ear. She nodded and tried to stop. She did a pretty good job.

Simms said, "All right. Do you want to report anything missing?"

She shook her head without looking at him, either.

"A lot of this stuff is ruined," he said. "You could maybe file a vandalism claim with the insurance, but only if we file a report, and only if we can't prove it's your husband. Okay, even if we forget your husband, the detectives still gotta come out here and file a vandalism report. That's the insurance company, see?"

"You're okay, Simms," I said.

He ignored me. Ellen blew her nose on a little bit of Kleenex and shook her head again. "I'm very sorry for the bother," she said.

Simms frowned around the room. "Husband, huh?"

Janet Simon said, "Ellen, you should have this for court." I felt Ellen Lang tighten like a flexed muscle.

"Forget that," I said.

Simms stood there a second longer, breathing heavily, then nodded and walked out.

Nobody moved for a long time. Then Janet Simon pulled out another cigarette. "You're a dope."

Ellen Lang began to tremble. I felt it deep in my chest and up through my arm, a high-strung from-the-lonely-place resonance that left the tips of her collar shaking like leaves in a chill breeze. "You want me to stay?" I asked. "I can bunk on the couch."

Ellen lifted off her glasses, wiped at the wet around her eyes, and sniffled. "Thank you, no. We're going to stay the night with Janet."

I gave Janet a look. "Gosh, I was hoping I could. I'm into pain." Janet ignored me, but Ellen Lang smiled. It wasn't much of a smile, but it was real.

I told her I'd be back tomorrow to look over the bills and bank statements and that she should gather them. I let myself out. The chill had a bite to it now and I could smell a eucalyptus from a neighbor's yard along with the jasmine. There were times when I thought it might be nice to have a jasmine and a eucalyptus to smell. But not always.

6

I woke up just before nine the next morning and caught the tail end of *Sesame Street*. Today's episode was brought to us by the letter D. For Depressed Detective. I pulled on a pair of tennis shoes and went out onto the deck for the traditional twelve sun salutes of the hatha-yoga, then segued smoothly to the tai chi, third and eighth cycles, Tiger and Crane work. I started slow the way you're supposed to, then increased the pace the way you're not until the tai chi became a wing chun *kata* and sweat trickled down the sides of my face and my muscles burned and I was feeling pretty good again. I finished in *vrischikasan*, the second-stage scorpion pose, and held it for almost six minutes.

The cat was waiting in the kitchen. I gave him the big smile and a cheery hello. "Held the scorpion for six minutes," I said. Proudly.

The cat thought about that, then licked his scrotum. Some people you can never please.

I made us eggs. His with tuna, mine with a couple of shots of Tabasco. We ate in silence. After the meal I phoned General Entertainment Studios.

A young woman's voice said, "Casting."

"Patricia Kyle, please."

"Who's calling?"

"Elvis Cole."

"Pardon me?"

"Don't be cruel," I said.

"I'm not. I—oh." A giggle. "*That* Elvis. Hold on."

Patricia Kyle came on the phone, voice loud enough to be heard in Swaziland. "You got me pregnant, you bastard!" That Patricia. What a kidder.

I said, "I need to pump you."

"Oh, ho!"

"For information."

"That's what they all say." She told me that she would be

30

there until lunch, that there would be a drive-on pass at the main gate, and that I should come by anytime.

"That's what they all say," I said. And hung up.

Forty minutes later, showered, dusted, deodorized, and dressed, I was on the GE lot walking toward the casting offices.

GE has one of the few remaining old-time studio lots. Huge gray sound stages packed belly-to-butt with bunkerlike offices, navigable only by a grid of narrow streets usually fouled with the big semis production companies employ to carry cameras and lights and costumes to location. On any given day you could see almost anyone walking those slim tarmac streets. As a tour bus passed I waved and the people waved back. Ah, the land of make-believe.

I went in a door that said Emergency Exit Only and took the first flight of stairs I came to, turned down a short hall and passed seven of the most beautiful women on Earth, strolled past the casting office receptionist like I owned the place, went through a glass door and down another short hall past a man and a woman who were arguing softly, and stopped outside Patricia Kyle's door. She was on the phone.

I said loudly, "Have the abortion. It's the only way." I looked at the man and the woman. "Herpes." Then a hand yanked me into Patricia Kyle's office and the door slammed amid a gale of red-faced laughter.

"You nut, that's my boss!"

"Not for long."

She picked up the phone and cupped the receiver. "Business. I'll just be a second."

I took a seat in a chair beneath a wall-sized poster of Raquel Welch from the movie *1,000,000 Years B.C.* Someone had taken a Magic Marker and drawn a voice balloon over her head so that Raquel was saying, "Mess with me, buster, I'll gut you like a fish!!!"

Patricia Kyle is forty-four years old, five-four and slim the way a female gymnast is slim, all long, lithe muscle and defined curves, with a pretty Irish face framed by curly auburn hair. When we met four years ago she weighed in at one seventy-three and had just gotten out of the world's worst marriage. Only her ex didn't see it that way. He'd show up all hours, drunk and stumbling around, knocking over the garbage cans, doing Stanley Kowalski. To prove how much he loved her, he put a brick through the rear window of her BMW and used an ice pick on the tires and that's when she called me.

I took care of it. She dumped the weight and quit smoking and took up Nautilus and started running. She got the job at General Entertainment. Things were looking up.

She apologized into the phone, told whoever it was that GE and the producers really wanted their actor but couldn't pay more than Top of the Show, that she knew the actor's wife had just had a baby and so he'd probably want the work and the money, and that he'd be just so *right* for the part she really wished he'd do it. She listened, then smiled, said fine, and hung up.

"He's going to take the role?"

She nodded. "It's twenty-five hundred dollars for two days work."

"Yeah, but those guys earn it."

She laughed. I've never heard Patricia giggle. It's either a smile or a full blown laugh, but nothing in between. I gave her the once-over. "Nice," I said.

She put a thousand watts out through her teeth. "One-twelve," she said. "I ran in my first Ten-K last week, *AND* I've got a new boyfriend."

"He's just after your mind."

"God, I hope not."

"Tell me everything you know about an agent named Morton Lang."

She pushed back in her chair. "He used to work for ICM, I think, then he left about a year ago to start his own agency. He calls maybe once a month, sometimes more, to push a client or ask about upcoming roles."

"Talk to him anytime in the past week or so?"

"Unh-unh." She leaned forward, gave me dimples and an eager look. "What's the dirt?"

I tried to give her the sort of look I'd always imagined Mike Hammer giving to dames and broads who got out of line. "It's the game, doll. You know that."

Her left eyebrow arched. "Doll?"

I spread my hands. "Let's pretend you didn't commit this major gaff by asking about a client, and continue. Mort had business with a producer named Garrett Rice."

"Garrett Rice. Yuck."

"Crepey skin, lecherous demeanor, sour body odor. What's not to like?"

She looked at me as if she were trying to think of a concise way to say it. "When you're in high school, and you first start thinking you'd like to work in this business and you tell your parents and they freak out, they're freaking out because they're thinking of men like Garrett Rice."

"Can you think of any reason why he might need a bodyguard?"

"You're kidding me."

"Nope. Guy named Cleon Tyner. He's pretty good. Not world class, but okay in a bar. Somebody put a couple of marks on Mr. Rice and scared him. Ergo, Cleon."

Patricia thought about it, then laid a finger alongside her nose. "I've heard there's some of this."

"Cocaine."

"Just talk. I don't know for sure. Garrett has this reputation. He came on to one of the girls here by offering her a toot, that kind of thing."

I saw him closing the drawer, closing the briefcase. "Mort, too?"

She looked surprised. "I wouldn't think so."

"Okay, that's Garrett's problem. Mort ever mention any friends, anyone he might've been close to?"

"Not that I remember. I can ask the other people here. I'll call a friend at Universal Casting and he can ask around over there."

I unfolded the 8 × 10 of Kimberly Marsh. Patricia looked at it, turned it over and read the résumé, then shook her head. "Sorry."

"If Mort Calls, will you try to get a number and let me know?"

"You going to tell me what this is about?"

"Mort's peddling government secrets to the Arabs."

She stuck her tongue at me.

"Tell me the truth," I said. "Do I look like John Cassavetes twenty years ago?"

"I didn't know you twenty years ago."

Everyone's a comedian. I stood up and went to the door.

"It's too bad about Mort," she said. "I remember when he was with ICM. He was well-placed. He had a fair clients list." She leaned back, putting her feet on her desk. She was wearing dark blue Espadrilles and tight Jag jeans. "You only start dealing with a Garrett Rice when you're scared. It's the kiss of death. A guy like Garrett Rice, he rents space over at TBS but he couldn't get a deal with Warners or Columbia. Nobody wants him around." She frowned. "I met Mort twice maybe a year and a half ago when he was with ICM. He seemed like a nice man."

"Yeah, they're all nice men. This business is rife with nice men."

"You're a cynic, Elvis."

"No, I've just never met anyone in this business who believed in anything worthwhile and was willing to go the distance for it."

"Oh, foo," she said. That's one of the reasons I like her, she said things like "oh, foo." She slapped her desk, then got up and came around and punched my arm. "Hey, when are you going to come to the house for dinner?"

"Then I'll have to meet your boyfriend."

"That's the idea."

"What if I don't approve?"

"You'll lie and tell me he's the greatest thing in the world."

I squeezed her butt and walked out. "It works like that, doesn't it."

7

I pulled up at Ellen Lang's house at ten minutes before noon. She came to the door in cutoffs, bare feet, and a man's white-with-blue-stripes shirt tied at the waist. Her hair was done up in a knot. "Oh, God," she said. "Oh, God."

I smiled serenely. "To some, yes."

"I wasn't expecting you. I'm not dressed."

I went past her into the living room. The books and records were back on their shelves and most of the furniture was righted and in some semblance of order. There was a staple gun and packaging tape by the big couch, which was still upside down. Too heavy for her. I whistled. "You do all this by yourself?"

"Of course."

"Without Janet?"

She flushed and touched her hair where it was wispy out from the knot. "I must look horrible."

"You look better than yesterday. You look like someone who's been working hard and had her mind off her troubles. You look okay."

She flushed some more and turned back toward the dining room. Half a sandwich was laid out on a paper towel on the table. It looked like a single slice of processed chicken loaf on whole wheat, cut diagonally. There was half a Fred Flintstone glass of skim milk beside it.

She said, "I want to apologize to you for last night. And to thank you for what you did."

"Forget it."

She looked away, picking at the knot that held the shirttails together. "Well, you came all the way out here and I was so silly."

"No, you weren't. You were upset. You had a right to be. It would have been smart to keep the cops but you didn't and now it's past, so forget it."

She nodded, again without looking at me. Habit. As if she

had never been quite strong enough to carry on a conversation in person. "Why did you let the police leave?"

"You wanted them to."

"But you and Janet didn't."

"I don't work for Janet." Ellen Lang went very red. "When you hire me I work for you. That means I'm on your side. I act in your behalf. I respect your confidences. My job doesn't mean cribbing off what the cops dig up. So if you don't want the cops then I'll try to live by that."

She looked at me, then remembered herself and glanced away. "You're the first private investigator I've ever met."

"The others aren't as good looking."

A little bit of a smile came to one side of her face, then left. Progress. She turned and handed me a small stack of white and green envelopes from the table. "I found these by Mort's desk." There were phone bills, some charge receipts from Bullocks and the Broadway and Visa, and some gas receipts from Mobil. All neatly sorted.

"There's only two phone bills here," I said.

"That's all I found."

"I want everything for the last six months, and the check-book and the passbooks and anything from your broker if you have one, including ILA accounts and things like that."

"Well, like I said—" The awkward look was back. "Mort handled all the money."

"I'm so bad with figures. I'm sorry."

"Unh-huh." I pointed at the sandwich. "Why don't you fix me one of those, only put some food on mine, and when I come back we can talk."

I went back through the living room and down the hall to the master. The mattress had been pulled back onto the box spring. The clothes and personal items had been picked up and folded into neat piles on the bed, his and hers, outer garments and underwear, all waiting to go back into the drawers. The drawers were back in the chest and dresser, and the room, like the rest of the house, looked in order. She must have started at 3 A.M.

Two shoe boxes and the Bekins box were on Mort's desk, filled with envelopes and file folders and actors' résumés and more of those glossy 8 × 10's. On the back of each 8 × 10 someone had stamped The Morton Lang Agency in red ink. I went through his rolodex, pulled cards for the clients I recognized, and put them in my pocket. In the second shoe box I found registration papers for a Walther .32-caliber automatic pistol purchased in 1980. Well, well. I stood up and looked at the room but didn't see the gun sticking out of any place conspicuous. Halfway down the Bekins box, under a three-year-old copy of *Playboy,* I found an unframed diploma from Kansas State University in Morton Keith Lang's name. It was water-stained. The bills and receipts and bank stuff were near the bottom of the box. Grand total search time: eight minutes. Maybe the box had hidden from Ellen when she came into the room. I have socks that do that.

When I got back to the dining room, a full-grown sandwich sat on a black china plate atop a blue and gray pastel place mat. The sandwich was cut into two triangles, each sporting a toothpick with an electric blue tassel. Four orange slices and four raspberries and a sprig of parsley offset the tassels. A water goblet sat to the right of the plate. To the left was a matching saucer with sweet pickles and pitted olives and Tuscan peppers, and a little gold fork to spear them with. A blue and gray linen napkin was rolled and peaked and sitting above the plate.

Ellen Lang sat at her place, staring out through the glass doors into her backyard. When she heard me she turned. "I put out water because I didn't know what else you might want. We have Diet Coke or milk or Pabst beer. I could make coffee if you'd like."

The table was perfect. "No, this is fine," I said. "Thank you."

She shifted in the chair. I sat and ate a Tuscan pepper. I prefer chili peppers or serranos, but Tuscans are fun, too.

"Did you find what you were looking for?" she said.

"In the box on the desk." I showed her the stack of paper.

She closed her eyes. "Oh, God. I'm sorry. I put those things in there this morning. I don't know why I didn't see them."

"Stress. You give a person enough stress and they begin to fog out. People start having little fender benders in parking lots. People forget their keys. People can't see things right under their noses. It happens to everybody. Even Janet Simon."

She took a nibble of her sandwich, then rearranged it on the plate. "You don't like her very much, do you?"

I didn't say anything.

"She's my friend. She's a very strong lady. She understands."

Sit, Ellen. Speak.

"She's your anchor," I said. "She is that because she's abusive and insulting and she reinforces your lousy self-image, which is what you want. If she's right about you, then Mort's right about you. If Mort's right about you then you deserve to be treated the way he treats you and you shouldn't rock the boat which is something you do not want to do." Mr. Sensitive. "Other than that, I like her fine."

"You made a joke."

I had said a very hard thing and she wasn't angry. She should've been, but she wasn't. Maybe enough years of Janet Simon will do that to you. Or maybe she hadn't heard.

I shrugged. "Being funny, that's one way to deal with stress. Investigators, cops, paramedics. Paramedics are the funniest people I know. Have you in stitches."

She looked at me. Blank.

"Paramedics are the funniest people I know. *Have you in stitches.*"

"Oh."

"Another little joke."

We smiled at each other. Just your basic lunchtime conversation.

"Did you mean that, what you said about Janet?"

Maybe she had heard. Maybe, deep down, she was even angry. "Yes."

"You're wrong."

"Okay."

She took another microscopic bite of her sandwich, then pushed it away. Maybe she absorbed nutrients from her surroundings. "You must like being a private investigator," she said.

"Yes. Very much." I took the top off one of the sandwich halves, pulled the stems off two of the peppers, put the peppers on the sandwich, sealed it up again.

"Did you go to college for that?"

"University of Southeast Asia. Two-year program."

"Vietnam?"

"Unh-huh." I finished the first half of the sandwich, put three peppers on the remaining half, and started on that one.

"That must have been awful," she said.

"There were some very real disadvantages to being there, yes." I swallowed, took a sip of water, patted my lips with the napkin. "But adversity has a way of strengthening. If it doesn't kill you, you learn things. For instance, that's when I learned I wanted to be Peter Pan."

She didn't quite frown. She quizzled. "You're quizzling."

"Pardon me?" Confused.

"Me being funny again. I learned to be funny in Vietnam. Funny is a survival mechanism. I started yoga. Pranayamic breathing is a great way to keep your mind right. We'd be in a bunker, six of us, breathing in one nostril, out the other, *om*-ing to beat hell as the rockets came in. You see how this gets funny?"

"Of course."

"Yoga led to tai chi, tai chi led to tae kwan do, which is Korean karate, and wing chun, which is an offshoot of Chinese kung fu. All very centering, stabilizing activities." I spread my hands. "I am a bastion of calm in a chaotic world."

Blank eyes.

"I learned that I could survive. I learned what I would do to keep breathing, and what I wouldn't do, and what was important to me, and what wasn't. Just like you're going to learn that you can survive what's happening to you."

She pursed her lips, looking away to pick at a bread crumb on her milk glass.

"If I can survive Vietnam, you can survive Encino," I said. "Try yoga. Be good for you."

"Yoga."

Apparently she didn't consider yoga an appropriate substitute for a husband. "Mrs. Lang, do you know where Mort kept his gun?"

She looked surprised. "Mort didn't have a gun."

I showed her the receipt. "Well, this is years ago," she said.

"Guns tend to hang around. Keep an eye out for it."

She nodded. "All right. I'm sorry."

"You say that a lot. You don't have to be sorry. You look away a lot, too, and that's something else you don't have to do."

"I'm sorry."

"Quite all right."

She took a sip of her milk. It left a moustache on her upper lip. "You are funny," she said.

"It's either that or be smart." I killed the rest of the sandwich and sorted the paperwork: bank stuff together, credit card billings together, phone stuff by itself. Without Janet Simon around, she was much more relaxed. You could look past the frightened eyes and mottled face and slumped shoulders and get glimpses of her from better days. I said, "I'll bet you were the third prettiest girl in eleventh grade."

Happy-lines came to the corners of her eyes. She touched at her hair again. "*Second* prettiest," she said.

It was good when she smiled. She probably hadn't done a lot of that lately. "You meet Mort in college?"

"High school. Clarence Darrow Senior High in Elverton. That's where we grew up. In Kansas."

"High school sweethearts."

She smiled. "Yes. Isn't that awful?"

"Not at all. You go to college together?"

Her eyes turned a little wistful. "Mort was in theater arts and business. His parents had quite a large paint store there, in Elverton. They wanted him to take it over but Mort wanted to act. No one can understand that in Elverton. You say you want to act and they just look at you."

I shrugged. "Mort didn't have it so bad."

She looked at me.

"He had the second prettiest girl at Clarence Darrow Senior High, didn't he?"

She looked at me some more until she realized what I was doing, then she grinned, and nodded, and finally gave a short uncertain laugh. She told me I was terrible.

I pushed the paperwork across the table to her. "Be that as it may, I want you to go through and notate all the phone numbers that you can identify. Go through the credit card billings and see if the purchases make sense to you. Same with the bank statements and the check stubs."

She looked at the stacks of paper. The smile disappeared. No happy-lines around the eyes. "Isn't that what I'm paying you for?" she said softly.

"We're going to have to take care of that, too. So far, you're not paying me anything."

"Yes, of course." Awkward and uncomfortable.

I sighed. "Look, I could do this, sure, but it's faster if you do it. I won't know any of these phone numbers, but you will, and that will save time. I don't know what you people bought from the Broadway or on Visa. I see a Visa charge from The Ivy for a hundred dollars a week every week, I don't know you and Janet make a regular thing of it there every Thursday."

"There's nothing like that."

"There might be something else."

She was looking at the paper like it was going to jump at her. "It's not that I don't want to," she said, "it's just that I'm not very good at these things."

"You'll surprise youself."

"I'm so bad with figures."

"Try."

"I'll mess it up." I leaned back in the chair and put my hands on the table. At the Grand Canyon, I'd seen a man with acrophobia force himself toward the guardrail because his daughter wanted to look down. He almost made it, both hands on the rail, leaning forward in a lunge with his feet as far back as possible, before the cold sweats cut his knees out from under him and he collapsed to the pavement. Ellen Lang's eyes looked like his eyes.

She tried to smile again, but it came out broken this time. "It really will be better if you do it, don't you see?"

I saw. "Mort really did it to you, didn't he."

She stood quickly and scooped up what was left of her sandwich and the Fred Flintstone glass. "You stop that right now. You sound just like Janet."

"Nope. With me it was just an observation."

She stood breathing hard for a second and then she went into the kitchen. I waited. When she came back out she said, "All right. Tell me what to do again."

I told her. "Now, about my fee."

"Yes, of course."

"Two thousand, exclusive of expenses."

"I remember."

I looked at her. She looked at me. Nobody moved. After twenty or thirty years I said, "Well?"

"I'll get it to you."

I took the checkbook out of the stack of bank paper and pushed it across the table to her. "What's wrong with now?"

A tick started on her right eye. "Do you . . . take Visa?"

It was very still in the house. I could hear a single-engine light plane climbing out of Van Nuys Airport to the north. Somewhere down the street a dog with a deep, barrel-chested voice barked. There was a little breeze, but the jasmine was soured by the smog. I slid the checkbook back and looked at it. Most of the couples I know have the husband's name printed out, with the wife's name printed beneath it, two individuals. Theirs read: *Mr. and Mrs. Morton K. Lang*. There was a balance of $3426.15. All of the stubs were written in the same masculine hand. I said quietly, "Go get a pen and I'll show you how."

She went back into the kitchen. When she didn't come out

for a while I went to see. She was standing with one hand on the counter and one hand atop her head. Her glasses were off and her chest was heaving and there was a puddle of tears on the tile counter by the glasses. Streamers of mucus ran down from her nose. All of that, but you couldn't hear her. "It's okay," I said.

She broke and turned into my chest, sucking great gasping sobs. I held her tight, feeling the wet soak through my shirt. "I'm thirty-nine years old and I can't do anything. What did I do to myself? What did I do? I've got to have him back. Oh, God, I need him."

I knew she wasn't talking about Perry.

I held her until the heaving stopped and then I wrapped some ice in a dish towel and wet it and told her to put it on her face.

After a while we went back out to the dining room and I showed her how to fill in the check and how to maintain the balance on the stub. She was fine with the figures once she knew where to put them.

When the check was written she tried to smile but all the life had gone out of her. "I guess I'll need to do this to pay the bills."

"Yes."

"Excuse me."

She went down the hall toward her bedroom. I sat at the table for a while, then brought the dishes into the kitchen. I washed both glasses and the plate and the saucer, and dried them with paper towels, then I went back out, gathered together the bank records, and went into the living room by the overturned couch. She'd done a fair job of stapling the bottom cloth back on, but she would have a helluva time righting it. I listened, but couldn't hear her moving around. I turned the couch over and put it where I thought it should go and left.

8

Forty minutes later I was back at my office. It was nicer there. I liked the view. I liked the Pinocchio clock. I liked my director's chairs. I arranged the rolodex cards I'd taken from Morton Lang's desk neatly on top of his bank statements. I took out my bankbook and the two thousand dollar check Ellen Lang had written. Her first check. I filled out a deposit slip, endorsed the check, stamped *FOR DEPOSIT ONLY* over my signature, put it all in the bankbook, put everything back in my desk, closed the drawer, and put my brain in neutral, a relatively easy task.

The outer door opened and Clarence Wu stuck his grapefruit head and thin shoulders into the little waiting room. "Is now a bad time?"

Pinocchio's eyes went side to side, side to side.

Clarence came in with his briefcase. Clarence owned Wu's Quality Engraving on the second floor, above the bank. I had stopped in a week ago to see about the business cards and stationery, telling him I wanted a more businesslike image. "I made up the samples," he said. "You had some wonderful ideas."

I didn't remember having any wonderful ideas, but there you go. He put the briefcase on the desk, took some cards out of his shirt pocket, and laid them out on the case like a blackjack dealer. I looked at Pinocchio. Clarence frowned. "You seem preoccupied," he said.

"A small loss of faith in the human condition. It'll pass. Continue."

He turned the case around. "*Voilà.*"

There were four cards, two white, one sort of light blue, and one cream. One of the white ones had a human eye rendered in charcoal in the center with *The Elvis Cole Detective Agency* arced above it and the legend *on your case* beneath. "Businesslike," I said. He beamed. The other white card had my name spelled out in bullet holes with a smoking machine gun

43

underneath. Had I thought of that? The sort-of-blue card had a magnifying glass laid over a deerstalker hat in the upper left corner and the agency's name in script. "Victorian," I said.

"A certain elegance," he nodded.

The cream card had my name centered in modern block letters with the word *detective* beneath it and a .45 Colt Automatic in the upper right quad. I looked at that one the longest. I said, "Get rid of the gun and you've got something."

He looked confused. "No art?"

"No art."

He looked confused some more and then he beamed. "Inspired."

"Yeah. Gimme five hundred with my name and the *detective* and another five hundred that say The Elvis Cole Detective Agency. Put the phone number in the lower right corner and the address in the lower left."

"You want cards for Mr. Pike?"

"Mr. Pike won't use cards."

"Of course." Of course. He nodded and beamed again, and said, "Next Thursday," and left.

Maybe I could find Mort by next Thursday. Maybe I could find him this afternoon. There would be advantages. No more trips to Encino. No more Ellen Lang. No more depression. I would be The Happy Detective. I could call Wu and have him change the card. *Elvis Cole, The Happy Detective, specializing in Happy Cases*. Inspired.

I went down to the deli, bought an Evian water, drank it on the way back up, then went through Mort's finances. As of two weeks ago Monday, Morton Lang had $4265.18 in a passbook savings account. There was one three-year CD in his name worth $5000 that matured in August. I could find no evidence of any stocks or other income-producing investment in either his name, Ellen's name, or in the names of the children. Irregular deposits totaling $5200 had been made into savings over the past six months. During the same period, $2200 was transferred to checking every two weeks. Figure $1600 note and taxes, $800 food, $500 cars, another $200 gardener and pool service, another $500 or $600 because you got three kids and you live in Encino. Forty-five hundred a month to live, next to nothing coming in. *You only start dealing with a Garrett Rice when you're scared*.

I dialed ICM. They gave me to someone in the television department who had known Morton Lang when he worked there fourteen months ago. He had known Mort, but not very well, and if I was looking for representation perhaps he could help me out, ICM being a full-service agency representing artists in all media. I dialed Morton's Lang's clients. Edmund Harris wasn't home. Kaitlin Rosenberg hadn't spoken to Mort in three weeks, and I should tell him the play was going fine. Cynthia Alport hadn't heard from him in over a month and why the hell hadn't he returned her calls? Ric-with-no-K Lloyd hadn't returned Mort's call of six weeks ago because he'd changed agents and would I please pass that along to Mort? Darren Fips had spoken with Mort about two weeks ago because the contracts had never arrived but Mort hadn't gotten back to him and Darren was getting damned pissed. Tracey Cormer's line was busy. Fourteen minutes after I started, the rolodex cards were back in their stack and I still had no useful information. I dialed Kimberly Marsh, thinking maybe she hadn't run off with Mort after all, and got her answering machine. I called Ellen Lang, thinking maybe she'd found something in the phone bills, or, if not, maybe she just needed a kind word. No answer. I called Janet Simon, thinking maybe Ellen Lang had gone over there, or, if not, Janet might know where she had gone. No answer. I got up, opened the glass doors, and went out onto the balcony to stand in the smog.

All dressed up and no place to go.

The phone rang. "Elvis Cole Detective Agency. Top rates paid for top clues."

It was Lou Poitras, this cop I know who works out of North Hollywood Division. "Howzitgoin, Hound Dog?"

"Your wife's here. We're having a Wesson oil party."

There was a grunt. "You workin' for a guy named Morton Lang?"

"His wife. Ellen Lang. How'd you know?"

It got very still in the office. I watched Pinocchio's eyes. Side to side, side to side. "What's going on, Lou?"

"'Bout an hour ago some Chippies found Morton Lang sittin' in his Caddie up near Lancaster. Shot to death."

There was a loud shushing noise and my fingers began to tingle and I had to go to the bathroom. My voice didn't want to work. "The boy?"

Lou didn't say anything.

"Lou?"

"What boy?" he said.

9

I parked in the little lot they have next to the North Hollywood
Police Department headquarters and went around front to this
big linoleum-floored room. There were hardwood benches on
two of the walls, a couple of Coke and candy machines,
and a bulletin board. A poster on the bulletin board said
POLICE FUND RAISER—A NIGHT OF BOXING ENTERTAINMENT—
COPS VERSUS FIREMEN! SPECIAL EXHIBITION BOUT: BULLDOG
PARKER AND MUSTAFA HAMSHO. Beside the poster a skinny
white kid with stringy hair spoke softly into a pay phone. He
leaned against the wall with one foot back on a toe, his heel
nervously rocking.

I went around two Chicano men in Caterpillar hats with
green jackets and dirty broken work shoes and through a
reinforced door, up one flight of stairs, and down a short hall
into the detectives' squad room. Also known as Xanadu.

The detectives live in a long gray room with all the desks
against the north wall and three little offices at the far end.
Across from the desks are a shower, a locker room, and a
holding cell. *Days of Our Lives* was going on the locker room
TV. Two brown hands were sticking out through the holding
cell bars. They looked tired. Poitras' office was the first of the
three at the far end.

Lou Poitras has a face like a frying pan and a back as wide as
a Coupe de Ville. His arms are so swollen from the weights he
pumps they look like fourteen pound hams squeezed into his
sleeves. He has a scar breaking the hairline above his left eye
where a guy who should've known better got silly and laid a
jack handle. It lent character. Poitras was leaning back behind
his desk as I walked in, kielbasa fingers laced over his belly.
Even reclined, he took up most of the room.

He said, "You didn't bring that sonofabitch Pike, did you?"

"I'm fine, Lou. And you?"

Simms was sitting in a hard chair in front of Lou's desk.
There was another chair against the wall, but it was stacked

high with files and folders. First come, first served. Simms wore street clothes: blue jeans and a faded khaki safari shirt with an ink stain on the pocket and tread-worn Converse All Stars. "You get promoted?" I said.

"Day off."

Lou said, "Forget that. Gimme the kid's picture."

I handed him the little school picture of gap-toothed Perry Lang. He yelled, "Penny!" and flipped the photo over to read the back, jaw working.

Penny came in. There was a lot of dusty red hair and tanned skin. She had to be six feet tall. "Sheena, right?" I said. She ignored me. Lou gave her the little picture. "Color-copy this, front and back, and have a set phoned up to McGill in Lancaster right away." When she left, Simms looked after her. So did I.

"She's new," I said.

Simms smiled. "Uh-huh."

Poitras looked sour. "You two try to control your glands."

"You get anything new on the cause of death?" I said.

"I called the States up by Lancaster after we talked. They say four shots, close range. ME's out there now."

"What about the boy?"

"McGill up there, he's okay. McGill said there was nothing in the Caddie to indicate the boy was in the car when his old man got it. They put some people out to search the roadside, but it's gonna be a while before we hear."

"Okay."

Poitras leaned forward and looked at me, his forehead wrinkling up like a street map of Bangkok. "Simms says you're in on this."

I started from the beginning, telling them how Ellen Lang had hired me and why. I told them about Kimberly Marsh and said her address twice so Lou could write it down, and then about Garrett Rice and what Patricia Kyle had given me as background information. I told them what I knew about Mort from Kansas and his failing business and his heavy monthly note and his midlife crisis. It didn't take long. Somewhere in there Simms went out and came back with three coffees. Mine was cold. When I finished, Lou said, "All right. You come up with any angles on Lang?"

"No."

"Enemies?"

"No."

"How about connections?"

"Unh-uh."

Simms liked that. "Sounds like you been busting your ass."

Lou drummed his fingers on the desk. It sounded like firecrackers going off. I'd once seen Lou Poitras dead-lift the front end of a '69 Volkswagen Bug. "Simms said somebody went through their house last night."

"Simms knows what I know. The wife figures the husband did it. I don't figure it that way, but it's possible. I think somebody went in there looking for something."

Simms cracked a knuckle. "You think the wife's holding out?"

"No."

Lou said, "What would somebody want?"

"I got no idea."

A tall thin man in a dark gray three-piece suit walked in and gave me the checkout. He had a tight puckered face that made me think of Raid Ant & Roach Killer. He said, "This asshole works with Joe Pike?"

I smiled at Poitras. "You two rehearse this?"

Lou said, "Wait outside, Hound Dog."

Simms got up so the new guy could sit down, and Poitras shut the door behind me. It made me feel left out. The squad room was empty. Tail end of the lunch hour, all the dicks were still out scoring half-price meals. The big redhead came back with a sheaf of color copies and stopped when she saw the closed door. I was sitting behind one of the desks with my feet up, reading a *Daily Variety*. Half the desks on the floor sported show business trade papers. One of the desks even had *American Cinematographer*. These cops. She looked at me. I said, "Conference with Washington. Very hush-hush." Then I wiggled my eyebrows. She stared at me a half a heartbeat longer and walked away.

I got up and wandered into the locker room for more coffee. An older cop with a bad toup and lots of gold around his neck was watching *Wheel of Fortune*. The place smelled like a ripe jock but he didn't seem to mind. I poured two cups and brought one out to the holding cell but it was empty.

I was standing by myself in the middle of the squad room with a cup of coffee in each hand when Poitras' door opened and Simms looked out. "I always take two," I said. "One for me. One for my ego."

"Inside. Bring a chair."

I put the coffees down, took a chair from beside one of the squad desks, and went in. Lou said, "Elvis, this is Lieutenant Baishe. He took over from Gianelli a couple months ago."

Baishe said, "He doesn't need my pedigree."

I looked at him.

Baishe was leaning into the corner behind Poitras' desk, looking at me like he'd had to scrape me off the bottom of his shoe. Without waiting he went on, "I know about you. Big deal in the Army, security guard at a couple of studios, sucking around town with that bastard Joe Pike. They say you think you're tough. They say you think you're cute. They also say you're pretty good. Okay. Here's what we've got. The highway patrol up by Lancaster finds Morton Lang shot to death behind the wheel of his car, an '82 Cadillac Seville. He's got three in the chest and one in the temple, close range." Baishe touched his forehead. Wasn't much hair there to get in the way. "No shell casings in the car, but the people up there say it looks like a 9mm. There's blood, but not a whole lot, and some peculiar lividity patterns so maybe he wasn't popped there in his car. Maybe he got it somewhere else and he was put there. No sign of the kid. Car's been wiped clean. Robbery's out. He's still got his wallet and the credit cards and forty-six bucks and his watch. Keys are in the ignition. You got all that?"

"I'm watching your lips, yes, sir."

Baishe looked at me, then at Lou. Lou said, "Cole has a brain imbalance, Lieutenant."

Baishe unwrapped his arms, came out of the corner, leaned on Poitras' desk and looked at me. He looked like a Daddy Longlegs. "Don't fuck with me, boy."

I pretended to be intimidated. After a bit he said, "How do you fit into this?"

I went through it again. Baishe said, "How long have you known the wife?"

"Since yesterday."

"You sure it hasn't been longer?"

I looked from Baishe to Poitras to Simms and back to Baishe. Poitras and Simms were looking at Baishe, too. I said, "Come off it, Baishe. You got nothing."

"Maybe we dig into this we see a bigger connection. Maybe you two are pretty good friends, so good you decide to get rid of her old man. Maybe you rig the whole act and you pull the trigger. Setup City."

"Setup City?" I looked at Poitras. His mouth was open. Simms was staring at a spot somewhere out around the orbit of Pluto. I looked back at Baishe with what we in the trade call "disbelief." He was looking at me with what we in the trade call "distaste."

I said, "*The Postman Always Rings Twice*, right? 1938?"

"Keep it up," Baishe said.

"That's a real good thought, Lieutenant," Lou said, "only Cole here is known to me personally. He's a good dick." I expected Baishe to laugh maniacally. *Only the Shadow knooowwzz.* I was getting tired and just a little bit cranky. I said, "Is that it?"

Baishe said, "We'll tell you when that's it."

I stood up. "Screw that. I didn't come down here so you guys could work out. You got any other questions, book me or call my lawyer."

Baishe went purple and started around the desk. Lou stood up, just happening to block his way. "Lieutenant, could I talk to you a sec? Outside."

Baishe glared at me. "Have your ass in that chair when I get back, peep."

"Peep. You're really up on the patois, aren't you?"

Baishe's jaw knotted but they went out. I glared at Simms. He looked bored. I glared at Lou's desk. Behind the desk on a gray metal file cabinet were pictures of a pretty brunette and three children and a three bedroom ranch-style home in Chatsworth. One shot showed a couple of comfortable lawn chairs in the backyard beneath a poplar tree, just right for drinking a beer and listening to a ball game while kids played in the backyard. There was a picture of Lou doing just that. I had taken the picture.

Lou came back in alone. "He expects your continued cooperation."

Simms laughed softly.

I said, "You notify the wife yet?"

"Not home. We got a car there waiting for her." I could see a couple of street monsters parked in her drive, scratching their balls and waiting for a fadeaway woman in a light green Subaru wagon with two little girls in the back. Sensitive guys. Guys like Baishe. *Sorry, lady, your old man caught four and he's history.* I said, "Maybe I'd better do it."

Lou shrugged. "You sure you want to?"

"You bet, Lou. Nothing I want more than to sit down with this woman and give her the news her husband's dead and her nine-year-old son is missing. Maybe I'll even break the word to the two little girls, too, for the capper."

"Take it easy."

"I'm taking it easy," I said. Simms had stopped smiling.

The redhead came back in with the color copies and the little picture. She put the copies on Lou's desk and the little picture on top of the copies. She looked at me. "What, no cracks?"

"They broke my spirit."

She smiled nicely. "Penny Brotman. Studio City." And swayed away. Simms said, "Sonofabitch."

I took the little picture and put it in my pocket. I sneered at Simms, then gave Lou a flat look. "If we're finished, I want to get out of here."

He looked at his hands. "I didn't know he was gonna pull that, Hound Dog. I'm sorry."

"Yeah."

I went back along the short hall, down the flight of stairs and out through the reinforced door. Nothing had changed. The Chicano guys still stood by the front desk, the white kid still murmured into the phone. People came in and went out. A fat woman bought a Coke; it wasn't a diet drink. A black cop with heavy arms led a man past the desk and through swinging doors. The man's fragile wrists were cuffed. There were knots in my trapezius muscles and in my latissimus dorsi and my head throbbed. I went up behind the kid on the phone and stood very close. He looked at me. Then he murmured something into the phone, hung up, and sat on one of the wooden benches with his head in his hands. I dialed Janet Simon and let it ring. On the thirty-second buzz she answered, breathless. I said, "Does Ellen Lang have any close relatives nearby? Sister or mother or something like that?"

"No. No, Ellen doesn't have any relatives that I know of. She's an only child. I think there could be an aunt back in Kansas, but her parents are dead. Why?"

"Can you meet me at her house in twenty minutes?"

There was a long pause. "What is it?"

I told her. I had to stop once because she was crying. When I was through I said, "I'm on my way," then I hung up. I stood with my hand on the phone for several seconds, breathing deeply, in through the nose, out through the mouth, making my body relax. After a while, I went over to the kid on the bench, said I was sorry, and put a quarter on the bench beside him. It was shaping up as a helluva day.

10

At twenty minutes before three I pulled into Ellen Lang's
drive and parked behind Janet Simon's Mustang. Ellen's
Subaru wasn't there. I went to the front door and knocked.
Out on the street, cars driven by moms went past, each
carrying kids home from school or off to soccer practice. It was
that time of the day. Pretty soon Ellen Lang would turn in with
her two girls. She'd see the Corvette and the Mustang and her
eyes would get nervous.

I knocked again, and Janet Simon opened the door. Her hair
was pulled back and large purple sunglasses sat on top of her
head. Every woman in Encino wears large purple sunglasses.
It's *de rigueur*. She held a tall glass filled with amber liquid and
ice. More ice than liquid. She said, "Well, well. The private
dick." It wasn't her first drink.

Ellen Lang had made the house spotless for Mort's return.
Everything was back in its place, everything was clean. The
effort had been enormous. Janet Simon brought her drink to
the couch and sat. The ashtray beside her had four butts in it. I
said, "You know when she'll get home?"

Janet Simon fished in her pack for a fresh cigarette, lit it, and
blew out a heavy volume of smoke. Maybe she hadn't heard
me. Maybe I'd spoken Russian without realizing it and had
confused her.

"In a while. Does it matter?" She took some of the drink.

"How many of those have you had?"

"Don't get snippy. This is only my second. Do you want
one?"

"I'll stay straight. Ellen might appreciate coherence from
the person telling her that her husband is dead."

She looked at me over the top of the glass, then took some of
the cigarette. She said, "I'm upset. This is very hard for me."

"Yeah. Because you loved Mort so much."

"You bastard."

The leaders on either side of my neck were as tight as

54

bowstrings. My head throbbed. I went out to the kitchen, cracked ice into a glass, and filled it with water. I drank it, then went back into the living room. Her eyes were red. "I'm sorry I said that," I said. "I've done this before, and I know what it's going to be like, so my guts are in knots. Part of me wants to be up in Lancaster trying to get something on the boy, but I've got to do this first. The rest of me is pissed because the cops had me in so an asshole named Baishe could give me a hard time and feel tough. He did, it wasn't fun, and I feel lousy. I shouldn't have taken it out on you."

She listened to all that, then quietly said, "She always runs a couple of errands after she picks up the girls. They might go to Baskin-Robbins."

"Okay." I sat down in the big chair opposite the couch. She kept looking at me. She brought the cigarette to her mouth, inhaled, paused, exhaled. I got up and opened the front door to air the place out.

She said, "You don't like me, do you?"

"I think you're swell."

"You think I ride Ellen too hard."

I didn't say anything. From where I was sitting I could see the street and the drive through the big front window. And Janet Simon.

She said, "What the hell do you know," then finished off her drink and went into the dining room. I heard glass against glass, then she came back in and stood at the hearth, staring out the window.

I said, "She's your friend, but you don't show her any respect. You treat her like she's backward and you're ashamed of it, like you've got some sort of paradigm for modern womanhood and it burns your ass that she doesn't fit it. So you put her down. Maybe if you put her down enough, what she wants will change and she'll begin to fit the paradigm."

"My. Don't we have me figured out."

"I read *Cosmo* when I'm on stakeout."

She took a long sip of the drink, set it down on the mantel, crossed her arms, and leaned against the wall to stare at me. "What shit."

I shrugged.

"Ellen and I have been friends since our kids were in nursery. I'm the one she cries to. I'm the one who holds her when she breaks down in the middle of the morning. I'm the only goddamned friend she has." More cigarette, more drink.

"You haven't seen the bags under her eyes from the sleepless nights or heard the horror stories."

"And you have. I respect that."

"All right."

"The problem is that you're shoving too hard. Ellen has to move at her own rate, not yours. I'm not talking about where you want to go. I agree with that. I'm talking about how you get there. Your method. I think it weakens the one you're hoping to strengthen."

She raised an eyebrow. "My. Aren't we sensitive. Aren't we caring."

"Don't forget brave and handsome."

She cupped her hands around her upper arms the way you do when you're standing in a draft, the way Ellen Lang often did.

"Maybe you're too close," I said. "Maybe you're so close and hurting so much you can only know how you'd react and that isn't necessarily the way Ellen should react. You're not Ellen."

"Perhaps I used to be."

I shook my head. "You were never Ellen Lang."

She stared at me a little longer, then shrugged. "I was alone, and it was rough. I was taken advantage of. Even my women friends deserted me. Their husbands were business friends of Stan's. They went with the money."

"But you'll stick with Ellen."

"I'll help any way I can."

"It must've been worse than rough."

She nodded, barely moving.

"You should've called me," I said. "I'm in the book."

She put her eyes on mine and left them there. "Yes. Maybe I should have." She bent down to stub out her cigarette in a little ceramic ashtray one of the kids made in school. She was wearing tight jeans and a clinging brown top that was cut just above the beltline and open-toed strap sandals with a medium heel. When she bent over, the top pulled up to show tanned skin and the ridge of her spine. A good looking woman. She picked up the drink, drained half the glass, and took a deep breath. It was a lot of booze. "What was all that crap you gave Ellen about yoga and karate and Vietnam?"

"You guys tell each other everything?"

"Friends havta stick together." You could hear the booze in her voice. "You look too young for Vietnam."

"I looked old when I got back."

She smiled. You could see the booze in her smile, too. "Peter Pan. You told Ellen you wanted to be Peter Pan."

"Unh-hunh."

"That's crap. Stay a little boy forever."

"It's not age. Childhood, maybe. All the good things are in childhood. Innocence. Loyalty. Truth. You're eighteen years old. You're sitting in a rice paddy. Most guys give it up. I decided eighteen was too young to be old. I work at maintaining myself."

"So at thirty-five, you're still eighteen."

"Fourteen. Fourteen's my ideal age."

The left corner of her mouth ticked. "Stan," she said, face soft. "Stan gave it up. But he doesn't have Vietnam to blame it on."

"There are different kinds of war."

"Of course."

I didn't say anything. She was thinking. When she finished, she said, "How'd you get a name like Elvis? You were born before anyone knew who Elvis Presley was."

"My name was Phillip James Cole until I was six years old. Then my mother saw The King in concert. She changed my name to Elvis the next afternoon."

"Legally?"

"Legally."

"Oh, God. And you've never changed it back?"

"It's what she named me."

Janet Simon shook her head, putting her eyes back on mine. With her face relaxed and the booze taking the edge off, she seemed stronger. Sexier. She crossed her ankles and rocked. She took more of the drink. "Have you ever been shot?"

"I caught some frag in the war."

"Did it hurt?"

"At first it feels like you've been slapped, then it starts to burn and the muscle tightens up. With me, it wasn't too bad so I could take it. Other guys who had it worse, it was worse."

"So it probably hurt Mort."

"If the head shot was first, he didn't feel a thing. If not, he hurt a lot."

She nodded, then put the glass back on the mantel. It was empty except for the ice. "If Ellen asks, please don't tell her that."

"I wouldn't."

"I forgot. Sensitive and caring."

" 'Prove yourself brave, truthful, and unselfish, and someday you will be a real boy.' The Blue Fairy said that. In *Pinocchio.*"

She looked at me a very long time, then her eyes got red and she turned toward the window. Past her, I could see three little girls walking north down the middle of the street, one of them skipping. They were laughing, but we were too far away to hear them. The house was quiet. "Ellen's never home before four," she whispered.

It was five minutes until three.

"Did you hear me?" Still facing the window.

"Yes."

Janet Simon began to shiver, then tremble, then cry. I went over to her and let her sob into me like Ellen Lang had done. This time I got an erection. I tried to ease away but she pressed against me. Then her head came up and her mouth found me and that was that.

She squeezed hard and bruised my lips with her teeth and bit me. She was as lithe and strong as she looked. I lifted her away from the hearth and the big window and put her on the floor. She pulled off her clothes while I closed and locked the door. Her body was lean and firm and tan with smallish breasts and definition to her abdominals with nice ribs.

She came twice before I did. She bit my shoulders and scratched me and said "Yes" a lot. When it ended we lay on our backs, wet and breathing hard, staring at the ceiling. She got up without a word, picked up her clothes, and disappeared down the hall. After a moment I heard water running.

I dressed and went into the kitchen for a glass of water. When I went back out to the living room, Janet Simon was there. "Well," she said.

"Well," I said.

The phone rang. While Janet answered it, I took a peek out the big window. No light green Subaru. No Ellen Lang. No boys on bicycles or little girls in the middle of the street. Everything was on this side of the door.

Janet hung up and said, "That was the girls. They're still at school. Ellen never picked them up."

My watch showed three twenty-two.

"What time does school let out?"

"Two forty-five." She looked uneasy. "The girls want me to go get them."

"Can you drive?"

She gave me a small tight smile without a lot of humor in it. "I've been sobered."

I nodded. "I'll stay here for Ellen."

"What do I say to them about Mort?"

"Don't say anything. We wait for their mother for that."

"But she didn't pick them up."

"She's got a lot on her mind."

We stood there for a while, neither moving toward the other. Then Janet nodded and left. I went back to the chair and drank my water. Then I got up and went back to the big window and watched the drive. Ellen Lang didn't turn in.

11

Janet Simon was back with the two girls in less than forty minutes. The older one came in first, sullen and red-eyed, and went straight back to her room, slamming her door. Janet and the younger one came in together. Janet gave a little shake of her head, meaning that she hadn't told them anything. She said, "Did Ellen call?"

"Nope."

The younger one dropped her books on the long table they have in the entry, then ran past me to the TV, turned it on, and sat on the floor about two feet from the screen. *3-2-1 Contact* was starting. It was the episode about directions and map-making. I'd seen it before. "My name's Elvis. What's yours?"

"Carrie."

She inched closer to the set. I guess I was making too much noise.

Janet Simon sat on the hearth, as far from me as she could get and still be in the room. I went over and sat by her. She didn't look up. I went back to the couch. Here were these two children and their father was dead and here were we, faking it, holding back The Big News.

We watched *3-2-1-Contact* until five, then switched channels for *Masters of the Universe* until five-thirty, then switched again for *Leave It to Beaver*. It was the one where Eddie Haskell talks Wally into buying a watch so Wally can make like he stole it to get in solid with some tough kids. I'd seen that one before, too. Halfway through *Leave It to Beaver*, Janet went back to see the older girl, Cindy. I heard a door close, then muffled screaming, Cindy shrieking that they were both crazy and she hated them. She hated him and she hated her mother and she wished she lived in Africa. Carrie inched closer to the television. I said, "Hey, you hungry?"

She shook her head. Even with the lousy angle I had I could see her eyes swelling.

"Listen, you think you could help me find something? It's your kitchen, right? You know where things are." She turned up the volume. I said, "I could really go for a donkeyburger. Or the hairball soup. Or the breast of puppy." She looked at me. "Or the stuffed toad au gratin with duck fuzz." She giggled and said, "I can make soup."

In the kitchen, we couldn't hear Cindy. The kid got a three-quart pot from beneath the sink, a large spoon from the drawer beside the refrigerator, a glass measuring bowl, and a packet of Lipton chicken noodle soup mix. She put the pot on the stove, filled the measuring bowl with three cups of water, then put the water in the pot. She covered it and put the heat on high. She put the packet of soup mix on the counter with the spoon beside it and the measuring bowl in the sink. "We have to wait for the water to boil," she said.

"Okay."

We stood there a while, sneaking glances at each other. Finally she couldn't stand it anymore. "You got a gun?"

"Yeah."

"Can I see it?"

"It's in the car. I don't carry it when I don't have to. It weighs a lot."

"What if you get jumped?"

I looked over my shoulder. "Here in the house?"

She said, "You see *Bateman and Evans?*"

"What's that?"

"This TV show. You know, *Bateman and Evans*. It used to be on Wednesday nights."

"No."

"Why not?"

"I don't watch much nighttime TV."

"Why not?"

"I think it promotes cancer."

"You're silly."

"I guess."

She said, "My daddy used to represent Evans. I met him once. He was a detective and he always carried a gun."

"You see, if I carried my gun I'd probably be on television."

"Well, you have to be an actor, too." Wouldn't know it from watching most of those guys.

"I got to meet Lee Majors that time, too, and this other time my daddy got this actor a job on *Knightrider* and brought me over to Universal and David Hasselhoff was standing there and I got to meet him, too."

"Unh-huh."

"Are you going to find my daddy?"

Something long and thin and cold went in just below my stomach and up into my chest. "Soup smells good," I said.

She said, "I bet I know where he is."

I nodded. "You want a bowl or a cup?" Some big-time private cop, you want a bowl or a cup?

She said, "We've got soup cups in that cabinet there. Blue ones. If I tell you, you can't say I told you, okay? Cause nobody knows this but me and Daddy and he wouldn't like it if I said, okay?"

"Okay." My voice was hoarse.

"Wait here."

She ran out of the kitchen, then ran back thirty seconds later with a thick green photo album. It was the older kind, with heavy cardboard covers and black felt paper and the pictures held to the pages by little corner tabs. On the front of the album it said, *"Home."*

On the first page there were faded sepia pictures dated June 1947 of a man and a woman and a baby. Mort. Adult faces changed or disappeared, but the child's face grew. Mort as a toddler. Mort riding his bike. Mort and a skinny, long-tongued dog emerging from an infinite field of Kansas wheat.

"My momma made this book up and gave it to my daddy when they moved out here. You see, these are all of my daddy back in Elverton, that's where Daddy and Momma are from in Kansas. It's got pictures of Gramma and Grampa and their house and Daddy in school and this dog my daddy had named Teddy and this girl named Joline Price that Momma used to tease Daddy about and all this stuff."

She flipped the pages for me, taking me on a guided tour of Morton Lang's life. She would point. I would nod. Isn't that nice? Mort in grade school. Mort at the paint store in a clerk's apron. Mort and three buddies sitting around a bedroom, laughing. Crew cuts one year, duck's ass pompadours the next. Mort in a '58 Dodge. Mort looking good and strong and proud. Mort in a play. Mort and Ellen. Their prom. She was pretty. Very pretty. Isn't that nice?

Carrie was saying, "I got up real late to go to the bathroom one night and Daddy was sitting in the living room. He was looking at this book and he was crying, looking at the pictures and crying and I started crying, too, so we looked at the book together and he said, 'I don't know what any of this is.' I said, 'That's Gramma and Grampa, that's Teddy, that's Joline Price.' He always says how much he hated Kansas and how he doesn't even want to go back there to visit, but I'll bet that's where he went. I bet if you went back to Elverton, Kansas, and looked you could find him and make him come home."

I said, "I think the soup's ready."

I ladled out the soup into two blue mugs while she got two spoons and two napkins. Out in the dining room you couldn't hear Cindy anymore. We sat down and ate, Carrie with the book beside her on the table. Her last meal believing her daddy was alive, could walk in the door and make it better. I got up and found the dark stuff Janet Simon had been drinking and brought it back to the table. Carrie's nose wrinkled. "Yuck."

Yeah, kid. After a while Janet came out of the back of the house and asked to see me in the kitchen.

When we were in there she stood well away from me. "It's after six, Elvis. Ellen wouldn't stay out like this." Her face was white.

"Okay," I said, feeling cold. I picked up the phone and called Lou Poitras.

12

I told Poitras that I had been at Ellen Lang's since I'd left him earlier that day and that she hadn't come home. I told him that Ellen had failed to pick up her children from school and that there had been no messages. I told him I was worried. There was a long pause on his end, then some noise I couldn't make out, and then he asked questions. I gave him Ellen Lang's description and the make and model of her car. Janet Simon knew the license number, KLX774. He told me to stay put and hung up. I think I caught him going home to dinner.

Janet said, "What do we do?"

"Cops are on the way. Is there someplace we can put the kids so they don't have to hear it?"

There was. Mrs. Martinson's, across the street. While Janet walked the girls over—Carrie scared and Cindy sullen—I found directions for a Toshiba automatic coffee maker and fresh Vienna cinnamon beans in the freezer and put on a pot. Then I went out to the Corvette, took the Dan Wesson out of the glove box, put it on, and got out a pale blue cotton jacket I keep in the trunk to wear over it. Made me feel like I was doing something. Maybe I should go across to Mrs. Martinson's and show the Dan Wesson to Carrie. Maybe it would make her feel like I was doing something, too.

I stood out on the drive until Janet came back across and the western sky began to pinken and the first chill of the night settled through Encino.

"Are you just going to stand here?" Janet said.

"For a while. I made coffee."

She looked like she wanted to say something, then turned and went into the house.

Poitras pulled up at twenty minutes to eight. It was dark enough for the first wave of jasmine to be filtering into the air and for drivers to begin using their headlamps. Poitras had brought an older dick with him, gray-haired and crew cut with a face he'd left out of doors a couple centuries too long, named

Griggs. When he saw me, Griggs feigned surprise and said, "You still got a license?"

Griggs is a scream.

We managed to get Poitras through the door and into the living room without tearing out a wall. After we were settled with coffee and some little biscuits Janet found, I went through it all again, from when I left Poitras earlier in the afternoon until now. There wasn't much to tell. Poitras took out a little pad and a gold Cross pen and gave them to Janet and asked her to list all the places Ellen frequented: where she got her hair done, where she did the marketing, where she bought clothes, that kind of thing. Janet took the pad and pen into the dining room. After she was gone Lou said, "This guy, Lang, he was into something."

I nodded. "Unh-huh."

Poitras gave me empty cop eyes. "And you got no idea what."

"Mere unfounded speculations."

Griggs grunted. "Our favorite kind."

"What?" Poitras said.

"Lang was going broke. He needed five grand a month to keep this place going but in the last eleven months he's only made fifty-two hundred. His savings were depleted. He might've tried going to a bank, but a bank wouldn't let him refinance the house because he was effectively unemployed. He could've gone to someone less reputable for some carry-over cash and been unable to pay the vig."

Poitras thought about it. "You welch on ten, fifteen grand, they maybe only break you up. They don't put four in you."

I shrugged. "I told you. Speculation."

Poitras was still thinking. "Not anyone sane, at any rate." He looked at Griggs and Griggs got up and went into the kitchen to use the phone.

I said, "Did you guys follow up on Kimberly Marsh?"

"We rolled by and had the manager let us in. Looks like she took off. But it looks like she's coming back, too. Talked to some fat guy there with a little dog. He said you told him you were Johnny Staccato. Shit."

Griggs came back in and sat down.

"How about Rice?"

"Couldn't reach him. Left word at his studio and a card on his front stoop."

Griggs spread his mouth in a strictured smile. "Yeah. We're hell with those calling cards."

Lou shrugged. "You do what you can."

Griggs said, "Hey, you happen to find out where Lang bought his gas?"

"Missed that, somehow."

"Yeah, be a hot shot. That's how the feds busted Carlo "The Hammer" Peritini, mouthing off to the guy at the Exxon station pumped his gas. Peritini, shit, all his millions, head of a whole goddamned family, he had to be a big shot to the guy who pumped his gas, told him everything."

Poitras and I were staring at him. Griggs spread his hands. "That's how they got The Hammer."

"You'll do well with Baishe," I said.

"Up yours."

Janet Simon came back and handed Poitras the note pad. "This is all I can think of."

There were nine places listed, some under headings. *Hair: Lolly's* on Ventura at Balboa. *Food: Gelson's* at Ventura & Hayvenhurst, *Ralph's* on Ventura (Encino). *Fashion Square*, Sherman Oaks. *Saks*, Woodland Hills. *Books: Scene of the Crime* in Sherman Oaks. Like that.

I would've thought her writing would be strong and measured and connected, only it wasn't. She wrote in a small, uneven hand in lines that curved up. She wrote the way I thought Ellen Lang would write, only Ellen Lang didn't write that way. Ellen wrote the way I had thought Janet Simon would write.

Griggs took the pad into the kitchen to make another phone call. When he came out again he had a fresh cup of coffee and another plate of the biscuits.

Poitras asked Janet to run through it from her point of view, from the last time she'd seen Ellen Lang. He watched her as she did, with that flat, impassive face of his that says maybe the sun comes up tomorrow, maybe not, maybe he'll hit the Pick Six at Santa Anita for two mil, maybe not. Janet's hand was resting on the arm of the sofa by me. I patted it. She pulled away. Ah, romance.

Poitras said, "You and Mrs. Lang seem to be pretty close."

Janet nodded. "She's my best friend."

"So if she's gonna tell anybody anything, it's going to be you."

"I guess. Yes. It would be me."

"A guy doesn't get it in the chest for no reason."

I sat forward. "Hey."

Poitras' eyes shifted to me. There was a little bit of a smile there, but maybe not. "I'm just asking her to think back and think hard."

"I know what you're asking her and I don't like the way you were asking it."

Janet Simon snapped, "I don't need you to defend me," then went eye-to-eye with Poitras. "What is it you mean, Sergeant?"

Poitras said, "It doesn't have to be right now, but I'd just like you to see if you can remember anything Mrs. Lang or Mr. Lang might've said, that's all. Okay?"

Janet said, "Of course," but she was a little stiff when she said it.

The phone rang. Janet got up and went into the kitchen to answer it. Griggs grinned at me. "She's a fine looking woman," he said.

"There's something between your teeth."

He tried to laugh it off but when he looked away I could tell he was sucking at his teeth.

Janet came out a moment later and looked at Poitras. "It's for you."

He went into the kitchen, stayed about a minute, then came out. Same frying-pan blank face. "They found her car," he said to me. "You wanna come?"

I nodded.

Janet stood very still, then said, "I'd better pack for the girls. They can sleep at my place until she's back." She went out of the living room and down the hall without looking at us. Griggs stayed at the house while I rode over with Poitras.

Ellen Lang's light green Subaru wagon KLX774 was under a streetlamp at Ralph's supermarket on Ventura in Encino, the third place on Janet Simon's list. Ralph's had closed at eight-thirty, so the lot was empty except for the Subaru, a radio car, and a sun-faded Galaxy 500 belonging to the night watchman, an old geez who stood out on the tarmac talking cop-shop with the uniforms. We pulled up to them and got out, Poitras flashing his shield, making sure the watchman saw it.

Poitras said, "You got any idea how long it's been here?"

The old man jerked his head once, to the side. His white hair looked purple in the streetlight. So did my jacket and so did Poitras' white Hathaway shirt. Twenty feet above us the

lamp buzzed like an angry firefly. "It's been here since before I
come on," he said.

"Okay. You got the manager's number?"

The old guy jerked his head toward the store. "It's inside."

"Get it. Call him and have him come out here. I wanna talk
to his bag boys and stock clerks and anyone else who might've
been out here."

The old guy looked scared he was getting cut out of the
action. "What's up, Sarge?"

"Go call."

The old man frowned but nodded his head and gimped
away. Walter Brennan. Out on Ventura, traffic had slowed to a
crawl, drivers looking our way to see what was going on. I
walked over to the car. Four bags of groceries were lined up on
the back deck behind the rear seat. She'd done her shopping,
then come back, and was probably approached while she
loaded the bags. "Okay to try the door?"

Poitras said yeah. One of the uniforms drifted over and
stood behind me. Young guy, muscled arms, Tom Selleck
moustache. I pulled on the rear door handle and it lifted. The
tailgate swung out and me and the uniform stepped back.

"Bad milk," Poitras said. He walked over, dug through the
bags. Wilted lettuce. Wrinkled strawberries. A burst tomato.
It gets hot in a sealed car on a sunny afternoon in Los Angeles.
Hot enough to kill someone. Poitras finally came out with an
opened pint of skim milk, like she'd had a little, just a sip while
she was shopping, then sealed it up again to bring it home. I
said, "Probably been here since early afternoon. Could've
been here since I was with you."

Poitras grunted. He opened the driver's side door and stuck
his head in. When he leaned against the little car, it settled on
its springs. Then he dropped down into a push-up position on
the ground. He got up, went to the tail end of the car, and
dropped down again. This time he reached under the car and
came out with a pair of white and lavender glasses. The left
temple was broken.

"Ellen Lang's," I said.

Poitras nodded and watched the cars go by on Ventura. He
set the glasses on the Subaru's hood, leaned against the fender,
and stared at me, eyes empty. The streetlamp was suddenly
much louder. "Old Mort," Poitras said slowly, "he was into
something all right."

13

Later, Poitras had one of the uniforms drive me back to Ellen Lang's for my car. Janet Simon was sitting on the ottoman when I walked in, the little blue ashtray beside her full and the living room cloudy with smoke. I didn't make any cracks. She said, "Well?"

"Looks like someone grabbed her."

She nodded as if it were unimportant and stood up. There were two small suitcases by the entry, one light blue, the other tan. She said, "I'd better get the girls."

"Are you sorry it happened between us?"

She went ashen around her lips as if she were very angry. Maybe she was. As if in opening herself she had violated a promise she held very dear. Maybe she had. "No," she said. "Of course not."

I nodded. "Want some help with the girls?"

"No."

"Maybe some company, when you tell them?"

"No. I'm sorry, but no. Do you see?" She was a pale, creamy coffee color beneath her tan, her lips and nostrils and temples touched with blue. She wasn't making eye contact. She was at a place like Ellen Lang, where putting your eyes to someone else's cost too much, only Janet Simon wasn't used to it.

"Sure," I said. "You've got my number."

She nodded, once, looking down at her cigarette.

I left.

I stopped at a Westward Ho market to pick up two six-packs of Falstaff, the best cheap beer around, and went home and put George Thorogood on loud and drank beer with the cat and thought about things. Ellen Lang and Janet Simon. They weren't so very different. Maybe Janet Simon *had* been Ellen Lang. Maybe Ellen Lang would one day be Janet Simon. *If* she were still alive. I drank more beer, and cranked the speakers up to distortion when George got to *Bad to the Bone*. I listen to that song, I always feel tough. I drank more beer. At some point very late that night I became a flying monkey, one of thousands chasing Morton Lang toward the Emerald City.

The next morning I hurt, but it was manageable. The cat was on the floor beside me, belly up. "Have something ready when I get back, okay?" He ignored me. I stripped down to my shorts, went out onto the deck, and went from the twelve sun salutes to the tae kwan do. I took air in deep, using my stomach muscles, saturating my blood with oxygen until my ears rang. I pushed hard, spinning through low space to mid space to high space, using the big muscles in my back and chest and legs the way I'd been taught, working to burn out the Bad Things and finding a proof of it in the pain singing in my muscles.

After I shaved and showered and dressed I made soft-boiled eggs and raisin muffins and sliced bananas. While I ate them I made four sandwiches, brewed a pot of coffee, and poured it into the big thermos. I took out a six-pack of RC 100, two Budweisers, and a jar of jalapeño-stuffed olives. I put all that in a double-strength paper bag on top of a couple books by Elmore Leonard, *Hombre* and *Valdez Is Coming*. I took my clip-on holster out of the closet, put the Dan Wesson in it, and selected a jacket to go with my khaki Meronas. By eight-twenty I was staking out Kimberly Marsh's apartment. I was cranky. If the fat guy brought his dog out today, maybe I'd shoot it. They'd probably arrest John Cassavetes, and wouldn't Gena Rowlands be surprised.

There were still letters in Kimberly Marsh's mail drop and still bulk-rate flyers in the big open bin. I walked back past the banana trees to number 4 and let myself in. The rest of the petals had fallen from the dead daisies. A guy named Sid had left a message on the machine saying they'd met at Marion's and how much he'd like to get together with her because his planets were rising in the lower quadrant and if she was a happening babe she'd give him a buzz. I let myself out, closed the door, and locked it. The walkway continued past number 4, turning right to pass a laundry room, then down one flight of stairs to the underground parking. I went down and found one other stair at the opposite side of the garage that opened out into the complex. That was it. Anybody wanted to get to number 4 they'd have to go past me through the entry, or down the parking drive, also past me. All I had to do was stay awake and I had the place covered.

I walked back to the Corvette, pulled the top up, and

climbed into the passenger side. I was armed, supplied, and ready for siege. I could hang in as long as it took. Even until lunch.

Seven minutes later the dark blue Nova with the bad rust spot on its left rear fender rolled past and pulled to the curb about six cars ahead of me. Same two Chicano guys. Curiouser and curiouser. The driver got out and trotted across the street to disappear behind the banana trees. He was back there a long time. Maybe Pygmies got him. Just when I got my hopes up he came back, still scowling, still trying to look like Charles Bronson, still not making it. It's tough to look like Charles Bronson when you got no chin. He walked into the street in front of an elderly lady driving a big bronze Mercury. She had to stop. He scowled at her. Tough, all right. I heard his car door slam, then a minute later faint Mexican music. These guys were good.

A couple minutes before nine, two cars eased up out of the garage, a little metallic-brown Toyota Celica and a green LTD. About nine-fifteen a beige Volvo sedan turned in. Kimberly Marsh wasn't driving and probably wasn't hiding in the trunk. At ten-fourteen the fat guy came out with his little dog. I held my fire so as not to tip the guys in the Nova. The little dog didn't have any better luck than last time. At ten fifty-five the mail was delivered. Kimberly Marsh got a couple more letters. At six minutes before noon the Nova cracked open again and a different guy walked back past me on the sidewalk, heading toward Barrington. This one was taller, with a relaxed face and prominent Adam's apple. This one, maybe you could talk to. I scrunched down onto the floor, no easy feat in a '66 Corvette, and counted to forty before I looked up. Thirty-five minutes later he came back, whistling and carrying a white paper bag with grease stains at the bottom. Tacos or burritos, one. I ate a salami sandwich, followed it with a turkey, and drank a warm Budweiser. Bud holds up better warm than any other beer. Great for that tailgate party when you're on stakeout.

At ten minutes after three, a dirty red Porsche 914 double-parked in front of the Piedmont Arms and a good-looking kid the size of a tree got out and went to the mailboxes. Kimberly Marsh's mailbox, in particular. Then I had him. The beach picture in Kimberly Marsh's dresser drawer. Six-three. Two-fifteen. Brown-almost-blond hair and toothpaste-commercial features. I lifted myself up in the seat and tried to see the guys in the Nova. They didn't seem to be paying any attention, the

driver talking and gesturing and the passenger nodding his
head and the Mexican music going with a lot of trumpet. The
big kid cleaned out the box, dug through the bin, then went
back to his car. Sonofabitch, stay with the Nova or follow the
kid? The Mexican driver was still explaining something with
his hands. The passenger fired the wadded-up white paper bag
into the shrubs around the apartments. They turned up the
music. Marimbas. I went with the kid.

He cruised back toward Barrington, then left on San Vicente
to Wilshire and the San Diego Freeway, north. I stayed three
or four cars back up through the Sepulveda Pass into the valley
and onto the Ventura Freeway, east. He took the Woodman
exit and headed to Burbank Boulevard where he pulled into an
auto parts store, running in like he was in a hurry. I swung the
Corvette into the Shell station across the street and stopped by
the pay phone. I kept one eye on the parts store, fed money
into the phone, and called Joe Pike.

A man's voice said, "Gun shop."

"Joe Pike, please."

Five seconds. Ten, tops. "Pike."

"It's warming up. You feel like work?"

I could tell Pike covered the mouthpiece. When he took his
hand away the background at his shop was quiet. "What do you
want me to do?"

"There're two Mexicans sitting in a dark blue Chevy Nova at
412 Gorham, just above San Vicente in Brentwood. Bad rust
spot on the left rear fender behind the wheel well. I want to
know where they go."

"You want me to clean and dress them after?"

"Just the address." With Pike you had to be careful. You
never knew when he meant it.

I followed my man back down Woodman to the freeway
again, up and east until the Universal City exit, then down to
the boulevard and climbed almost at once into the hills above
Universal Studios. The streets there are old and narrow, built
back when hill streets were poured cement and curbed for cars
with high, skinny wheels. The houses are pink and yellow and
gray and white, stucco and wood, old Spanish and new
Ultramodern, little places jammed together on tiny lots, some
bare, some shaded with old, gnarled trees and knotted vines.
The 914 pulled into a small wood and stone contemporary on
the mountain side of the street. I continued past around the

curve, then reversed in someone's drive and parked at the curb.

I took the .38 out of the glove box and clipped it onto my waistband over my wallet. I got out and pulled on the jacket, then dug around under the seat until I found a roll of nickels. I slipped the nickel roll in my right pocket and walked back to the house.

The 914 was ticking in a little carport dug into the side of the mountain. The flat-roofed house sat on top of the garage and spilled to the right, nestling in an ivy bed as did so many houses in Los Angeles. There was a big plate glass window to the right of the door and a dormer window a little beyond that. The landscaping was uneven and shabby. Dead vines twined with live; lonely Saint Augustine runners purchased in bare spots along the unmaintained slope, outlining just as lonely sprigs of ice plant and cactus. Everything looked dusty: the 914, the carport, the brick steps leading up to the house, the house, the plants, the bugs crawling on the plants. Classy.

I crept up the steps to the door and listened. Murmurs, maybe, but impossible to tell if it was people or TV. I left the stoop and went to the right, creeping along on all fours under the big window and hoping the local rent-a-cops didn't pick now to cruise by. I raised my head and looked. Living room. Big and empty and open all the way through to the back of the house. There was a kitchen in the back on the left and a freestanding fireplace just to the right of the big window. A shabby couch covered with something that looked like a bedspread stood next to the kind of bookshelves college kids make out of boards and cinder blocks. No books; just a stereo and some records and a big aquarium with green sides and too many plants and green around the water line. In the back, off the kitchen, there was a round dining table with spindly legs and two chairs. Newspaper sections were spread across the table, pinned there by a glass, a quarter filled with something I couldn't identify. I was staring at the glass when Kimberly Marsh walked out of the kitchen and into the living room without a stitch of clothes. When she saw me she said, "Hey!" so loud I could hear her through the glass.

I waved at her and smiled. Then the front door opened and the Son of Kong appeared.

14

Up close, he was shorter than I had guessed, but his thighs and calves were thicker than in the picture and there was maybe a little more muscle across his chest. He'd changed clothes. His shirt was off, and he was wearing a pair of red gym shorts, so old and faded I couldn't make out the name of the school. He was barefoot. There was a four-inch crescent-shaped scar on the front of his left shoulder and two long ugly zipper scars bracketing his left knee. The girl appeared in the doorway behind him, holding a sheet around herself. There were stains on the sheet. I said, "Hi, Kimberly. My name's Elvis Cole. I want to talk to you about Morton Lang."

She said, "Larry."

Larry flicked his fingers back toward the house without taking his eyes off me. "Go pack. I'll take care of this." Larry's voice had a whiny quality, as if he were a rich kid from a small town who'd been Mister Everything in school and was spoiled by it.

I ignored him. "I'm a private investigator, Kimberly. Morton Lang is dead."

"Dead," she said.

I nodded. If she was ready to collapse with grief, it didn't show. "Yeah. We need to talk about it."

Larry gestured to the house again. "Go on, Kimmie." Kimmie. Okay, Jody. Let's go, Buffy. He sort of nodded to himself, making a big deal out of sizing me up. "I got this guy by forty pounds. He's mine."

I said, "Larry, you wanna be dominant male, that's okay by me. But it's important that Kimberly and I talk about this."

He shook his head. "Beat it, asshole."

I pushed my jacket back so he could see the gun. "This ain't like playing football, boy."

He blinked, and the hard lines around his eyes softened, making him look even younger, then he yelled and came at me, leading with his face like a lot of ballplayers do. It only

74

took him two hard strides to get to me, but moving so fast on the crumbly slope, his footing was weak and he was off-balance. I took one step uphill, planted, then hit him as hard as I could with the roll of nickels, getting some umph into it from my hips and carrying it up through my shoulder. His nose burst in a red and pink spray and he folded, stumbling and sliding downhill before the ivy and ice plants snagged him. He flopped around for a while, then grabbed his face and moaned. "Come on, Kimmie, " I said, "help me get him inside."

We put him on the couch with his head back over the arm and gave him ice wrapped in a wet towel to hold on his face, then she went into the back to dress. While she was gone I filled a small pot with water, cracked in some ice cubes, and brought it to the dining room table to soak my hand. Larry stirred and looked at me out the corners of his eyes, trying not to bend his head much. "You hit me with something." Sort of accusatory, like, *You cheated*.

Kimberly came back wearing a faded pair of cut-off jeans and a black POLTERGEIST tee shirt cut just below her breasts so her belly was exposed. Her body was lean and firm but she didn't look as good as the 8×10. Take away the lights and the makeup and the pose, her nose had an uncomplimentary bend to it and her eyes said nothing. Even with the tan and the dimple in her chin, she looked puffy and worn. Life in the fast lane.

I said, "Why are two Mexicans sitting on your apartment and what does that have to do with Morton Lang?"

She glanced sort of vaguely at Larry, who stirred on the couch, then struggled up and gave me the eye. I took out the Dan Wesson. "If you come off that couch," I said, "I'll shoot you in the chest."

He stayed where he was, both hands holding the red-splotched towel to his face. Kimberly positioned herself between me and the kitchen door, thumbs hooked down in the top of her shorts. Posing. She said, "Are you the police?"

I put the gun on the table, took out the photostat of my license with my dry hand and held it up. I said, "Think back five minutes, when we were outside, what I said." Beneath the smell of kitchen grease and fishbowl was the burned tar scent of marijuana and sandalwood. And maybe the metallic after-smell that ether leaves from freebasing.

She didn't look at the license. "Oh, yeah, private investigator."

"Right. That means I don't have to be nice. I don't have to read rights. I don't have to wait for your lawyer. I can kick the shit out of people and nobody can say dick." Mr. Threat.

She shook her head and used her right foot to scratch her left. "I don't know who they are."

"Mort dropped out of sight last Friday. You with me, Kimmie?"

"Unh-hunh."

"He took his son with him. Perry. You ever meet Perry?"

"Unh-unh."

"Yesterday, the cops found Mort dead up by Lancaster. He was shot to death. The boy's missing. Now Mort's wife is missing. Maybe kidnapped. Those two Mexicans, maybe they want to make you missing, too."

Larry grunted. "Spics."

"What was the trouble about?" I said.

"I don't *know*," she said, picking at her fingernail polish.

I looked past her to Larry. "Bullshit, Kimberly. Mort loved you. He would've said something to you."

She followed my eyes to Larry and tried to remember how to look offended. "Mort was my mentor and my friend," she said. I think she *moued*.

I looked back at Larry. "You her mentor, too?"

"Fuck off."

I could see Mort's card hanging by the thin wire from the wilted flower: *For the girl who gives me life, all my love*. Right, Mort. Asshole.

She paced in a small circle with her thumbs back in her shorts, then stood in the middle of the room. Show-and-tell time. "I'm scared."

"With good ol' Larry here?"

Larry gave me his tough look. She said, "Mort took me to this party to meet some guy. A guy from Mexico. A Financier." She said financier like it was Duke or Earl or Governor. "Mort's friend Garrett found him. Garrett's a producer. When you're starting out you have to meet producers and directors and the power people."

"When was this?"

"Early last week. Tuesday." Tuesday, Mort was still living at home, Ellen wasn't yet being badgered into seeking a private investigator, the Lang children's lives were shaky but still intact.

"Okay."

"Mort said that Dom was thinking about backing one of Garrett's movies, so it'd be good if they knew me for parts."

"Yours or theirs?"

"Hunh?"

"Is Dom the Mexican?"

She nodded. "All they said was Dom. I don't know his last name." She giggled. I hate women who giggle. "He's an older man. Really neat. Sort of old-fashioned, you know. He called me Miss Marsh." She giggled again. "He used to be a bullfighter, only now he's got oil and stuff."

"Good connection," Larry agreed.

I frowned at him.

"It was a big deal," Kimberly said. "Mort told me to dress sexy and be real nice, you know, laugh at their jokes and smile a lot and follow his lead. Mort knew just what to do, you know. He's great at getting with the right people and making the right connections."

I thought of Mort sitting in his chair, looking at his photo album, crying. I thought of his steadily shrinking bank balance, all out and no in. I thought of Mort with four bullets in him. "Yeah, his strong point. Where was the party?"

She looked confused and gestured somewhere off into outer space. "Somewhere over the hill. I dunno. It was dark."

"All right. What happened?"

"It was rad. We were hanging out, talking, doing lines. Everyone was very sophisticated. The dope was first-rate."

"Mort, too?"

"What?"

"Doing coke."

"Sure."

I could see it: palatial living room, marble coffee table, crystal bowl with the white powder, everybody playing Pass the Mirror. Old Mort right in there with them direct from Elverton, Kansas, by way of Oz, laughing when they laugh, nodding when they nod, eyes nervous, darting, wondering if they accept him or if they're just faking it. I couldn't make the pictures fit. I couldn't clip Mort out of the snapshot in his pool with the three kids, color in Versace threads, and drop him around that marble table with this woman and Garrett Rice and that life. Maybe Mort couldn't make the picture fit, either. Maybe that had been his problem.

Kimberly giggled. "Dom really liked me, you know."

I was getting tired of 'you know.' Larry took the towel away and grinned, but there was no humor in it. "It's the business, man." His nose was a mess.

"You're going to need a doctor," I said. "It's broken."

He stood up, wobbled, then went to the shelves by the slimy fishbowl. He took a slender blue cigarette from a little painted box and lit up, pulling deep. "For the pain."

"Was anyone else there?"

"These people from Italy. They said they might want to get into movies, too. You know—"

"Yeah. Financiers. How much did Dom like you, Kimberly?"

She tried to look embarrassed but they probably hadn't covered that in acting school. "Dom, you know, wanted to get to know me." Giggle. That made four.

"How'd Mort feel about that?"

A shrug. "You know."

"No, I don't know," I said carefully. "If I knew I wouldn't be here with you and him listening to this."

Larry giggled.

Kimberly focused on me like she wasn't quite sure what I had said and gave me a pout. "Mort had to act like such an asshole. Dom is *rich*. Dom said he might make a three-picture deal and I could be in *all* of them."

Larry giggled again. "The old spic fucked her brains out."

I looked at him. "Shut up."

Larry frowned and stared at the slime in the fish tank.

"When Dom and I came back, Mort got all upset and Dom started yelling in Spanish and Garrett was yelling and this Italian woman just kept laughing. Then Garrett got everybody calmed down and they went off and talked for a while and then Mort came back and we left. It just went all wrong. Mort had to act like such an asshole."

Her story could explain Garrett Rice. A guy like Rice, he'd get pissed if his friend blew a deal just because he didn't want his girlfriend humping for dollars. Guy like Garrett Rice, that'd be a pisser, and Rice certainly had been pissed.

"Mort tell you what they talked about when they went out?"

"We didn't talk on the way home. I was so mad."

"Sure," I said. "Who could blame you."

She cocked her head and gave me that sort-of-confused look again. "The next day he calls me and says we're in trouble. He says he can't talk because his wife is in the next room, but if anybody comes around the apartment I wasn't to answer the door and that he'd call when it was okay again. I got so scared I called Larry and came up here."

Larry sat up straighter and nodded. Defender of damsels. "Did Mort say anything about the boy?"

"Unh-unh." Kimberly started to sniffle. "I kept checking my answer machine but Mort never called back. Now you say he's dead and there's guys watching my apartment and I'm scared."

Larry smirked. It didn't look like much, considering his nose had evolved into a rutabaga. "Coupla spics. Let'm come and see what happens."

"Yeah. Like with me."

He frowned. "You hit me with something."

"Mort got hit with four 9mm Parabellums, stupid." I was at my limit. "A cop named Poitras is going to come around. Talk to him. He won't hassle you about things that don't matter. Just don't try to act tough. He's not as nice as me."

I walked out through the living room past the fishbowl. It smelled like a toilet. Algae were thick and furry around the sides and on top and over the big rocks at the bottom, and there was a dense mat of seaweed that looked like colonic polyps. A white fish of indeterminate genus lay bloated and belly-up at the surface. I stopped at the front door and looked back at them. Larry took a toke on his joint and the tip glowed.

"Kimberly?"

She turned toward me, putting her hands in her back pockets and letting me see her body. It was nice. A long time ago she could've been a cheerleader or even the homecoming queen in Elverton, Kansas. Every boy's desire. "Hunh?" she said.

"Mort was an asshole because he loved you."

She put her right hand up under her Poltergeist tee shirt and scratched her right breast.

I went out and slammed the door.

15

The next morning I woke with brilliant white sunlight in my face, smelling coffee. The sliding glass doors were open and Joe Pike was out on the deck. He was wearing faded jeans and a gray sweat shirt with the sleeves cut off and blue Nikes and government issue pilot's sunglasses. He rarely takes the glasses off. He never smiles. He never laughs. I'd known Joe Pike since 1973 and he has never violated those statements. He's six feet one with short brown hair and muscled the way a fast cornerback is muscled, weighing in somewhere between one eighty-five and one-ninety. He had a red arrow tattooed on the outside of each shoulder when he was in The Nam. They pointed forward.

Pike had the rail section out and was sitting on the edge of the deck. The cat was in his lap. I pulled on a pair of sweat pants and went out. I said, "Goddamnit. If you broke the alarm again, you pay for it."

"Slipped the latch on the sliding doors with a hacksaw blade. You didn't arm the system. You don't arm the system, it won't keep out the bad guys." Pike stroked the cat along the top of the shoulders, using slow, careful passes the way the cat likes.

I said, "I don't like to keep out the bad guys. I like to let'm in and work out on them."

"You should get a dog. A good dog, properly trained, you don't need to arm him. He's always armed."

"What? You don't think I'm tough enough?"

Pike sat silently.

"I got the cat."

Pike nodded. "That is a problem." He put the cat down. The cat flattened his ears, hissed, grabbed Pike's hand and bit him, then darted away to the other side of the deck to crouch under my grill. He growled deep in his throat. Helluva cat. Pike stood up. "Come on," he said, "I've got breakfast, then we can take a ride."

Pike had put out plates and napkins and flatware. There was

a bowl of pancake batter beside the stove and four eggs and a small pot of water simmering on a back burner. The big skillet was greased and waiting for the batter. I said, "How long you been here?"

"About an hour. You want eggs?"

"Yeah." About an hour, doing all this. I might just as well have been on the moon.

Pike poured the coffee, then spooned the eggs into the simmering water and looked at his watch. It was a big steel Rolex. He said, "Tell me about it."

By the time we sat down, each with two soft-boiled eggs smushed atop six pancakes and syrup and butter, I had told him. Pike nodded, forked in some pancake and egg, swallowed. "We're not overburdened with useful intelligence."

"One might say that, yes."

"She say this guy Dom's a matador?"

"Yes." The pancakes were good. I wondered if he'd put cottage cheese in them.

"I put cottage cheese in these," he said, reading my mind. "What do you think?"

I shrugged. "Okay."

He ate. "You know what matador means?"

"Bullfighter."

He shook his head. I could see little images of me in his glasses. "Bullfight is an American concept. It has no relevance to the actual event. Not only is the term irrelevant, it's insulting. If a matador fights a bull, then they're adversaries. That's not what it's about. The matador has to dominate the bull, not be equal to it. The bull's death is preordained. The matador's job is to bring him to it."

What a thing to wake up to. I said, "So what does it mean?"

The corner of Pike's mouth twitched. That's the closest he comes to a smile. "Means 'bringer of death.' Nifty, huh?"

I sipped the coffee. Bush coffee, bitter and black, made by putting grounds in a pot, adding water, and boiling it down. Amazing, what you can grow to like. "How do you know so much about it?"

The twitch again. "I'm into ritualized death. You know that."

I ate more pancake. "Is this your contribution to the case?"

"What'd you have in mind?"

"A small clue, perhaps. A small note, a small eyewitness. Anything, really. I'm easy to please."

"We'll see."

I got up, found two bananas in the living room, and brought them back to the table. I put one by Pike and sliced the other over my pancakes. Pike didn't touch his. He said, "I don't see how you stand dealing with these screwups."

"People didn't screw up, we'd be out of a job. Screwups are our business." I liked the sound of that. Maybe I should call Wu, have him put it on the cards.

Joe said, "Guy like Mort, laughing when they laugh, nodding when they nod, sucking up the slimeballs." The cat came in off the deck, hopped up onto the table, and stared at Pike. He held out a bit of egg. The cat ate it with delicate bites. "I know this Mort. I've known men like him. I don't like people with no will and no commitment and no pride."

"Your problem is your lack of a clear-cut opinion."

Joe stopped feeding the cat, so the cat walked across the table and sat beside me. I ignored him.

"It's never that simple," I said. I told him about Carrie, about the photo album, about the pictures of Mort and Ellen and the kids around the pool.

Joe said, "Everybody's got pictures. People *pose* for pictures. I've got pictures of me and my old man with our arms around each other, smiling, and I haven't spoken to the sonofabitch in twelve years."

I didn't say anything. I had pictures, too. I finished off the pancakes and the eggs and speared the last slice of banana. "Mort gave himself up," I said.

Joe Pike sat erect at the table, chewing, mirrored lenses immobile, lean jaws flexing, one veined, muscled arm in his lap, the other against the table, elbow not touching. He swallowed, finished his coffee, wiped his mouth. Impeccable. He said, "No. He gave nothing. He lost himself. The distinction is important."

After a while I gathered the dishes, brought them into the kitchen and rinsed them. When I finished, Pike was back out on the deck, holding the cat, staring off toward Hollywood. I went out to the rail. He didn't turn around. "Somebody screws up, I clean up after them. That's why people come to the agency. That's what I'm good at. You're good at it, too."

"Hell of a way to make a living," he said.

"Yeah," I turned and went back inside. "Come on, Yukio. Let's take that ride."

16

Pike had parked his red Jeep Cherokee off the road by the carport. It was one of the older, full-size models, blocky and tall and resting on immense knobbed tires. It dwarfed the Corvette. Three years ago we'd taken it north into the mountains, fishing. I'd used the fender for a shaving mirror. You still could. I shook my head. "Hate a man lets his car go to hell."

Joe nodded, looking grim. "Me, too." He wiped a finger along the Corvette. It came away dark.

"The wind," I said. "Blows the dirt right through the carport. Hell on the rolling stock."

Joe stared at his finger like it was something from Jupiter, then grunted and said, "You amaze me."

We dropped down Laurel Canyon and swung east on Hollywood Boulevard. It was warm and sunny and Hollywood was in full flower: a wino sat on a bench eating mayonnaise from a jar with his finger; four girls with hair like sea anemone smoked in front of a record store while boys in berets and red-splattered fatigue shirts buzzed around them like flies; young men with thick necks, broad backs, and crew cuts drifted in twos and threes past the shops and porno parlors—marines on leave, come up from Pendleton looking for action.

Ah, Hollywood. *Down these mean streets, a man must walk who is himself not mean. How mean ARE they???? So mean . . . well, just ask Morton Lang . . .*

We turned north at Western and climbed past Franklin toward Griffith Park, then right on Los Feliz Boulevard, winding our way past the park into the cool green of the Los Feliz hills. On a clear day, when the sun is bright and a breeze is in from the sea and the eucalyptus are throwing off their scent, Los Feliz is one of the finest places on earth. The hills are lush with plants and the right houses have a view all the way to the ocean. Hollywood legends lived and died here in homes built by Frank Lloyd Wright and Richard Neutra and

Rudolf Schindler. People who made fortunes in oil or off the railroad built mansions that are now bought by gay couples, renovated, and resold for fortunes themselves. But with poor Hispanic areas to the south and east and the Hollywood slimepit to the west, New Money now buys above the Sunset Strip and points west. Los Feliz has seen its day.

Pike left Los Feliz Boulevard for a narrow, overgrown street that wound its way higher in tight curves, climbing steeply in some spots, leveling or dropping in others. Traffic thinned to nothing, just us and a woman in a champagne-colored Jaguar. Then she turned off. Three quarters of a mile from where we'd left the boulevard we cruised past the sort of stone gateposts I had always imagined guarding Fort Knox. Pike pulled to the curb and killed the engine.

It was so quiet the engine's ticking sounded like finger snaps. Pike got out and walked to the gate. It was black and ornate and iron. It probably weighed as much as the Corvette. There were crossed swords over some kind of coat of arms centered on the gate. The tips of the swords were bent. Sometimes I felt bent, too. Maybe it was phallic.

I got out, opening the door easy, like when I was a kid sneaking out to do something bad and not wanting anyone to hear. This place did that to you.

An eight-foot-high mortared stone wall grew off the gate-posts. It was overgrown with ivy and followed the street both uphill and down to disappear around the curves. There were eucalyptus and scrub oak and olive trees inside the wall and out. Old trees. Gnarled and gray and established and quiet. I walked over to the gate and stood by Pike. The drive rose rapidly and disappeared behind a knoll. You couldn't see the house. You couldn't see anything. The trees were so thick it was dark. Ten o'clock in the morning and it was dark. "That does it. From now on I carry a crucifix and a sharpened stake."

Pike said, "The Nova came here. Other side of that knoll there's a motor court and the main house. Garage for eight cars. There's a pool in the back with a poolhouse, a tennis court to the northeast of it, and a guesthouse. Main house has two levels. These walls follow the topography. This gate is the only way in or out, unless you go over."

I looked at him. Pike shrugged. "I took a look."

"I suspect you went over."

"Unh-hunh."

"You get the Nova's tag number?"

"Unh-hunh." He handed me a slip of paper with a license number written on it.

"I suspect the guys driving the Nova, they don't own that place."

"Unh-unh. Had a few other guys walking around in there. Big necks."

We walked back to the Jeep. I leaned against the fender. Pike didn't mind. "Dom," I said.

"Unh-hunh. On the gate, that sword with the bent tip. It's called an *estoque*. It's what the matador uses to kill the bull."

I looked at him.

"I checked the address. Domingo Garcia Duran."

I looked at him some more.

Pike's mouth twitched. "You said you wanted a clue."

17

Joe dropped me back at the house to pick up the Corvette, then I drove in to the office. I parked in the basement and rode up alone, listening to an instrumental rendering of *Hey, Jude* that John probably would not have liked. I unlocked the outer door and went in. Nobody sapped me. Nobody stuck a gun in my face. I went to my desk, put the Dan Wesson in the top right drawer, sat, and stared out the glass doors.

Other detectives have partners with whom they could discuss the case. Me, I get dropped off in my driveway, grunted at, and left to fend for myself. Did Percival drop off Galahad? Did Archer drop off Spade?

Garrett Rice had mentioned a party. Kimberly Marsh said Morton Lang had taken her to a party. The party had been at the home of a Mexican gentleman named Dom. Dom had grown angry with Morton, probably about Kimberly Marsh, so Mort and Kimberly had left. The next day Morton Lang phoned Kimberly Marsh and told her he was in trouble and not to answer the door. A large dark man, possibly Mexican, was reported asking for Kimberly Marsh. Later, two men of Hispanic descent in a blue Nova spent hours outside Kimberly Marsh's apartment. Joe Pike followed them to a home belonging to Domingo Garcia Duran. Men with thick necks were observed.

I tapped the desk. I shifted from my right side to my left. My stomach growled and produced a vision of myself riding down to the deli for a lean corned beef with hot Chinese mustard on rye. Maybe I would sit at a little table for one they have down there. Maybe the slim blonde behind the register liked John Cassavetes. Maybe a lot of things.

It did not seem credible that Morton Lang had been murdered because he objected to Kimberly Marsh sleeping with Domingo Duran.

Men with thick necks.

I picked up the phone and called Eddie Ditko at the *Examiner*. He said, "What? I'm busy. What?"

"That's why I like talking to you, Eddie. Always anxious to share a human moment."

"You want a human moment? I got bowel trouble. I'm worried I gotta get cut and wear a bag the rest of my life."

That Eddie. Class all the way. I said, "You got any clippings on a guy named Domingo Garcia Duran?"

"Shit, know him from when I used to work sports. Bullfighter. A Mexican. Right up there with El Cordobes and Belmonde, those guys, when he was young. Made millions. Got himself into oil, Acapulco beachfront, hotels. Liked the high life. Always something on the wire about him hanging with the guys from Phoenix, Jersey, Bolivia, like that. I think he retired around '68, '69, something."

"He step over the line himself?"

"He supposed to be worth, what?, a couple hundred million? You flip up the rock, he's in bed with the wrong people somewhere. His name came up in a laundering scheme once, then again with some assholes who were transporting dope up from South America. No indictments. No convictions. Shit, he's always on Rudy Gambino's yacht, that kind of thing. What, Rudy's gonna have him around because he likes tacos?"

We shot the breeze a little longer, me trying to cadge some freebie Dodgers tickets for the upcoming season and him pretending not to hear, then we hung up. I tapped the desk some more. Cocaine. Organized crime. Rudy Gambino. Murder was beginning to seem more credible.

I picked up the phone and punched the numbers for the North Hollywood P.D. A voice said, "Detectives."

"Lou Poitras, please."

"He's out. Take a message?"

"Ask him to call Elvis Cole. He's got the number."

I hung up.

Outside, a brown gull floated on the breeze. He looked at me. I made my left hand into a gun and pointed it at him. He banked away from the building and disappeared. I called Janet Simon. She answered on the sixth ring. "How are you doing?"

"Okay." Her voice was flat.

"Was it rough?"

A hesitation. "I couldn't tell them."

I nodded, but she probably didn't see it. "What'd you tell them about Ellen?"

"I really can't talk now."

"Why don't I pick up some sandwiches or some chicken and come over?"

"No."

"I guess I'm calling at a bad time."

"Yes."

"Well, you have my number."

"Yes, that I do."

We hung up. It's always gratifying to be appreciated.

I called the deli, ordered a lean corned beef with Chinese hot mustard, told them I'd be down in ten minutes, and went out onto the balcony. There was a slight haze to the south and west and a thin band of cirrus clouds up high over the Santa Monica mountains to the north. The air felt glassy and damp. It hadn't turned hot yet, but it would soon. That was L.A.

I thought about Mort, wearing his *U.S.S. Bluegill* tee shirt in the little snapshot. Mort from Kansas. Mort of the paint store. Mort with his traditional wife and his traditional kids and his not-so-traditional life. *Don't look now, Toto, but this ain't Kansas. . . .* Would Mort be stupid enough to try to move some dope? *Laugh when they laugh, nod when they nod.* Partners with Rice, not on a movie deal, but on a dope deal that had gone bad? Had Mort picked up the boy from school, then been kidnapped on the way home? That would explain why Mort's clothes were still at the house and why he'd left no note. But with Mort dead, why grab Ellen and tear up the house? Because somebody thought Mort had something and thought Ellen Lang knew about it. Maybe that somebody was Domingo Garcia Duran. Maybe Ellen and the boy were up at his place now.

I was thinking about the big walls and the big gate and the big swords with the big bent tips when the outer door opened and the biggest human being I'd ever seen off a playing field walked in. If anything, I am consistent. First I thought Mexican, then Indian, then Samoan. Lots of Samoans come over to play middle guard for USC. He was six-eight easy and slim the way I'm slim, but on him that meant two-forty. When he moved I thought shark, sliding through the water. He had large, thick-fingered hands and big bones. His cheeks were high and flat. So was his forehead. So was his nose. His eyes were black and empty and made me think shark again. A shorter man came in after him, this one Mexican for sure. Shorter than me, but wider and heavier. About one-ninety.

Beer barrel body on little pin legs. You could tell he thought he was a hitter because he carried himself sort of hunched over with his arms away from his body. His hair was short and combed straight back the way Chicano kids do when they're in a gang. His right eyebrow was broken into three pieces by vertical scars. A long time ago someone had hit him very hard on the left side of his mouth and it hadn't healed right. I said, "Wrong door. Beauty supply is down the hall."

The big guy stopped just inside the inner door, but the Mexican came in all the way. He opened Joe Pike's door, glanced in, then closed it again. He turned in a full circle, looking at the cartoon characters on the wall and the clock and the stuff I keep around. His mouth was open. He said something in Spanish I didn't get, then shook his head and put his left foot on my desk and looked at me. I didn't like the foot on my desk. I also didn't like the lump in his windbreaker beneath his left arm.

The big one said, "Are you Elvis Cole?" Perfect diction with a slight accent I couldn't place. I was back to thinking American Indian.

"Sometimes. Sometimes I'm the Blue Beetle."

He said, "Domingo Duran wants to see you. You're to come with us." Talk about hard evidence.

I didn't move. "Navajo?" I'd just read Tony Hillerman.

"Eskimo."

"Some heat down here, huh?"

The Eskimo reached behind his back and came out with a black automatic. Looked to be a .380 but it could have been a 9mm. He held it loosely down at his side. "Come on," he said.

I stared at the Eskimo for a very long time. He let me. He was probably the guy who asked around at Kimberly Marsh's place. He may have been the guy who pulled the trigger on Mort. We started. I didn't like him and I didn't like what was happening.

The Mexican was handling one of the figures of Jiminy Cricket on the desk. I walked over, took it from him, put it back in its place. He said something in Spanish. "I don't speak it," I said.

"It's just as well," the Eskimo said. "Manolo doesn't like you."

"Tell Manolo to get his goddamned foot off my desk."

The Eskimo studied me for a while longer, then made a sighing sound and took a step back, taking himself out of it. He rested his gun arm on top of the file cabinet. He said something in Spanish. The Mexican's eyes narrowed and he smiled. One of his front teeth had a design etched into it. He said something back.

The Eskimo said, "He wants you to take it off for him."

"Tell him it'll hurt."

He did. The Mexican gave one barking laugh, then put his right hand under his windbreaker. I stepped in, swept his support leg out from under him, kicked him in the groin when he hit the floor, and followed it down hard, driving my knee in his chest. Something gave with a loud snap. I hit him twice on the jaw with my right hand. His eyes rolled back, shiny and black as marbles, he stopped trying to cover up, and that was it.

The Eskimo hadn't moved.

"He'll need a doctor," I said. "Maybe for the groin shot, but more likely for the chest. A couple of ribs went. Could be some liver damage."

Manolo rolled onto his side and coughed. The Eskimo looked at him with bottomless eyes. Maybe your eyes get that way from looking down through thin ice to see killer whales looking back at you. I read somewhere that in the Deep Ice Tribes young kids still have to kill polar bears to pass into manhood. By themselves. With sticks.

The Eskimo turned the eyes to me, nodded at whatever he saw, and made the .380 disappear. "Let's go."

"I didn't want you guys to think I was too easy."

"No problem."

He picked up Manolo like I'd lift an overnight bag. Manolo moaned. I said, "Those ribs are probably grating together."

"No problem."

We went out my office, along the hall, down the elevator, across the lobby, and out the side of the building.

18

A black Cadillac limo waited in the service alley. The Eskimo put me against the car, patted me down, then said, "Okay." He shoved Manolo into the front, then he and I got into the back. There was an Asian guy at the wheel. I said, "Hey, just like the Green Hornet."

The Asian guy glanced at me in the mirror. The Eskimo said, "Shut up," then settled back and closed his eyes. I nodded and did what I was told.

We went east on Santa Monica, then north on Highland to pick up the Hollywood Freeway north, passing Universal Studios with its ominous black tower and skyscraper hotels and array of sound stages so numerous it looked like a breeding ground for airplane hangars. In the San Fernando valley we looped onto the Ventura Freeway and rolled west for a long time. The big Cadillac was whisper quiet. The Eskimo was to my left, slouched down on his spine, eyes still closed. Maybe sleeping, maybe faking it and waiting for me to make my move. A lot like seal hunting, I guessed. The driver never looked back, never moved, just drove. Manolo shifted every once in a while, a lump in the front seat ahead of me. Quiet. I whistled the opening bars to *The Bridge on the River Kwai*.

The Eskimo said, "Shut up."

Yassuh.

We passed Woodland Hills and Reseda and Thousand Oaks. Pretty soon we left the west valley and were moving toward Camarillo. Manolo coughed twice, groaned, then sat up. He rubbed at his face, then shrugged his shoulders and rolled his head from side to side. He twisted around and looked at me. There wasn't any threat in his look; it was more like he'd discovered a new species of rhododendron.

The sprawl and clutter of the valley gave way to hilly pasture land, green from the winter rains. There was the occasional scrub oak and the occasional dirt road and Jersey and Hereford cattle spotted on the steeper slopes. In summer, the same hills would be brown and dead and would look like desert. A few minutes past Camarillo we left the freeway. There was nothing around but a Union 76 station and an old two-lane state road running to the northwest and what was maybe a grain elevator from the forties. I said, "If you guys are lost we should ask."

The Eskimo said nothing. Maybe I was wearing him down.

We went northwest. Ten minutes later we turned through an arched metal gate that said *Cachon Ranches* and followed a well-maintained composition road about a mile up into the hills until we came to what I guessed was the ranch. A maze of steel pipe corrals, one wooden main office, and three corrugated metal buildings. A heavy-duty livestock truck was backing up to the corrals as sweaty men in worn jeans and work shirts and broken fiber cowboy hats waited to receive it. Another limo was parked by the wooden office and there were three or four dusty pickups by the largest metal building. We pulled up beside the pickups and got out. The Eskimo said, "Come on." Manolo fell out of the front seat. No one rushed to help him.

Domingo Garcia Duran stood at one of the smaller corrals, his back to us. He was standing next to a fat man. Duran was about five-ten, slim and strong-looking with narrow hips and wide shoulders and black hair shot through with silver. He was wearing tan Gucci loafers and dark slacks and a cream-colored pullover shirt that showed his build. He stood erect, much like Ricardo Montalban. He looked wealthy, also like Ricardo Montalban. Maybe if I said, "Boss! Boss! De plane! De plane!" he'd think I was funny. He and the fat man were watching a black cow walk in slow circles about the corral. Every once in a while the fat man said something and pointed at the cow and Duran would nod. Duran was holding a slender sword in his left hand. About three feet long, with a bent tip. Ixnay on the Villechaise.

The Eskimo said something to them and the fat guy went away. The black cow was short and squat and nervous. She saw us, lowered her head, then twitched and jumped away to resume her walk. No resemblance to Elsie. Duran looked at me and said, "We will talk. I will ask you questions, you will answer. I will give you instructions, you will act on them. First, do you know who I am?"

"Karl Malden."

Something hit me hard in the left shoulder blade. I grunted and bent over but didn't fall. The Eskimo stared at me.

Duran said, "He will hit you as many times as I wish. There are others who will hit you, also. After they are done, still others will put your body there," he pointed the sword into the hills "so that it will never be found. Do you understand these things?"

"Do I get penalized for questions?"

The hard thing hit me again and this time I went over, my left arm dead from my shoulder blade out. He should have hit me in the head. In the head, he would've broken his hand and knocked some sense into me. Somebody lifted me and held me up before Duran. Life as a puppetoon. I said, "Do you have Ellen Lang or Perry Lang or know of their whereabouts?"

I tensed for the next shot but it didn't come. Duran looked at me like he was looking at a retard. He said, "A man named Morton Lang came to my home. I did not know this man, yet I welcomed him and allowed him in as a guest. He repays my hospitality by stealing from my home two kilograms of cocaine. Very special cocaine. Not easy to get. Medical quality, you see, the cocaine they study in laboratories and hospitals. Now I'm told you have it."

I looked at Duran. I looked at the Eskimo. I looked back at Duran. He looked at the cow. "She's beautiful, no?"

"Somebody told you I had your cocaine?"

"Come. I show you something."

The Eskimo shoved me after Duran toward the bigger corral. The truck had backed to the loading ramp and killed its engine. The ranch hands were swarming around the rear gate, pulling chains and metal latchbars. Duran said, "Do you know *toreo?*"

"No." *Toreo.* Next it would be Thai cuisine or decorative macramé. A guy like Duran, you've got to let him run his course. Especially if you don't want to get hit a lot.

"To the shame of the United States. It's an art of great passion and beauty."

"Yeah, all that red."

He shouted something to one of the men working at the truck, then turned back to me. "Much of what happens between the man and the *toro* grows out of *jurisdicción*. To cite the *toro*, to make him charge, you must place yourself in his *jurisdicción*. You invade his place. You offer yourself to his horn." He looked at the sword, then touched it to my chest. The point curved down. If he shoved it in, the blade would follow the curve to my heart. "The most courageous matador, he offers his balls."

I looked at the Eskimo, who was staring off across the yard, probably watching for narwhals. My back hurt, but feeling had returned to my arm. Maybe I could take him. Maybe I could do something to his eyes, then put him down on the ground to neutralize his size and go to work on his throat and groin. Sure. I looked back at Duran. "You mean the whole idea is that the bull is coming for your balls."

"Yes."

I shook my head. "Dumb." I think the Eskimo smiled, but I wouldn't swear to it.

The ranch hands slammed open the truck's gate. A brown and gray steer looked out, then trotted slowly down the ramp and into the pen. He didn't look like much. Then, almost as if in slow motion, a heavy black bull not quite the size of Godzilla came down the ramp to stand beside the steer. He stood very still, feet squarely placed, head up, looking first at the ranch hands, then at us. A Russell sculpture. It was impossible to imagine a chest and shoulders more powerfully formed. His horns came up and out then curved back in. They were very sharp. Duran nodded. "See how he carries his head, see the way he looks about. This is *pundonor*. Great pride, a very great jealousy of his *jurisdicción*. He accepts the duty of protecting what is his."

Maybe Duran was thinking about adopting him. I said, "Why the steer?"

"*Cabestros*. To calm the bull for the journey. The herd instinct, you see? They are friends." He looked at me again. "Would you offer yourself to such an animal?"

"Maybe with a rocket launcher."

"Imagine standing before his charge, watching him come, waiting for him." Duran smiled, maybe remembering. "We will breed them, the bull and the cow. The young one will inherit the looks of the father, the courage of the mother. She is very brave. She killed a man in the Pampas."

I said, "I don't have your cocaine. I don't know anything about your cocaine."

"I am told you do."

"You were told wrong. I was hired to find Morton Lang. He's been found. I don't guess you guys know anything about that. Now I'm looking for his wife and his little boy. I think you've got them."

He touched me with the sword again. I wondered if I could take it away from him before the Eskimo nailed me. I said, "Maybe Morton Lang didn't steal your cocaine. Maybe somebody else did."

"No."

"Maybe Nanuk here took it."

"No."

"Look, if Mort had taken the dope and now I had it, wouldn't I be trying to sell it back to you?"

Duran touched a button on my shirt with the point of the sword. He pressed. The button split. "Return my property. Perhaps then you'll find the woman and the boy."

The ranch hands began to chatter. When I looked, the bull had lifted his snout and begun to trot around the pen. The hands scurried to open a gate on the far side, but Duran snapped an order and they stopped. The bull made a coughing sound and lowered his head. There was drool streaming out of his mouth. The steer, eyes wide and rolling, edged away.

Duran said, "He smells the female."

The bull charged the steer. When they hit, it sounded like a mortar round, *whump*. The bull caught him in the gut by the hindquarters, then lifted and twisted, ripping forward into the ribs. You could hear them pop like green wood. The steer brayed and went down. The bull stayed with him, lowering the thick neck and hooking his horns two lefts and a right like a boxer throwing combinations, once almost lifting the steer off the ground. Then Duran nodded and the hands threw open the far gate, shouting and waving their hats. The bull backed away from the steer. His horns glistened red. He pawed the ground then ran through the gate. The steer flopped around for a while, then managed to gain its feet. When it did, most of its intestine fell out onto the ground. It wobbled and staggered but stayed up. Some friend.

Duran looked at me, then vaulted the fence. I was dismissed. The Eskimo led me back to the limo and opened the door. A full-service thug. Kato was still behind the wheel. The Eskimo said, "He'll take you where you tell him."

"What if I tell him the police?"

"He'll take you there."

"That easy."

The Eskimo shrugged. "Play it the way you want. Mr. Duran was lunching at the Marina today. He can prove that. If

you consider what has happened and what could, he won't
have to. You will do as he tells you."

"I don't have the dope."

He looked at me.

I said, "The woman and the boy, they'd better be all right."

Something like a grin touched the Eskimo's lips. He said,
"Nanuk," then turned and walked back toward the corrals.

I got into the car. The last thing I saw was Domingo Garcia
Duran approach the steer and drive the sword to its hilt down
through the steer's shoulders at the base of its neck. The steer
dropped, the ranch hands cheered, and I shut the door.

19

When I got back to my building I went to the deli to pick up the corned beef sandwich. They'd saved it and weren't happy about it. I wasn't so happy about it myself. I snapped at the blonde behind the register to prove I was still tough, then brought the sandwich and three bottles of Heineken up to my office. I was so tough I forgot I didn't have an opener and had to ride all the way back down to the deli to buy one of theirs. Buck sixty-five for a piece of tin.

I let myself into the office and locked the outer door. There were two messages on my machine: the first from an auto parts store letting me know that the genuine 1966 Chevrolet Corvette shifter skirt I'd ordered four months ago was finally in, the second from Lou Poitras, returning my call. I reset the machine, opened the balcony doors for air, sat down behind the desk, opened the first Heineken, and drank most of it.

The smart move would be to call the cops. That's what I'd advised Ellen Lang. More often than not, the cops crack the case, the cops get their man, the kidnapped come back alive when the cops are involved. The Feds will supply you with statistics that bear this out. Lots of neat black lettering on clean white sheets that don't have much at all to do with some dead-eyed psychopathic sonofabitch saying that if the police come in a little kid and a woman get dead. *Well, no, Your Honor, he didn't actually* say *it, but he* strongly hinted *that that would be the case. . . .*

I finished the rest of the Heineken, dropped the bottle into the trash, opened another, and unwrapped the sandwich. It was cold and the bread was stale. My back hurt where the Eskimo had hit me and my hand hurt from hitting Kimberly Marsh's boyfriend and the thick-necked Mexican. I ate some of the sandwich and drank more of the beer and thought about all this.

I couldn't see Morton Lang ripping two keys of cocaine off Domingo Garcia Duran. Trying to set up a deal and blowing it, that's one thing. But to shove two plastic packs of dope in your jockeys right in the man's house and walk out, unh-unh. That took *cojones*. There was Garrett Rice, but he didn't strike me as being particularly well-endowed either. Maybe someone else. Anyone else. The Eskimo, the guys in the Nova, Manolo, the fat guy at the ranch. Maybe the rich Italian Kimberly Marsh had mentioned. I drank more beer and ate more sandwich. What did I know? Maybe Mort had swiped it and Ellen knew about it and that's why she hadn't wanted the cops involved. Maybe she'd known all along and right now the dope was buried in a coffee can under the swing set in her back yard. I killed the second Heiny and opened the last one.

No chance. Maybe Mort had ripped off the dope but there was no way Ellen had known about it. Mort, I hadn't met, hadn't touched, hadn't sat with. Ellen, we'd breathed the same air. If Mort had ripped off the Crown jewels of London, Ellen hadn't known it. She'd been enduring, going through the necessary chore of shopping for groceries to feed her kids, probably wondering why life had turned so unfair since leaving Kansas when a man or men approached to show her just how unfair life could get. They would take her somewhere and ask her about the dope and maybe hurt her. And she would cry and maybe be angry but mostly be scared. After a while, when the fear wasn't so new and her head began to work, she'd think of me. Mr. White Knight. Dragons slain. Maidens rescued. She'd say, "Mr. Cole has it," because that would take the heat off her and maybe bring me into it and I could help. Maybe.

I finished the sandwich and the third Heineken and put the wax paper in the waste basket and the empty bottle beside the other two. Okay, Ellen, I'm your guy. Shield shined and charger shod. I got up and fished around in the little cooler by the file cabinet and found a Miller High Life. The Champagne of Bottled Beers. Domingo Garcia Duran has a couple of thugs deliver me and lays it out like he's talking to a dog who can't repeat it or report it or use the information in any way. Not that I had anything to repeat or report. I could tie Mort to Duran's little party through Kimberly Marsh and Garrett Rice, but Duran had admitted that much and would probably be willing to admit it again. He hadn't admitted offing Mort or holding Ellen and the boy. All I had for evidence was a phone call from Mort to Kimberly where Mort said he was in trouble with someone named Dom. Big deal. Still, I could run to the cops and let them worry about digging up the evidence. Maybe

Duran didn't care. Maybe he was so connected he could take the heat and shut off or divert an investigation. Maybe if he couldn't, his friend Rudy Gambino could. Rudy Gambino. Christ. I had seen Rudy Gambino once in Houston before I became an op. He was being led through the lobby of the Whitworth Hotel, surrounded by a swarm of attorneys and state marshals, on his way to face charges of statutory rape, rape, mayhem, assault, and sodomy against a twelve-year-old girl. Quite a guy, that Rudy. The charges were later dropped.

I finished the Miller and put it with the other empties. Saturday during a Dodgers game the pile would look respectable. Midweek during a case made me look like a drunkard. I dialed Lou Poitras. "You ever hear of a guy, Domingo Garcia Duran?"

"Runs a bodywork shop on Alvarado."

"Different Duran. This guy used to fight bulls. Now he's rich, has investments, friends, like that."

"This got anything to do with Lang?"

I ignored him. "This guy, he's seen around with Rudy Gambino and those guys. Think you could ask around, see what kind of weight he could handle?"

"You mean like, can he get a ticket fixed? Like that?"

"Like that."

"You didn't answer me, Hound Dog."

"No, it doesn't have anything to do with Lang."

There was a pause. "Okay," he said, and hung up. I frowned at the phone. Galahad lying to Percival. It made me feel small.

I brought my typewriter from its little stand in the corner over to the desk and typed up a complete report from the time Ellen Lang hired me three days ago until Kato brought me back to the building. When I finished, it was four single-spaced pages long. I corrected the typos, numbered, dated, and signed each page, then brought them to the insurance office across the hall. The secretary there lets me use their copy machine whenever the boss' door is closed. It was closed. I made two copies and tried not to breathe in the secretary's face. I took the copies back to my office, signed and dated each sheet again and wrote in longhand that there should be no erasures or deletions from any page. The original and one copy went into my office file. The other I sealed in an envelope, stamped, and addressed it to my home. Then I went down, put the letter in the drop outside the bank, and went back into the deli. I bought a bottle of aspirin and a large black coffee to

go. I chewed four of the aspirin while the blonde watched,
then took the steps, two at a time, all the way up. For every
sin, there must be penance.

Back in the office I ate two more aspirin, sipped the coffee,
and thought about what I might do. Ellen and the boy would
be safe as long as Duran thought he could trade them for the
dope, only I had no dope to trade. Maybe I could break into
his manse at three in the morning, ram a gun in his mouth, and
demand their release. Unh-huh. Maybe I could kite some bad
checks, score a hundred grand worth of dope, and pull the
trade that way. Unh-huh. The problem was that once Duran
had the dope, Ellen and Perry had to disappear. Wouldn't
matter how connected he was, he couldn't buck eyewitness
testimony. And that meant Elvis had to disappear, too. I
watched Pinocchio's eyes move back and forth. Portrait of the
investigator: young man in search of a plan.

Maybe I could poke around and trip over some heretofore
unknown bit of evidence. I dug out the rolodex card with
Garrett Rice's phone numbers and dialed his office. A woman
answered, "Mr. Rice's office," and told me he'd gone for the
day. I asked if Mr. Tyner was about. She said he had gone with
Mr. Rice. I dialed Rice's home number and waited while it
rang. Maybe Garrett Rice knew something he wasn't telling.
Maybe I could use some form of nonlethal persuasion to find
out. On the fifteenth ring I hung up. Not home. Some plan, all
right.

I took out my wallet and looked at the license number that
Joe Pike had copied off the Nova, then called a lady at the
Department of Motor Vehicles. I identified myself, gave her
the number of my PI license, and asked for the Nova's
registration. She told me to wait, then came back with a name
and an address. I thanked her, hung up, then finished the
coffee. The beer and the aspirin had helped my back. I pulled
on the shoulder rig without too much pain, got the Dan
Wesson out of my desk, put on the cotton jacket, and went out.
It was eight minutes after four.

I still didn't have a plan. Maybe the guys in the Nova,
maybe they had a plan. Maybe I could borrow it.

20

Forty minutes later I turned down a small residential street in an older part of Los Angeles between Echo Park and Dodger Stadium. The houses were flat-topped stucco bungalows, mostly off-white or sand or yellow in color. Most had porches and most of the porches had tricycles and big potted geraniums and old Chicano women sitting in lawn chairs. You could smell chili sauce and *machaca* simmering and the doughy scent of fresh, hand-thrown flour tortillas. It was a good, clean smell.

The DMV had said that the dark blue Nova belonged to a man named Arturo Sanchez who lived in the fourth house from the corner on the north side of the street. It was a light brown bungalow with a two-strip drive, a porch, and four ratty rose bushes. The Nova wasn't in the drive, nor was it parked on the street. I cruised past the house to the end of the block and turned into a little street-corner shopping center. There was a laundromat and a 7-Eleven and a taco stand and a billboard advertising Virginia Slims. *¡Hiciste mucho progreso, chiquita!*

I parked under the Virginia Slims sign, bought a taco and an iced tea, and sat with them at one of the little picnic benches in a place where I could watch Arturo Sanchez's house. It was a real taco, with chunk beef and chilis, fried in oil and doused with the sort of sauce that would bring a Taco Bell taco to its knees. Heaven. I had finished the first and started on a second when the blue Nova turned down the street and into Sanchez's drive. The poor man's Charles Bronson got out, looking sullen, kicked at something on the ground, kicked at it again, then entered the front door. Still tough, all right.

I waited.

The sun settled and the cars that passed began to burn their headlamps. It grew chill. Two teenage girls in tight pants and too much makeup walked past the taco stand and into the 7-Eleven. Cars pulled into the lot. Guys who looked like they worked hard for a living got out, went into the 7-Eleven and came out with six-packs or cartons of milk. It got dark. A beat-up station wagon discharged a short, thick-boned woman with two large baskets of clothes. The two baskets were almost as big as the woman. She edged sideways through the laundromat doors, set the baskets onto the floor near the closest machine, and sorted through her wash. She saw me watching her. I smiled. She smiled. She went on with her wash. Another close brush with dangerous inner-city life.

The guy in the taco stand was beginning to look at me, too, only he wasn't smiling. I threw the rest of my iced tea into a steel trash bin and went over to the 7-Eleven and pretended to make a call from the pay phone. The guy in the taco stand watched me. Four make-believe calls later I gave up, went back to the taco stand, and smiled in the little window. "Ever thought about licensing a franchise?" I said.

The guy never took his eyes off me. He had his right hand where I couldn't see it behind the Orange Crush machine. Probably embarrassed by a hangnail.

At ten minutes before eight Arturo Sanchez kicked open the screen door to his house and stormed out to his Nova. The porch light came on and a heavy woman appeared in the door, screaming something in Spanish. Arturo gunned the Nova, screeched backward out of the drive, and roared down the street away from me.

I caught up to him a block and a half down Elysian Park heading toward Dodger Stadium. With the baseball season still a couple of months off, traffic was light; two months from now with the Dodgers in a home game I might have had problems. We went up Stadium Way through Chavez Ravine and north on Riverside paralleling the Golden State Freeway. About a mile and a half up he swung right onto a crowded side street without signaling. Some guys are assholes all the way through.

The Nova pulled into a small apartment building. A man passed through his headlights and climbed in. It wasn't the same guy who'd been with Sanchez in front of Kimberly Marsh's place. This guy was shorter and built like an in-shape welterweight, compact and hard and mean. The kind of guy who just naturally wanted to make something of it. The Nova came back onto Riverside and continued north.

When we got to Los Feliz Boulevard they surprised me, turning west toward Hollywood instead of east toward Domingo Duran's. On Franklin they parked in front of a liquor store

and the welterweight got out. He went into the store, came
out with a bagged pint, and made a call on the pay phone.
Probably to his broker. They continued down Franklin to
Beachwood, then hung a right up into the Hollywood hills.
Halfway up they turned off Beachwood and climbed into a
little nest of cramped, winding streets beneath the Hollywood
sign. I killed my lights and backed off, guessing turns by
watching their lights bounce off the houses and trees above
me. We went higher, Hollywood and Los Angeles spreading
out below in a hypnotic panorama so wide and deep that you
could lose yourself in the lights.

When I saw their car again it was parked at the curb of a
little white clapboard bungalow. I eased to a stop, then let the
Corvette roll backward and swing into an empty drive. I took
my gun out from under the seat and held it at my side as I
walked up to the house. My heart was pounding. That really
happens when you're scared.

There were three men standing in the living room, Sanchez
and the welterweight and a third guy. The third guy was
holding a can of Budweiser beer in his teeth and pulling on a
white shirt. He had spiderwebs tattooed on each shoulder
along with assorted daggers and skulls and female breasts. He
also had a shoulder holster. Behind them was a short hall
running back to what looked like the kitchen. The welterweight peeled the bag off his pint, set it on the coffee table,
and laughed at something. Probably not the other guy's
tattoos.

I went around the side of the house and peeked in a window.
It was a little bedroom off the hall, decorated in early poverty.
Ellen Lang sat in a chair. Her hands were tied behind her back
and there was a Mayfair Market grocery bag over her head. I
went back to the front and around the other side, looking in
each window for the boy. I didn't see him. At the back of the
house, there was a wooden door off the kitchen, opened to
catch the breeze. I stood just outside the wedge of light, trying
to hear into the front room. The men were still laughing.
Maybe if I yelled *Fire!* they'd run. I eased back the hammer on
my gun and stepped into the house.

Alarms didn't go off. The Eskimo didn't swoop out of the sky.
The kitchen was dingy and yellow and hadn't been cleaned in a
long time. There was a roach trap on the floor under the
dinette, Taco Bell and Burrito King wrappers on the counter,
and the stink of old hot sauce. Someone had built a pyramid of

Coors cans on the dinette. From where I was standing I could look down the hall and see the back of Sanchez's head. I took one step out into the hall, then turned right into the bedroom with Ellen Lang. I could hear her breath hissing softly against the paper bag. She shifted once, then sat motionless. Out in the living room, the men talked and laughed and I heard a bottle clunk the table. I went to Ellen Lang and said quietly, "Don't speak and don't move. It's me."

I thought it would end then. I thought she would gasp or moan or stumble out of the chair but she didn't. Her body tensed and she drew up very, very straight. I slipped the bag off her head and untied her wrists. Her eyes were puffy and she had one small red mark in the left corner of her mouth but that was all. She stared at me without blinking.

"Can you walk?"

She nodded once.

"Is Perry here?"

She shook her head.

"I'm going to slip your shoes off. We're going to go out that door, turn left, and go out through the kitchen. On the deck, we'll turn right and out to the street. You'll go first so I can cover our backs."

She nodded. I slipped her shoes off and handed them to her. Just as she stood up, a toilet flushed and a door across the hall opened and a fourth man came out of the bathroom. He was shorter than me and fat, carrying a *Times* sports section. He said something in Spanish to the living room and then he saw me. I shot him twice in the chest and he fell sideways. There were shouts and a thump like a chair hitting the floor. I yanked Ellen Lang toward the hall.

The welterweight came around the corner, firing as fast as he could pull the trigger. One of his slugs caught the doorjamb and kicked some splinters into my cheek. I shot him in the face, then shoved Ellen through the kitchen and half carried her around the house and out onto the street. The Tattooed Man popped out of the front door and fired five shots— *bapbapbapbapbap*—then dove back into the house.

Porch lights were coming on and someone was yelling and Wang Chung was coming out over somebody's radio. I shoved Ellen into the Corvette, fired up, and ran over two garbage cans pulling away. I was shaking and my shirt was wet with sweat and I wasn't having a great deal of luck seeing past the little silver flashes that bobbed around in front of my eyes. I drove. Slow. Steady. Just trying to get away from there. I think I ran over a dog.

At the bottom of Beachwood, I pulled into an Exxon station and waited for the shakes to pass. When they did I looked at Ellen Lang. She was drawn and pale in the fluorescent Exxon light, and sitting absolutely still. She didn't whimper and she didn't tremble but I'm not quite sure she felt anything, either. I touched her hand. It was cold. "Do you need a doctor?"

She shook her head once like back at the house, and looked at me with dulled eyes. I peeled off my jacket, put it around her shoulders, then leaned my head back on the seat. My heart was hammering. Outside on Franklin, night-time Hollywood traffic edged past. A tall skinny kid wearing an old Stetson and a threadbare Levi jacket thumbed for a ride. The Exxon attendant leaned against the gas pump, staring at us, probably wondering what the hell we were doing over in the shadows, probably thinking maybe he should walk over and see, probably deciding nope, this is Hollywood. The attendant went into a service bay.

I closed my eyes. I'd killed one man for sure and probably another. The cops would have to come in, and they wouldn't like it. I didn't much like it myself.

I heard her say, "Mort's dead, isn't he?"

I turned my head to see her. "Yes."

"Did he steal those drugs like they said?"

"I don't know."

She nodded once more, and that was it. We stayed in the shadows on the side of the Exxon station for a long time. Then I restarted the Corvette, pulled into traffic, and drove slowly toward Laurel Canyon.

21

The Corvette moved easily up the mountain. When cars came up behind us, I steered into turnouts to let them pass. At the far edge of the passenger seat, Ellen Lang sat huddled in the jacket, eyes forward, as I told her what I knew. She only spoke twice. Once to ask me about the girls, and once to answer "no" when I told her the girls were with Janet and asked if she wanted me to bring her there.

We pulled into the carport, killed the engine, and went into the kitchen through the carport door. When we were inside she asked me to please be sure to lock the door, so I had her watch me throw the bolt. I went out to the living room for a bottle of Glenlivet and a couple of glasses that looked like they were made for something besides jam. When I got back she was holding one of my R.H. Forschner steak knives. I put ice into each glass, filled them with the scotch, then pried the steak knife out of her hand and replaced it with a glass. "Drink this, then I'll show you what we have."

I dumped mine back, threw out the ice, then refilled the glass and downed that, too. You can't beat Glenlivet for the smooth mellow glow it gives you, especially after you kill some people. I felt my nose and eyes fill and something large in my throat and I thought I was going to burst. But I bit down on it and managed some more of the scotch and it passed. When she had taken half of hers I led her through the house, first the dining area and living room and powder room on the main floor, then the loft bed above and the master bath. The bottle of scotch went with us. I turned on every light in each room and left it on. We looked in closets and in the storage space under the platform bed. I showed her that the windows and the front door and the sliding glass doors were all locked and I showed her the red light that meant the burglar alarm was armed. When we finished the tour upstairs I refilled her drink and said, "You can bathe in here. I've got an oversized hot-water heater, so use all you want. There's buttermilk soap and shampoo in the cabinet and extra towels under the sink." I went out to the closet and brought back the big white terry robe. "You can wear this. If you'd rather have some clothes, I've got a sweat shirt and some jogging shorts that a friend left over. They should fit."

"Where will you be?"

"In the kitchen. I have to make a call, and then I'll make us something to eat."

She thanked me and shut the door. I waited until I heard the water running, then the scotch and I went back to the kitchen. I took off my pistol, put it on the counter, then went into the bathroom and plucked my face. It was like playing buried treasure with a needle and a bright light. I dug out six little pieces of wood, washed, dabbed on alcohol, then looked at myself in the mirror. No permanent damage. At least nothing that you could see.

Back out in the kitchen, I refilled my glass, then dialed Lou Poitras at home. He said, "Do you know what time it is? I got kids in bed."

"Ellen Lang's over here. To get her I had to kill a couple of guys up in Beachwood Canyon, in a house just under the Hollywood sign."

Lou said, "Hold on." There was a knocking sound, like the receiver had been put down on a table, then nothing, then some scuffing sounds as the phone was picked up, then a little girl's voice, giggling. "Judy bit my heiny."

An extension was lifted and Poitras yelled he had it. A hang-up, and it was just me and Lou again. He said, "You get the boy, too?"

"No."

"You home?"

"Yeah."

"Does this have anything to do with you asking about Domingo Duran?"

"Yes."

Another pause, this one the kind when the background static becomes real noise. Then he said, "You're an asshole, Elvis. I'm on my way."

He hung up. I hung up. I sipped the scotch. Asshole. That Lou. What a kidder.

I called Joe Pike. He answered on the first ring, a little breathless, as if he were finishing a long run or a couple hundred push-ups. "Pike."

I could hear his stereo system in the background. Oldies but goodies. The Doors. "It's gotten hot," I said. I gave him the short version.

Pike asked no questions, made no comment. "Button up," he said. "I'm coming in."

Pike thinks Clint Eastwood talks too much.

I took eight eggs, cream, butter, and mushrooms out of the refrigerator. I got out the big pan, put it on the stove, and was opening three raisin muffins when Ellen Lang came down and stood in the little passageway between the counter and the wall.

She was wearing the terry robe and a pair of my socks. Her hair was damp and combed out and looked clean. So did her face. She looked good. She looked younger and maybe willing to laugh if you gave her something worth laughing at. "How are you doing?" I asked.

"You must be terribly tired," she said. "Let me do that." She moved to the stove.

"It's okay." I put the muffins face up in the toaster oven.

"Don't be silly," she said. "You've had a hard day. If you want to do something, you can make the coffee." Her eyes had turned to poached eggs. Her smile was weak but somehow pleasant, the sort of smile you get when you practice smiling because you think you have to. Like with Mort. Only now the poached-egg eyes were rimmed with something that could have been desperation.

I smiled as if everything was fine, and stepped back out of her way. "Okay."

She opened each cabinet, saw what was inside, then closed it and moved on. She looked over the food I had out, then put the cream back into the fridge and took peanut oil out of the cupboard. The oil and a little bit of the butter she put into the big pan. While they heated she beat the eggs with a little water, then placed the spoon neatly beside the bowl when the eggs were frothy. I could see Carrie in her. I said, "I always put in cream."

She chopped the mushrooms. "You men. Cream makes the eggs stick. Never put cream. Would you like to shower before we eat?"

"Later, thank you."

She moved around the kitchen as if I weren't there, or if I was, I was somebody else. We talked, but I didn't think she was talking to me. She was Barbara Billingsley and I was Hugh Beaumont. But not. I drank more of the scotch.

She got out two plates, forks, knives, and spoons, and brought them to the counter. She had to move the Dan Wesson to set out the plates, and stared at it before she did.

I went into the dining area to get placemats out of the buffet. When I looked at Ellen again she had picked up the gun. She held it like that, then brought it close and smelled it. I stood up. "There're placemats and napkins," I said.

She set the places even though I offered.

She put the eggs in the pan and turned on the toaster oven and put out butter and strawberry jam and salt and pepper, and then she told me to sit. She nursed the omelette, then eased it onto a serving plate, added a sprig of mint leaf as garnish, and brought it to the counter. A lovely presentation. She brought out cups and poured the coffee and asked me if I took cream and sugar. I said no. She said she hoped I would like it. I said it smelled wonderful. She asked if there was anything else I might want. I said no, this would be fine. She said it would be no trouble if there were. I said if I thought of something, I'd ask for it. I wanted to cry.

We didn't speak as we ate. She took one spoon of eggs and one side of a muffin. She ate that, then took some more. She ended up eating more eggs than me and half of the muffins. That was okay. I was happy with the scotch.

When she was finished she took a breath and let out a sigh like her body was trying to rid itself of ten years' accumulated poison.

I said, "A couple of friends of mine are on their way over. Joe Pike, who owns the agency with me, and a guy named Lou Poitras. Poitras is a sergeant with the LAPD. He's also a friend. We're going to have to talk to him and tell him what we know. Do you have any objection to that?"

She sipped some of the coffee and put down the cup. Her voice came out softly. "If I had let the police search the house when you wanted, would Mort still be alive?" Steam from the coffee crept around her hand like delicate vines. I watched the way the overhead light worked the planes of her face. She had a nice face when she didn't slump.

"No," I said. "Mort was already dead. There wasn't anything in the house that could've told us where he was."

She nodded. I drank more of the scotch. She drank more of the coffee. That's what we did until Poitras arrived.

22

Poitras said, "Okay, let's have it."

I told him everything from following the beach boy to Kimberly Marsh all the way up to what had just happened in Beachwood. He didn't laugh when I told him about Duran and the bull. He just chewed his lower lip and listened. Ellen Lang listened closely, too, as if she were taking notes on her own life. I kept my version of what Kimberly had said about Mort and the party at Duran's as brief as possible without leaving anything out. When I finished, Poitras went into the kitchen and used the phone.

I patted Ellen's arm. "You okay?"

She gave a little shrug. I drained the rest of the scotch, went to the cabinet for some more. Out of Glenlivet. Damn. I cracked a bottle of Chivas that a cheap client had given me as a present and brought it back to the couch. I drank some. Hell, it wasn't much different from the Glenlivet after all.

Ellen went into the dining area and came back with a coaster and a napkin. She put the coaster on the coffee table in front of me and the napkin on the arm of the couch by my hand. "There," she said.

Poitras came back and asked for her side of it. When he saw the Chivas bottle he gave me a look. I gave him a look back.

Ellen spoke slowly, in short, declarative sentences, describing how two men had approached her in the Ralph's parking lot, forced her into the backseat of their car, and taped a sack over her head. One of them was the tattooed man. They drove around for a while, Mexican music playing and one of them occasionally patting her rump, until they arrived at the Beachwood house. They told her that Mort had stolen cocaine from them and that they had killed him and would kill her, too, if she didn't tell them where Mort had hidden the dope. They wouldn't believe her when she told them she didn't know what they were talking about. They put a gun to her head and snapped the trigger and touched her breasts and between her legs and threatened to rape her, though they hadn't. One of them, the fat one, brought in Perry and slapped the boy repeatedly while the other asked her about the drugs. She screamed for them to leave Perry alone, but they wouldn't, and that was when she told them that Mort had hidden the cocaine but that now I had it. After that, another man came and they took the boy away and hadn't brought him back.

I watched her tell it and sipped at the Chivas and felt bad. Once when she mentioned Perry her voice broke. Other than that, she was fine. I decided she'd started out a pretty tough lady, back there in Kansas. So tough she took life-with-Mort on the chin for so long that it finally changed her into what Janet Simon had dragged into my office three days ago. I wondered if she could heal back to the person she had been. Could anyone, ever?

When she finished, Poitras ticked his fingers on his belt buckle and frowned at me. "Can you talk or are you incoherent?"

I sampled more of the scotch. Chivas ain't so bad no matter what they say. Probably just elitists, anyway.

Poitras excused himself to Ellen, then got up, and we went over to the kitchen. I brought my drink. He poured himself a cup of coffee and stared at me for a while. "You think Lang took the dope?"

I said, "I think Mort's lousy for it. I see him for the patsy. It's either inside or it's Garrett Rice or it's both. I'm thinking Duran's guys would be smarter than to try to screw the old man, so that puts it on Rice."

Poitras nodded. "We been trying to find him."

"Aha." My voice was loud.

Poitras looked at me. He didn't like what he saw a whole lot. "We talked with your friend Kimberly Marsh. Her boyfriend looked like he'd had a little trouble."

"Clumsy, that guy." It was getting tough to stand up straight, but I was doing okay.

Poitras said, "You think she had anything to do with it?"

"She'd go for it," I said. "Only she had no way to get away with it. Party like that, she'd be dressed sexy, showing as much skin as she could, no big pockets, no big purse, no way to hide four and a half pounds of dust."

He tapped his belt some more. "So now Duran has the boy."

I took more of the scotch and looked across the dining area out the glass doors. A police helicopter was pulling a tight orbit somewhere over Hollywood, its big spot tracking something on the ground.

Poitras said, "You asked me how much weight Duran could carry, remember? That was when I asked you if this had anything to do with Morton Lang, and you lied?"

I looked at him. He was angry. He was also out of focus.

"We've got files since 1964 connecting Duran to the Rudy Gambino family, operating out of Phoenix and Los Angeles," he said. "He's what the feds call a clean associate. Duran won't set up a dope deal or muscle into a business, but he invests through a guy like Gambino. The feds have been trying to bust Duran for years, only they can't because he keeps himself clean. They've got him placed as an investor with dope up from Colombia, with hotel kickbacks in Phoenix and Tucson. He owns a couple of banks in Mexico City and he's on the board of a bank in New Orleans. Gambino launders his Gulf Coast pornography take through Duran's New Orleans bank and gives Duran a cut. It goes on like that. This give you some idea what kind of weight he can handle?"

"Yeah."

"Yeah." Poitras walked away from me, back into the living room. "Mrs. Lang, who was the man who came and took your son?"

She said, "I don't think they called him by name. He spoke to the other men in Spanish, then he told Perry they were leaving. He said that in English with a different accent. It wasn't Spanish."

"That would be the Eskimo," I said.

Poitras said to her, "Did you see anyone who might've been Domingo Duran, or did any of the men in the house refer to him?"

She looked at me with a little bit of the fear back in her eyes. "What's wrong?" she said.

"He isn't liking it. He's coming in late in the game and we've got bad cards."

"You got no cards at all." Poitras looked big and grim and ominous, like the Michelin Man with a bad headache. He said, "You should've put me in on this as soon as you suspected, Elvis."

Ellen Lang said, "What're you talking about? What's wrong?" The first bright tinge of panic.

I said, "What's wrong is that Duran can beat what we have. He's kept himself away from it except for me and he can beat my story easy enough if people in the right place are willing to say the wrong thing. They will be. My statement gives the cops probable cause to go in to Duran's, but Duran won't have Perry in his home. He'll deny everything, and all we've done is jeopardize Perry with nothing but a guy named Sanchez to show for it." It came out harder than I liked, but I was angry with Poitras and too drunk to handle it.

Lou said, "That's about it."

Ellen Lang got white and the corner of her mouth with the red mark began to tremble. I put my hand over hers and squeezed. Her jaw clenched and the trembling stopped. "I'm all right," she said.

The phone rang and Poitras went back into the kitchen for it. I poured some of the Chivas into Ellen's coffee cup and put it in her hand. "It's going to be fine," I said. "Trust me. It'll work out." I gave her my everything-under-control smile. She didn't look convinced. Maybe it's tough for a drunk to look convincing. I saw the Eskimo put a size 18 hand on the boy's shoulder. I saw them walk out to the long black limo. I saw the limo disappearing into the high desert hills. I saw Domingo Duran, jabbing his sword toward the hills, saying *Then other men will come, and put your body there, where you will not be found.*

I spilled another inch of Chivas into my glass, then went into the kitchen so Ellen Lang couldn't see me drink it. Poitras was talking in that low mumble cops use that only other cops can hear and understand. After a while he hung up and said, "Okay. You left two in the house, like you thought. Fat guy in the hall and another one in the living room. The house is listed to a man named Louis Foley. The neighbors up there say Foley moved to Seattle two months ago and that the house has been up for sale. Your guys probably just pulled up the sign and cracked the lock box."

"That's great. They'll promote you to Lieutenant along with Baishe for this kinda work."

He looked at me. "You're pushing it, Hound Dog."

"And you're acting like an asshole with that woman in there. She's been through hell and all you got to say is a lot of bullshit about how I didn't call you in and how we got nothing. Negative bullshit that she doesn't need to deal with. She's missing a child, Poitras. She's lost her husband."

I was very close to him. His big face was calm. He said, "Take a step back, Elvis."

It was quiet in the kitchen with just his breathing and my breathing and the hum of the electric clock over the sink. The cat door clacked and the cat walked in. Staring at Poitras, I couldn't see him but I heard him growl, low and deep in his chest at finding a stranger in the kitchen. I heard the *snick-snick* of claws on the floor, then the crunch of hard food.

Poitras said softly, "You're drunk, man."

I nodded.

He said, "You found the lady and you went in and the boy wasn't there. You pulled the trigger. I know you, I know it's because you had to. You wouldn't have played it that way if you'd had a choice. But there weren't any choices. It was lousy that the kid wasn't there. You didn't lose the kid. He just wasn't there to be had."

I felt my eyes grow hot. I took more of the Chivas.

He made his voice quieter. "You always get in too deep, don't you? Always get too close to the client. Fall a little bit in love."

"Go to hell."

Poitras took the glass out of my hands and emptied it in the sink. He went out into the living room, bent over Ellen Lang, and spoke in that cop mumble. After a while she nodded and gave him a tiny smile. The cat walked over and sat by my feet. *Snick-snick-snick.* He stared up at me and purred. Sometimes a little love can be important.

Poitras came back and leaned against the counter with his arms crossed.

"Thanks," I said.

He nodded. "Even drunk you make a point."

I put on a fresh pot of coffee while Poitras made more phone calls, most local but at least one up to Sacramento. Between the calls we went through it again, and this time Poitras took notes. When the coffee was ready I poured fresh cups and brought one out to Ellen Lang. She had fallen asleep with the old cup in her hand. I went up to the loft, turned down the bed, then went back down. Ellen woke when I touched her arm, then followed me up and climbed into the bed still wearing the robe and the socks. She curled into a ball on her side, knees up, hands together under her chin. Fetal position, only with her eyes open. Large, liquid Bambi eyes. Something stirred in the empty part of my stomach, the part the scotch didn't fill.

"I'm scared," she said.

"Don't be," I said. "I never fail."

She looked at me and then she fell back to sleep.

I went downstairs and found Pike standing in the entry. Poitras was in the dining area, the coiled phone cord stretched taut from his coming out of the kitchen to see who had walked in. Poitras' gun was in his right hand hanging loose at his side. He stared at Pike a couple seconds, then went back into the kitchen to get off the phone.

Pike said, "You okay?" He was wearing a cammie Marine Corps field jacket.

"Good. You want something to eat or drink?"

Pike shook his head as Poitras came back out of the kitchen. The cat stuck his head out, saw Pike, made a wide arc around Poitras, and padded over to rub against Pike's legs. "Well, well. The big time cop," Pike said.

Poitras' face was empty the way a traffic cop's face is empty when he's listening to you try to talk your way out of a ticket. "You ever wanna work out, bo. You know where the gym is."

Pike's mouth twitched.

Poitras' shoulders flexed, filling most of the dining area with his bulk.

"Here's to good friends," I said. "Lemme see if I've got some Löwenbräu." Mr. Levity.

Pike's mouth twitched again, his dark glasses never moving away from Poitras. "You got the woman here?"

I said yes.

"You going to stay in all night?"

I said yes again. Poitras kept his eyes on Pike. Motionless. Two tomcats squaring off across a property line.

"You need me, I'll be around." Pike reached back to the door, looked at Poitras before he opened it. "We don't see each other enough anymore, Lou."

"Drop dead, Pike."

Pike's mouth twitched and he left, holding the door long enough for the cat to follow. The tension level dropped around three hundred points.

"I'll have to have you two guys over for lunch sometime," I said. "Or maybe a dinner party."

Poitras flexed his jaw, put .50-caliber eyes on me. "You tell me the next time that sonofabitch is going to be around."

"Sure, Lou."

Poitras went into the kitchen, made another phone call, then came back into the living room carrying a cup of coffee. His face was smooth and calm, as if Pike had never been. "There might be a way to work this Duran thing."

"Unh-huh."

"You willing to stay in it?"

I said, "Duran's expecting me to produce the dope. Maybe I can. Maybe I can put the dope and Duran and the boy together. If I can do that, we own him. If I can do that without tipping him to what's going on, we can get the boy back."

Poitras sipped more of the coffee. "Sometimes you think like a pretty good cop."

"We all have our weak moments."

Poitras nodded. "You think Duran wants the dope that bad?"

"I don't think he cares about the dope at all. He's pissed that someone would steal from him in his own home. He's got a highly developed sense of territory."

Poitras smiled crookedly. "Macho."

I nodded.

Poitras said, "Yeah, me and you are thinking along the same lines. Maybe I can help you with the dope. I'll see. I'll have to run it up the line and get it okayed."

"Up the line through Baishe?"

"You don't make it to lieutenant without something on the ball, Hound Dog. Even Baishe."

"My confidence is bolstered."

"That's all we care about down at the PD, keepin' you confident." He folded up his note pad, slipped it in his back pocket, and headed toward the door. "Come around first thing tomorrow and we'll work this thing out. If anything happens between now and then, let me know. When things start to break it'll be tricky. You'll have to play it our way."

"Can't we do it professionally instead?"

Poitras grinned hard and without humor. He said, "You know something, Hound Dog? It sounded to me like Duran maybe thought you and he had an understanding. Now you break out the woman and kill a couple of his soldiers. He's probably gonna be pissed. He might even come after you."

"There's Pike."

Poitras' face went dead. He opened the door and stepped out. "You got lousy taste in partners."

"Who else would put up with me?"

I stood in the door until Poitras drove away. Off to the left I heard the cat growl, and Joe Pike answer, "Good cat."

23

I showered and shaved, then went through the house dousing the extra lights that I had turned on for Ellen Lang. The house was quiet, warm in the gold light from the lamp beside the couch, and comfortable. There were books on the shelves that I liked to read and reread, and prints and originals on the walls that I liked to look at. Like the office, I was proud of it. Like the office, it was the result of a process and the process was ongoing. The house lived, as did the person within it. Upstairs, Ellen Lang shifted under the covers.

I got six aspirin from the powder room, ate them, then got my sleeping bag from the entry closet, spread it on the couch, and stretched out. My head rocked from side to side, floating on the scotch, and started to spin. I sat up.

It was too late for the final sports recap. Too late for Ted Koppel. Maybe I could luck into a rerun of Howard Hawks' *The Thing* with Ken Tobey. When I was a boy, Ken Tobey kept the monsters away. He battled things from other worlds and creatures from the bottom of the sea and prehistoric beasts and he always won. Ken Tobey fought the monsters and kept us safe. He always won. That was the trick. Any jerk can get his ass creamed.

The cat came in a little while later, jumped onto the couch next to me, stepped into my lap, and began to purr. His fur was chill from having been out. I petted him. And petting him, fell asleep.

I dreamed I was in a hot dusty arena and Domingo Duran, replete with Suit of Lights, was advancing toward me, little sword before him and cape extended. The crowd was cheering, and beautiful women threw roses. I figured I was supposed to be the bull, but when I looked down I saw my regular arms and my regular feet. Where the hell was the bull? Just then, Duran's cape flew up and a dark, satanic bull charged me. Not just any bull. This one wore mukluks and sealskin boots. When I dream, you don't have to hop the

Concorde to Vienna to figure it out. Just as the bull was about to horn me with something looking suspiciously like a harpoon, I felt myself spinning out of the arena, spinning up and up until I was awake in my still-dark house.

Ellen Lang stood at the glass doors, her back to me, arms at her sides, staring down into Hollywood. Beside me the cat shifted, out of it. Some watchcat.

I listened to the house, listened to my breath. She never moved. After a while I said, quietly so as not to startle her, "We'll find him."

She turned. Her face was shadowed. "I didn't want to wake you."

"You didn't."

She made a little sound in her throat and came over to the big chair by the couch. She didn't sit. I had fallen asleep on top of the sleeping bag and was cold but didn't want to move. I could see her face now, blue in the moonlight.

She looked out at Hollywood, then down at me. She said, "They wouldn't believe me. I told them I didn't know what they were talking about but they just kept asking. Then they brought in Perry. They kept saying I knew and I had to tell them, and they kept slapping him and feeling me and saying that they would rape me in front of Perry, and that I had better tell them. I thought of you. I told them I thought you had it."

"It's okay."

"I'm sorry."

"You don't have to be sorry."

"I'm ashamed of myself. It wasn't right."

I lifted the cat, sat up, then put the cat back down beside me.

She said, "Would you like coffee?"

"No, thanks."

"If you're hungry, I could make something."

I shook my head. "If I want anything, I'll get it. But thank you."

She nodded and curled up in the big chair across from me, her feet tucked under her.

I said, "Would you like me to turn on a light?"

"If it's what you want."

I left the light off.

After a while the cat stood up, stretched, turned in a circle, and lay back down. He said, *roawmph*. Ellen said, "I didn't know you had a cat."

"I don't. He lives here because I'm easy to sucker for beer and food. Don't try to pet him. He's mean and he bites."

She smiled, her teeth blue in the reflected moonlight.

"Besides that, he's dirty and he carries germs."

Her smile widened for an instant, then faded.

We sat some more. Outside, another police helicopter flew very low up the canyon and over the house. When I was little we lived near an air base and I was terrified that the airplanes and helicopters would scare away Santa Claus. Years later, in Vietnam, I grew to like the sound. It meant someone was coming to save me.

Ellen Lang said quietly, "I don't know if there's any money. I don't know if I can feed the children. I don't know if I can pay for the house or the school or any of those things."

"I'll check the insurance for you. If worse comes to worst, you can sell the house. You would sell Mort's car, anyway. The kids can go to public schools. You'll adapt. You'll do all right and so will the kids."

She sat very still. "I've never been alone before."

"I know." The helicopter looped back and disappeared toward the reservoir. I wondered if Joe Pike was watching it. "You've got the children. There's me. When it's over doesn't mean you never see me again."

She nodded.

"I'm a full-service op. I provide follow-up service and yearly maintenance just like Mr. Goodwrench."

She nodded again.

"Just like the Shell Answer Man."

She didn't respond. This stuff would kill'm in the Comedy Store. Maybe she only laughed at cat jokes. I looked at the cat. He offered little inspiration.

"There's even Janet."

"Who reinforces my lousy self-image?"

"Keep you humble."

She said, "You're sweet, trying to cheer me up like this. Thank you."

We sat. Ellen stared out the window. I stared at Ellen. Her hair was dry and brushed out and offset her small narrow face nicely. The pale light softened her features and I could see the girl back in Kansas, a nice girl who'd be great to bring to a football game on a cold night, who'd sit close to you and jump up when the home team scored and who'd feel good to hug.

After a very long time, she said softly, "It must be beautiful, living up here."

"It is."

"Are there coyotes?"

"Yes. They like the hills above the reservoir."

She looked at the cat. "I heard they take cats. I had a friend in Nichols Canyon who lost two that way."

I touched the cat's head between his ears. It was broad and flat and lumpy with scars. A good cat head.

She shifted in the chair. She was sitting on her feet, and when she moved she was careful to keep the robe over her knees. She said, "Tell me, how can you live with someone for so long and know so little about them?"

"You can know only what someone shows you."

"But I lived with Mort for fourteen years. I knew Garrett Rice for five years. I was married to Mort for eight years before I even knew there were other women. Now I find out about drugs. I never knew there were drugs." Her lips barely moved, matching the stillness of the rest of her. "He said it was me. He said I was killing him. He said he would lie in bed some nights, hoping I would die and thinking of ways to hurt me."

"It wasn't you."

"Then how could Mort be that person, and how could I not know? His wife. What does that say about me?" A whisper.

"It says you trusted a man who didn't deserve your trust. It says you gave of yourself completely because you loved him. It comments on Mort's quality, not yours."

"I've been so wrong about things. Everything's been such a lie. I'm thirty-nine years old and I feel like I've thrown my life away."

"Look at me," I said.

She looked.

"When you marry someone, and put your trust in them, you have a right to expect that they will be there for you. The marriage doesn't have to be perfect. *You* don't have to be perfect. By virtue of the commitment, your partner is supposed to be there. Without having to look around, you have to know they're there. When you looked, Mort wasn't there. Mort hadn't been there for a long time. It doesn't matter about his problems. He failed to live up to you. Mort lived the lie. Not you. Mort threw it away. Not you."

Her head moved. "That sounds so harsh."

"I'm feeling a little harsh toward Mort right now." I took short breaths, feeling the booze still there. The big room had grown warmer.

We sat like that for several minutes. I was slouched on the sofa with my abdominal muscles forming neat rows leading up to my ribs. My legs were extended, my feet on the coffee table. I looked blue.

"I don't mean to whine," she said.

"You hurt. It's okay."

She brought her feet out from under her with a soft rustle, and sat forward. I heard her draw a deep breath and sigh it out. She said, "You're a very nice man."

"Unh-hunh."

She said, "What happened"—she leaned forward out of the chair and touched my stomach—"here?"

When she touched me the muscles in my stomach and pelvic girdle and thighs bunched. Her finger was very warm, almost hot. I said, "I got into a fight with a man in Texas City, Texas. He cut me with a piece of glass."

She moved her finger about an inch along the scar. I stood up, pulling her to me. She held on tight and whispered something into my chest that I did not hear.

I carried her upstairs and made love to her. She called me Mort. Afterward I held her, but it was a long time before she slept. And when she slept it was fitful and without rest.

24

The morning sky was a rich orange when I left the bed. Ellen was up, wearing the socks and the big terry robe. She had the washing machine going, doing two towels and the clothes she had been in since Ralph's, and had started breakfast by the time I was showered and dressed.

"I called Janet," she said.

"What a way to start your day."

"I asked her to tell the girls that I was in San Francisco and that I'd have to be there a few days. Do you think that's all right?"

"It's smart if you don't go home."

She nodded.

"You could stay here."

She nodded again.

"That okay with Janet?"

The young pretty part of her momentarily surfaced. "I'll call her and ask." Definite progress.

The cat door clacked and the cat came in, his fur misted with dew. He saw Ellen, went to her ankle, sniffed, and started to growl.

I said, "Get away from there."

The cat sprinted back through his door. *Clack-clack.*

There was a knock, then Joe Pike walked in. He was misted with dew, also. "Couple of black-and-whites cruised you just before sunup. Other than that, nada."

I introduced him to Ellen.

She said, "You're the one in the pictures." There were pictures up in the bedroom of me and Pike after billfish off Cabo San Lucas at the tip of Baha.

"I'm the only one in the pictures," he said. Enigmatically. Then he left.

"He's like that," I said.

"Mr. Pike is your partner?"

"Unh-hunh."

"He was out there all night?"

"All night."

"Why?"

"To watch over us, why else?"

Joe came back with an Eastern Airlines flight bag and a brown leather rifle case and without the field jacket. He put the rifle case in the entry closet, took a Colt .357 Python in a clip-on holster from the flight bag, and put it on his hip. He took two boxes of .357 Softnose out of the bag, then rezipped it and put it in the closet next to the rifle. The boxes of extra ammo he brought to the coffee table by Ellen Lang. She watched every move the way a canary watches a cat, her eyes going from his tattoos to the gun at his waist—it was the big Python, with the 6-inch combat barrel—to the polished sunglasses. Pike was in uniform: faded Levis', blue Nikes, white sweat socks, steel Rolex, sleeveless sweat shirt. When he had everything where he wanted it, he looked at her again. "I'm sorry to hear of your trouble," he said.

She tried out a small, faltering smile. "Would you like something to eat?"

"It's nice of you to offer. No. Not right now."

He stood close, dwarfing her with his size and his energy and his capacity for violence. He did it without thinking about it. He could do it to almost anyone I knew, even men much taller and much heavier. Anyone except Lou Poitras.

Pike went into the kitchen. Ellen watched him, large-eyed and uneasy. "You'll be fine," I said. "The Amal militia couldn't touch you with him here."

She kept her eyes on Pike. Joe was standing in the kitchen, staring at a closed cabinet, unmoving. It was easy to imagine him standing all night like that.

"I'm going to swing by your house before I go to the cops," I said. "Can I bring back some clothes for you?"

"Yes. If you would. And my toothbrush. It's the green one."

"Would you like to come with me?"

She glanced at the floor. "I don't want to go back there right now."

The drive to Encino was easy. This early, traffic down the valley side of Laurel Canyon was light and the freeway west seemed empty. I parked in Ellen's drive and let myself in the front door. There is no quiet the way a house is quiet when its family is gone.

I found an empty Ralph's bag in the kitchen and brought it

back to the master bath. I packed her green toothbrush in it, along with a bottle of Almay roll-on that was probably hers, and a Personal Touch shaver. I opened the counter drawers and stared into them a while, wondering what she might want. I took out three little white Georgette Klinger face cream jars, two lip gloss tubes, a marbled plastic box of Clinique blush, a Clinique eye liner pencil, and two silver tins of Clinique eye shadow, and put them in the bag. You never can tell. Out in the bedroom, I selected panties, bras, a pair of white New Balance running shoes, three light tops, two pairs of cotton pants, and one pair of Jordache jeans. Mort's insurance policy was in the same box where I had found his banking papers. He had purchased a $200,000 policy three years before but had borrowed against past premiums. Its current value was written down to $40,000. Not a lot, but she wasn't broke. She'd have to plan. I put the policy back in the box and went through the room for Mort's .32. Nothing. I went through the living room, the dining room, the kitchen. Nothing. I went through the kids' rooms. Zip.

At twenty minutes after eight I parked beside the North Hollywood station house and went up to the detectives' squad room. Poitras was standing by a desk, talking to Griggs in a low voice. Griggs was sipping coffee from a mug that said #1 DADDY and nodding. When Poitras saw me he said something else to Griggs, then jerked his head back toward his office. He didn't look happy. "Come on," he said.

"Top of the morning to you, too, Louis."

A thin blond man sat in the hard chair in Poitras' office. He wore brown slacks and brand-new tan Bally loafers with little tassels and a brown coarse-knit jacket with patches on the elbows. He had a dark beige shirt and a yellow tie with little white camels. Silk. He glowed the way skinny guys glow then they get up early and play three sets at the club. I made him for Stanford Law. Poitras dropped into his chair behind the desk and said, "This is O'Bannon." When Poitras looked at O'Bannon his flat face hardened and his eyes ticked. "From Special Operations."

O'Bannon didn't offer to shake my hand. He said, "From the California Attorney General's office, attached to Spec Op."

Spec Op. Stanford Law, all right. "You say that to girls when you try to pick'm up?" I said.

O'Bannon smiled the way a fish smiles when it's been on ice

all day. "No, only to smart guys who've been tagged for two bodies up in Beachwood Canyon. You want to push it?"

They make'm tough up at Stanford.

"I thought not. Tell me about your encounter with Duran."

I started at the beginning, when Ellen Lang and Janet Simon came to my office. O'Bannon stopped me. "Poitras filled me in on the background. Just tell me about your contact with Domingo Duran."

I started again. I told him how the Eskimo and Manolo picked me up in my office and brought me out to the bull ranch, and I told him what happened out there. Listening to myself describe Duran and reconstruct the dialogue and sequence of events, I came out sounding pretty good. It's easy to sound good. All you do is leave in the parts where you act tough and forget the parts where you get shoved around. At one point we got up and went out into the squad room where they have a big map of L.A. and the surrounding counties so I could ballpark the ranch. O'Bannon wrote down everything I said. He reminded me of Jimmy Olsen, only nastier.

When I finished, O'Bannon stared at me like I was the biggest disappointment of his life. "That it?"

"I could make up more if you want."

"Did the Lang woman have any direct contact with Duran?"

"The Lang woman's name is Ellen, or Ms. Lang."

O'Bannon gave me you're-wasting-my-time eyes. I get those a lot.

"No, no direct contact."

He folded his note pad and put it in his inside jacket pocket, unconcerned that it might ruin the line. Daring, he was. Gotta be daring for Spec Op. He said, "All right. We may need to talk to her later."

I looked at Lou. "Later?"

O'Bannon nodded. "There a problem with that?"

"I figured maybe we could do a little better than later. You know, with her son missing and all."

O'Bannon pulled a brown briefcase from beside the hard chair. "There's no 'we.' This is a Spec Op case now. You're out. We're handling the investigation."

Poitras' jaw worked and he picked at something invisible on his desk. He said, carefully, "Somebody downtown decided Special Operations was better suited to cover Duran."

"What the hell does that mean?"

His voice came out ugly. "What the hell does it sound like,

Elvis? You took an IQ reducer since last night? We're out. You're out. That's the end of it."

I said, "O'Bannon, there's a nine-year-old kid out there. You don't need a goddamned investigation. I'm handing you the scam and the setup and the bust."

O'Bannon took a manila file folder off the end of Poitras' desk, put it in his briefcase, snapped the brass latches. It was a Gucci case. He hefted it, then turned and looked at me the way prosecutors look at jurors when they're showing off. "Spec Op will handle it, Cole. You're out. You're not to approach Duran, nor to proceed with this in any way. He's off limits. You go near him, I'll yank your license for violating the Private Investigators Act of California. You got that?"

"I'll bet you can't get it up, can you, O'Bannon?"

He tried to give me the sort of glare he'd seen fighters give on TV. Then he walked out.

The big redheaded secretary was talking to Griggs down by the rec room door. She watched O'Bannon pass and shook her head. I didn't move for a very long time and neither did Poitras. Then I got up, carefully shut Poitras' door, and went back to my chair. "Who shut it off, Lou?" I said, softly.

"It ain't been shut off. Other people are handling it, that's all."

"Bullshit."

Poitras' eyes were small and hard. Kielbasa fingers worked against each other with no purpose. Someone knocked at the door. Poitras went red. He yelled, "Beat it!"

The door opened anyway and Griggs came in. He closed the door behind him and leaned against it, arms crossed. Only a couple of hours into the morning and he already looked rumpled and tired.

I said, "It's still kidnapping, Lou. You can pass it to the feds."

Griggs said quietly, "You know the rules, bo. You pass it up the line, up the line has to refer it."

"Did Baishe bring them in?"

"Goddamn it, it wasn't Baishe," Lou said. "You got Baishe on the brain. Forget him. He was for it."

"What do I tell Ellen Lang?"

"Tell her it's a Special Operations bust. Tell her someone from Special Operations might come talk to her."

"Later."

"Yeah. Later."

"Is that what I tell Duran when he calls?"

"You're off Duran. That's the word. You go around Duran, O'Bannon will use those two bodies up Beachwood to grind you up."

"They grow'm hard up at Stanford Law," Griggs said. "Only a hard guy could wear a tie with little white camels like that, right, Lou?"

Lou didn't say anything.

I said, "This smells like buy-off, Lou. Like Duran picked up the phone."

Poitras leaned back in his chair and swiveled to look at the file cabinet. Or maybe he was looking at the pictures of his kids. "Get the hell out of here, Elvis."

I got up and went to the door. Griggs gave me sleepy eyes, then peeled himself away from the door and opened it.

I looked back at Lou. "The cops up in Lancaster happen to find a Walther .32 automatic in Lang's car?"

"How the hell do I know?"

"He had one."

"Good-bye."

I walked out. The door closed behind me, and I heard something heavy hit something hard. I kept walking.

The redhead was gone. I walked out past the rec room and the holding cell and into the stairwell. I met Baishe coming up. His face looked softer and older. He stopped me on the stairs. "I got a prowlcar making extra passes at Duran's place. That's the best I can do."

We nodded at each other, then he went up to the squad room and I went down and out to my car.

25

It was already hot out in the parking lot. I pushed down the top on the Corvette, climbed in, and sat thinking about Perry Lang and his mother and how O'Bannon might want to talk to her. Later. That was probably okay with Perry. He was probably having a good time. The Eskimo was probably showing him how to eat seal fat and Manolo was probably giving him piggyback rides and Duran was probably teaching him the correct technique for a *verónica,* with *temple.* Of course, when Duran called and I told him he was now a Spec Op, he'd probably get pissed and stop the lessons. Then it wouldn't be very much fun at all. I took out my wallet, looked at my license for a long time, then folded the wallet again and put it back in my pocket. Screw you, O'Bannon.

I peeled out of the parking lot and laid a strip of Goodyear rubber halfway down the street.

Ten minutes later I was parked across from the Burbank Studios and walking back toward Garrett Rice's office. The backhoe and the bulldozer were tearing up the little parking lot and kicking up a lot of dust that I had to walk through to get to the stairs. Rice's door was closed and locked. I knocked and looked through the glass panel next to the door. The outer office was dark, Rice's inner office darker still. I went to the next office.

The door was propped open, and an almost-pretty blonde in a green LaCoste shirt was fanning herself with a *Daily Variety* behind the desk. She raised her eyebrows at me, something my mother had done quite a bit. I said, "Has Mr. Rice been in?"

"I don't think so, today. Sheila left about a half hour ago."

"Sheila the secretary?"

"Unh-huh. You an actor?"

"Look sorta like John Cassavetes, right?"

She stuck her lips out and shook her head. "No, you just have the look, that's all. I know the look. Hungry."

"A man is defined by his appetites."

Her eyes smiled. "Unh-huh."

I gave her one of my better smiles and walked loudly back to the stairs, waited a few seconds to see if she'd stir, then eased back to Rice's door, picked the lock, and let myself in.

Nothing much had changed since the last time I was there. The furnishings were still cheap, the dead mouse stain still marked the couch, the plants still clung to life. There were crumbs beneath the couch cushions, along with three pennies, a nickel, two dimes, and a Winston cigarette. The top three drawers of the file cabinet held yellowing scripts and news clippings, and articles and short stories that had been snipped from magazines. The bottom drawer was actors' résumés and correspondence and interoffice memos. More than one of the memos warned Rice against any further evidence of copyright infringement.

Behind the memos there was a mason jar of marijuana, two packs of Zig Zag papers, and three porno magazines. One titled *Lesbian Delight*, another *Women in Pain*, and the last *Little Lovers*. *Little Lovers* was kids.

I took a deep breath and stood up and felt tired. You feel tired a lot in this business.

I shredded *Little Lovers* into a metal waste can and brought the can over to the window looking out at the water tower. There was a book of matches in the top drawer of the desk. I put the can beneath the window and burned away the images of the children and what some animal had made those children do. If Rice walked in, maybe I'd burn him, too.

When I finished with that I went through the rest of the desk. There was no cocaine. No clues to Garrett Rice's whereabouts. No unexpected or surprising evidence. In the middle drawer on the right side of his desk there was a small yellowed envelope postmarked June 1958. It was a handwritten note from Jane Fonda, saying how much she had enjoyed working with Garrett during a recent summer stock production and that Garrett was one of the most professional stage managers it had been her pleasure to meet. It was signed, *Love, Jane*. The edges of the note and the envelope were smudged and gray, as if Rice took it out and read it often.

I went out to the secretary's office and checked her calendar. There weren't any special notes or appointments scheduled for Mr. Rice. There weren't even any unspecial ones. I looked up Garrett Rice in her rolodex and pulled the card. It had his home phone, which I already had, but it also had his home address, which I didn't. I gave him a call, let it ring twenty-two times, then hung up. Maybe he was taking an early lunch.

I called my office and had the answer machine play back the messages. There weren't any. I didn't like that. After last night, the Eskimo should've called. I punched another line and dialed my house.

One ring. "Pike."

"There's an address book upstairs on the left side of the phone. I need Cleon Tyner's home number."

"Wait."

In a few moments the upstairs extension lifted and Pike gave me the number.

"Ellen okay?" I said.

"She likes to wait on people."

"It's all she knows how to do."

"She's cleaning the house. If you came back now, she'd probably wash your car."

"Have her check the Cherokee. It looked a little dirty on my way out this morning."

Pike gave me Hard Silence. Then: "How'd it go with the cops?"

I told him.

"Special Operations," he said. "That's shit."

"Close enough to smell bad."

"Poitras is good. Poitras won't shit you."

"Poitras doesn't like it any more than me. Someone up the line yanks the deal from Poitras, this asshole O'Bannon tells me to back away. Nobody knows anything. If it's a buy-out then they're selling the kid to let Duran handle us himself."

"What's Cleon got to do with this?"

"He was working for Garrett Rice. Only I can't see Cleon on the other side. I can't see him selling muscle to take down a dope deal. You know Cleon."

"People change."

"You haven't changed since 1975."

"Other people."

I hung up, then dialed Cleon Tyner. A woman with a hoarse bar singer's voice answered.

I said, "I was trying to get Eartha Kitt for the Sands, but everybody says Betty Tyner is sexier."

She laughed. "Oh? And how would everybody know?"

"Her walk, her talk—"

"The way she crawls on her belly like a reptile?"

I said, "Now you're embarrassing me."

She laughed louder, the strong healthy laugh of a woman at ease with herself. We spent a few minutes bringing each other up to date and trading friendly insults before she said, "Well, since you ain't asked me to marry you yet, I'll bet you're calling for that shiftless brother of mine."

"Amazing. The woman not only is fantastic in bed, but she mind-reads, too."

"How you think I got to be so fantastic?"

"Practice?"

She suggested an anatomical impossibility. "Cleon's working. He ain't been here for a couple of days."

"He go out of town?"

"I don't know, babe. He just said something about staying with the client. Said the man was walking sideways he was so scared."

We shot the breeze another few minutes, with me promising to give a call soon, and her saying I'd better, then we hung up. The door in the next office closed, and the blonde secretary walked by, carrying a large blue purse. She didn't glance in and she didn't see me sitting in the dark at Sheila's desk, staring at Garrett Rice's address.

I opened the door enough to see that no one was on the walk, then let myself out and drove to Garrett Rice's house in the hills above the Sunset Strip.

Rice lived in a low-slung white stucco modern on a little cul-de-sac off Sunset Plaza Drive. It was the sort of place that went for half a million plus today, but if you were lucky enough to be working in the sixties it didn't cost you more than eighty or ninety thou. I drove into the cul-de-sac, circled, then parked at the curb in front of Rice's house. Each house was set back enough to have some sort of gate and some sort of motor court and some sort of lush greenery, mostly ivy and banana trees and giant ferns. There were walls between each house and tall skinny cyprus so you wouldn't have to see the next guy's roofline, and none of the houses had very much in the way of windows looking out toward the street. Easier to forget the world if you didn't have to see it. They probably gave great block parties, though.

I walked up through the little motor court to Garrett Rice's door. There was a little white form envelope from the LAPD thumbtacked to the jamb. Inside there would be a little white form note informing *(Mr. Garrett Rice)* that *(officer's name written in)* wished to speak with him and requesting that *(Mr. Garrett Rice)* call *(officer's phone number)* at his earliest opportunity. I had seen these notes before. I wondered if Elliot Ness ever saw them. Probably what killed him.

I rang the bell. No answer. I knocked. Still no answer. Across the street a woman in pink frou frou slippers and a pretentious silver housecoat watched me from her drive as a Yorkie sniffed at the thick ivy in front of their house. I nodded at the woman and smiled. She nodded back but didn't smile. Probably too early to smile. Can't smile when you're still in the housecoat.

There was no car in the motor court, no way to see into the garage, and nothing parked on the street but my Vette. Cleon drove a black '83 Trans Am. I didn't know what Garrett Rice drove. I went back to my car, climbed in, and thought about it.

Poitras said the cops had tried to see Rice two days ago. That meant the little call-back note had been posted for two days and Rice hadn't seen it. Or maybe he had, but wanted the cops to think he hadn't, and left it there.

Or maybe Garrett Rice, who was so scared he asked Cleon Tyner, not the most social of people, to move in with him, had blown town. That made sense if he had had the dope, and then moved it. Cashed in and ran from Duran. He'd still be scared enough to want a muscle like Cleon along so he could sleep at night. He'd sport for the plane fare and head for parts unknown. Sure. That made sense. But Cleon being part of it, that didn't. Betty had once chased the dragon with a lounge owner from Riverside. Cleon found out when she ended the chase in the Riverside ER. The lounge mysteriously burned. The lounge owner's Caddie mysteriously blew up. The lounge owner himself mysteriously disappeared. Cleon Tyner suffered neither dope nor dopers. So. Dilemma, dilemma.

The woman in the silver lamé housecoat came out into the street and stared at me with her hands on her hips, then pointed at a little sign planted in the ivy by her drive. Every house on the street had one, a little red sign that said *Bel Air Patrol—Armed Response*. I stuck my tongue out at her and crossed my eyes. She gave me the finger and went back into her compound. Another close brush with dangerous, affluent-class life-forms.

I took a deep breath, let it out, and started my car. I was

26

At the bottom of Sunset Plaza I parked behind a gelato place and used the pay phone to call Pat Kyle at General Entertainment and ask her if she'd heard anything more about Mort or Garrett. She asked if she could call me right back. I gave her the number on the pay phone, then hung up, bought a cup of double chocolate banana, and enjoyed the extra butterfat.

The minutes ticked by, slow and heavy. I took small bites of the gelato and thought about the girl behind the counter to keep from thinking about Perry Lang and Ellen Lang and Domingo Duran and a guy named O'Bannon. She caught me staring and stared back. She couldn't have been more than sixteen, pretty despite yellow and black eyeshadow, yellow lip gloss, and yellow and black paint in her hair. The hair was spiked and stood out straight from her head like thick fuzz. The bumblebee look. She had a nice even tan and large breasts and probably two parents who wouldn't think kindly of a thirty-five-year-old man wondering what their baby looked like without clothes.

I said, "I'm John Cassavetes."

"Who?"

I said, "Tell me the truth, do I look more like John Cassavetes or Tony Dow?"

She cocked her head. "I think you look like Andy Summers, only bigger and more athletic-looking."

"Nah, I don't look like Andy Summers."

"I bet you don't even know who Andy Summers is."

"Useta play lead for The Police."

She grinned. Her teeth were even and white. "Yeah," she said, "You look like him. Thoughtful and smart and sensitive."

Maybe if everyone wore yellow and black makeup the world would be a better place. I sat up straighter and was considering marriage when the phone rang. Pat said. "Sorry. I had someone in the office."

"It's okay. I fell in love during the wait."

She made her voice cool. "Perhaps I should call back later. Give you time to consummate the relationship."

"It's as consummated as it's going to get. What's the word?"

"I didn't hear anything new about Mort, but I did confirm those rumors about Garrett Rice. He's a glad-hander with the weasel dust. He gets invited to parties because he always brings along a little something and he's willing to share it."

"Gosh, you mean what I hear about those Hollywood parties is true?"

"No. I mean what you hear about *some* of those Hollywood parties is true."

"How'd you confirm it?"

"Friend of a friend at another studio. Someone who is very much involved in that world and who knew firsthand."

I said, "Patricia, if I had two kilograms of pure cocaine that I wanted to sell and I was around the studios like Garrett Rice, who would I call?"

She laughed. "You're talking to the wrong person, Elvis. I'm into health and the perfect body."

"Would your friend of a friend know?"

"I can't tell you her name."

"Would you ask for me?"

She sighed. "I don't know. She might be scared."

"It's important, kid."

She said okay, then hung up. I went back to my seat at the table and looked at the counter girl some more. She said, "What's going on?"

I said, "Can you keep a secret?"

"Sure."

"A mobster from Mexico is holding a little kid ransom for two keys of cocaine. I'm trying to get the cocaine back so I can trade it for the kid and maybe nail the mobster at the same time."

She laughed. "What bullshit," she said.

"No bullshit. I'm a private detective."

"Yeah."

"Wanna see my gun?"

She put her hands behind her and gave me a look. "I know what you want to show me."

Such cynicism. Two women who were probably Persian walked in and the counter girl went over to them. The phone rang and I picked it up. Pat said, "My reputation may be ruined. I was just invited to a freebasing party."

"You get a name?"

"Barry Fein. He's probably the guy Garrett dealt with."

I thanked her, hung up, and called the North Hollywood PD. The same tired voice said, "Detectives."

"Lou Poitras, please."

"He ain't here."

"How about Griggs?"

There was a pause, then Griggs came on. "Griggs."

"It's Cole. You guys got anything on a guy named Barry Fein?"

"You got some nut, you know that. We don't run a goddamned library service here."

"Considering what I saw this morning, it ain't much of a cop house, either."

He hung up. I took a deep breath, let it out, called back. A different bored voice answered this time, "North Hollywood Detectives."

"Let me have Griggs, please."

"Hold on."

A minute, then Griggs picked up. "Griggs."

"I'm sorry," I said. "I shouldn't have said that. It was dumb, and I apologize. I know you guys don't like it any more than I did, and I know it's tougher for you than it is for me."

"You're fuckin'-A right it is, bubba. Lou's downtown raising hell right now, goddamnit. Even Baishe is down there, that sonofabitch. So we don't need any bullshit from you."

"Can you give me an address on Fein?"

"Hold on."

While I waited, the counter girl gave one cup of something light-colored to one of the women and a cup of something so brown it was almost black to the other. They took their gelato to a little table at the front of the shop and spoke to each other in Farsi. Two men entered, one wearing a conservative gray Brooks Brothers, the other something resembling a pale orange pressure suit. The spaceman looked intense, and snapped his fingers at the girl. I didn't like that.

Griggs came back on the line. "Fein's a goddamned dope dealer."

"Yeah."

"You're supposed to stay the hell away from this Duran thing."

"I know."

I could hear him breathing into the phone. In the background, I could hear other cops talking and phones ringing and typewriters tapping and a deep, coarse laugh. Cop sounds. The sort of sounds Griggs would miss if he had to stop hearing them. Griggs said, "Try 11001 Wilshire, Suite 601. That's in Westwood."

"Thanks."

"Cole, the wrong people find out I gave you this, it's my badge."

"Gave me what?"

Griggs said, "Yeah" and hung up.

The counter girl was holding a cup in one hand and a scoop in the other, waiting for the guy in the pressure suit to make up his mind. He kept asking to taste the different flavors, then making a big deal about a place in Santa Monica that made this place look like shit. The two Persian women glanced at him.

The counter girl put down her scoop, looked my way, and chewed her fingernail. I hung up, walked over, smiled at the counter girl, and said, "The double chocolate banana was excellent, thank you." Then I turned to Captain New Wave. I was very close to him. "Do you dance?" Smiling.

He had a healthy tan and coarse black hair and a gold Patek Philippe watch. There'd be the health club and handball and somewhere along the way he would've taken judo and been pretty good at it. His eyes flicked to the guy he'd come in with, wondering, what the hell is this?

"Not with boys," he said. Tough, but uncertain. In over his head and just beginning to realize it. He had walked through a door and now he was in something and it could go in any direction, and in any direction he'd lose.

I put my hand in the small of his back and pulled him close. He should've stepped back sooner, but he hadn't because he was tough. Now he couldn't. One of the Persian women stood up.

"Try the double chocolate banana," I said softly.

He wet his lips, again glancing at the man he'd entered with. The man hadn't moved. I pulled him tighter, letting him feel the gun.

"The double chocolate banana," I said.

"The double chocolate banana."

"To her."

"Chocolate banana." To her.

"Please."

"Please." To her.

"Good. You'll like it."

I let him go. He started to say something, wet his lips again, then stepped back.

The counter girl was frozen with wide bumblebee eyes. More scared now than when it started. Some days, you can't win.

"I'm sorry," I said. "It's been hell the past few days."

She nodded and gave me a shy, quiet smile, more young girl than grown-up woman, which is the way it should be when you're sixteen. Everything's gonna be okay, the smile said.

I leaned over the counter and put one of my cards by the cash register.

"If anyone ever bothers you," I said, shooting a glance at the guy in the spacesuit, "let me know."

I walked out the door, went to my car, and drove west along Sunset toward Westwood and Barry Fein.

27

11001 Wilshire is a nine-story high-rise done up quite nicely in gray and white and glass, what the big ads in the real-estate section of the *Times* call "a luxury address." There is a circular drive of gray cobblestone running up beneath a tremendous white and gray awning to the large glass lobby and two waiting doormen. A Rolls and a Jaguar were parked by the glass doors. In the lobby was a security officer behind an elaborately paneled security station who probably took great pride in collecting the mail and calling the elevator and giving the arm to peepers and process servers and similar social debris. It was not a place where you could go to a call box, press a lot of buttons, and count on someone buzzing you in.

I turned up one of the little side streets that ran north through a pleasant residential section, parked by a sign that said Permit Parking Only, and walked back to the high-rise. On the east side of 11001 there was a parking garage with a card key gate leading down, elegantly landscaped with poplar saplings and California poppies. I sat on the ground by the poplars. It was getting hotter, but the smog was manageable. After about ten minutes, the gate groaned to life, folded up into the roof of the building, and a long forest green Cadillac nosed out onto the street. By the time the gate closed, I was in the garage.

There were two cars parked in the slot for 601, a powder blue Porsche 928 and a steel DeLorean. Barry Fein was home. I looked for the elevator and found it on the other side of the garage, but it was one of those security jobs that didn't have buttons down in the garage, just another card key slot. There would be stairs, but the stairs would go up to the lobby and the guards and I wasn't ready for them yet. I went back to the gate, pressed the service switch, and let myself out.

It was a six-block walk to Westwood Village along elm-shaded sidewalks.

If you ignore the surroundings, Westwood Village could be

the center of a college town in Iowa or Massachusetts or Alabama. Lots of fast food vendors, restaurants, collegiate clothing stores, bookshops, art galleries, record stores. Lots of pretty girls. Lots of young guys with muscles who thought playing high school football and being able to lift 200 pounds made them memorable. Lots of bicycles. In a drugstore next to a falafel stand I bought a box of envelopes, a roll of fiber wrapping tape, a stamper that said PRIORITY, an ink pad, and a Bic pen. On the way out I spotted a little sheet of stick-on labels that said things like HANDLE WITH CARE. I bought that, too.

Back at the car I tore an old McDonald's Happy Meal box into strips, put it in an envelope, sealed it, and wrote *Mr. Barry Fein* on the front. I put the wrapping tape along all four edges, then across the flap on the back, making sure to keep the fiber bands even. Even in crime, neatness counts. I stamped PRIORITY twice on the front and twice more on the back, then put a sticker that said DO NOT BEND where you normally put the stamp. I looked at it. Not bad. I bent it twice, then put it on the ground and stepped on it hard. Better.

I walked back to 11001 Wilshire and went in to the guard at the reception desk. "Got something here for Mr. Barry Fein," I said.

The guard looked at me like I was somebody else's bad breath and held out a hand. "I'll take it." He'd crossed the line into his fifties a couple years back. He had a broad face and a thick nose that had been broken more than once, and eyes that stayed with you. Ex-cop.

I shook my head. "Unh-unh. Hand delivery."

"Hand deliveries are made to me."

"Not this one." I waved the envelope under his nose. "My ass is in the grinder as it is. Guy tells me, get this to Mr. Fein and be careful with it, right? Like a dope I drop it and some asshole kicks it and the wind picks it up and I gotta chase it half across Westwood against the traffic."

He was impressed. "This is as far as you go."

I put the letter in my pocket. "Okay, you're a hard ass and you don't give a shit if I get chewed. Call Fein. Tell him it's from Mr. Garrett Rice. Tell him that even though he wants this you've decided that he shouldn't have it."

The guard's eyes never moved.

I said, "Look, Sarge, either you call Mr. Fein now or Mr.

Rice is gonna call him when I bring this thing back, and then my ass won't be the only one in the grinder."

We stared at each other. After a while his mouth tightened and he picked up the phone and pressed three buttons. One of the doormen had come inside and was looking at us. The guard put down the phone and scowled at me, not liking it that I'd showed him up.

He said, "You think I'm letting you upstairs with the piece, forget it."

He was good. The way I'm built, most people never see the gun under the light jacket I wear. I grinned and spread the jacket. He reached across, fingered it out, and put it under his desk. "It'll be here when you come down," he said.

"Sure."

"When you get out of the elevator, turn right, then right again."

I took the elevator up to six, got out into the H-shaped hall, turned right, then right again by a little gold sign that said 601 & 603››. Blue-gray carpet, white walls, cream light fixtures, Italian moderne artwork. It was so hushed and so clean and so sterile, I wondered if people really lived there. Maybe just androids, or people so old they stayed in bed all day and fed from tubes. I thought of Keir Dullea as an old man in 2001.

At the end of the hall a blond man stood in the door to 601 waiting for me. He was blond the way straw blonds are blond, so light it was almost white. He wore a white LaCoste shirt and white slacks and white deck shoes, all of which made his dark tan look even darker. On the young side, maybe 24, with a boyish face, and built the way you're built when you lift for strength rather than bulk. Like Pike. Unlike Pike, he was short, not over five-eight.

"Mr. Fein?" I said.

"I'm Charles. Are you from Mr. Rice?" His voice was higher pitched than you would've guessed, and soft, like a sensitive fourteen-year-old's. Five-eight was short for this kind of work.

"Yeah. I'm supposed to give this to Mr. Fein."

Charles took the envelope, opened the door, and stepped to the side to let me in. The first two knuckles of each hand were large and swollen, the way they get doing push-ups on them and pounding sacks of rice and breaking boards. Maybe five-eight wasn't so much of a problem for him.

We went through a blue-tiled entry, down two steps, and into a room not quite the size of Pauley Pavillion. It was very bright, the outer wall all glass and opening out on a balcony lush with greenery. The glass was open and, very faintly, you could hear the cars below like a whisper. The place was done in pastels: gray and blue and raspberry and white. The tile gave way to carpets, and ultramodern Italian furniture sprouted up out of the carpet. Barry Fein was sipping cognac at a hammered-copper bar. The copper clashed horribly with the pastels. So did Barry. He was short and skinny and dark, with close-to-the-skull hair and furry arms and furry, bandy legs. He was wearing red plaid Bermuda shorts and a dark blue tee shirt that said *RKO Pictures*. There was a hole in the shirt on his left shoulder. He was barefoot.

He said, "You the guy from Gary?" Charles gave him the envelope.

"Indiana?"

He looked at me, cocking his head. "Garrett Rice, stupid. Gary. Jesus fuckin' Christ."

"Well, not really."

"Whattaya mean, not really?" He finished the cognac, then refilled the snifter from a bottle of Courvoisier. There was a hard pack of Marlboros and a heavy Zippo lighter beside the bottle and a large marble ashtray filled with butts. Maybe I could introduce him to Janet Simon and they could have a smoke-off.

Barry Fein opened the envelope and looked in and saw Ronald McDonald. "What the fuck is this?"

I said, "Can I get my wallet out and show you something?"

Charles put his fists on his hips and stared at me thoughtlessly. Barry said, "Aw, shit, you ain't a cop, are you?"

"Unh-unh." I got out my wallet, went over to the bar, and showed him my license. "It's very important that I find out if Garrett Rice has tried to sell you two kilograms of cocaine."

Barry grinned at me and looked at Charles. "Is this guy serious or what?"

Charles smiled benignly. Perhaps repartée was beyond him.

I said, "Listen to me. I'm sorry I used a ruse to get up here, but I didn't think you'd see me if I played it straight. I'm not here to bring you trouble. Garrett Rice may have stolen two kilograms of lab-quality cocaine from a very bad man. Now that man wants it back and he's holding a little boy hostage. I think if Garrett stole the dope he'll try to move it. You're a guy he might move it through."

Barry Fein shrugged and jerked his head at Charles. "Get rid of'm."

I looked at Charles. "I'm in a rush here, Barry. He won't be able to do it."

Barry shrugged again. Charles whistled sharply between his teeth, and a moment later another Charles walked in from the balcony with a watering can. Five-eight, blond, muscled, white shirt and pants and shoes. Twins all the way down to the big knuckles.

Barry said, "Jonathan, we got some trouble here."

Jonathan set the watering can down and came over to stand a little in front of me, Charles a little behind. They stood with their feet spread for balance and their hands loose at their sides. Jonathan had the same perfect skin and vacant eyes as Charles. Idiot angels. The two of them reminded me of the kids down in Westwood who thought they were tough. Only these guys weren't down in Westwood. And they probably were tough.

"Attractive, Barry," I said. "Bet they're great in bed, too."

Charles said, "It's time to leave," and stepped in to take my arm. I threw Barry's snifter of Courvoisier on Charles. Jonathan hit me hard twice, not as hard as he should've because I was moving, but hard enough to hurt. I shoved Barry off his stool, making Jonathan hop back to keep from getting bowled over. Charles was coming at me sideways and planting for a spin kick when I grabbed the big Zippo and set him on fire. The Courvoisier went off with a blue alcohol whoosh. Charles screamed and slapped at his face and dropped to the carpet. Jonathan yelled, "Hey!" and forgot about me. He tried to turn Charles onto his belly to smother the flames. I broke one of the barstools across Jonathan's back. He was tough. He tried to get up, tears leaking down along his nose, then fell over and moaned.

Barry was down on his hands and knees where he'd fallen, staring at me, saying, "Jesus fuckin' Christ" over and over. I grabbed his hair and pulled him up. He said, "Jesus fuckin' Christ."

I shook him. "You think I'm playing with you, Barry? Tell me about Rice."

Barry looked at me with eyes like pissholes in fresh snow and tried to scramble away. I slapped him. "Stand still!"

"Jesus fuckin' Christ, you set the sonofabitch on fire."

"What about Rice?"

"No, no. I ain't heard from Rice in a couple of weeks."

"He hasn't tried to sell any dope to you?"

"I swear to Christ."

"He ask you where he could?"

"No. No." He looked over my shoulder at Charles, then at me, then back to Charles again. "Jesus fuckin' Christ."

I shook him again. "Your card key."

"What?"

"Your card key. What you use to open the gate downstairs. Give it to me."

We went to the near end of the bar and took the card key out of a brass tray where it sat with keys and change and a black alligator wallet.

I said, "Rice had two keys of lab-quality cocaine. Not all that common, so if he tried to shop it around, people would remember. Ask around. I'm going to come back here tomorrow, and you're going to have something for me. Right, Barry?"

"Jesus fuckin' Christ."

I bent down and checked Charles. His shirtfront was browned and his hair was singed and he was starting to blister in a couple of spots, but that was about it. Cognac burns off fast. His eye flickered open and he looked at me. His lashes were gone.

"You've got to be a lot better than you are to get away with a spin kick, Charles. They look great on the mat, but in real life they take too long."

I stood up.

"Remember this, Barry," I said. "Don't fuck with the Human Torch."

Barry said, "Jesus fuckin' Christ."

I went back along the hall, down the elevator, and collected my gun from the guard, who nodded and told me to have a nice day.

28

Until I heard from Barry Fein, there weren't a whole lot of options left for me to pursue. I could go back to my house and brood about things there. I could cover ground I had already been over and brood. Or I could go to my office and brood, and maybe be there when the Eskimo or Duran called. I drove to my office.

The fourth-floor hall was empty. Office doors were closed the way they always were; none was cracked open, no one peeked out of the broom closet. I went down the hall as quietly as I could, not even making the little shushing sound shoes will make on carpet. I took my gun out, held it down along my thigh, and keyed the office lock with my left hand. Wouldn't this be a sight for the insurance secretaries across the hall. *Oh, look, Elvis is scared someone's going to shoot him again!* When the knob turned I pushed open the door and went in low. No one shot me. No one was pressed along the ceiling, waiting to drop down. The Eskimo wasn't crouching under the desk. Safe again.

There was one call on the answering-machine. The auto parts clerk, telling me that if I didn't want the shifter skirt he knew plenty of guys who did. I turned off the machine, opened the balcony doors, and sat at my desk to wait. Sooner or later Duran would call or send the Eskimo. He'd have to. He lost two men last night and the woman and he wouldn't like it. Maybe Poitras was right and he'd like it so little he'd just say *aw fuck it* and send somebody to blow me away. Or maybe he'd just say, *Give me the dope* now *or I'll kill the kid*. Then what would I do?

The air was warm and moist and a small breeze was blowing in from the south. Down the coastline, toward San Pedro and Newport Beach, there were a couple of dark cumulus out over the water. Looking at them, I smiled. Where I grew up, there was much rain of the beating, pounding, falling-in-sheets variety that Southern California almost never enjoys. I missed it. Rain was a Good Thing. If there were more rain, there would be less smog.

I took out the Dan Wesson, checked the load, then laid it on the desk. If the Eskimo came in, maybe he'd think it was one of those fancy office lighters and ignore it.

I settled in and I waited.

Three hours later the phone rang. "Elvis Cole Detective Agency, we find more for less. Check our prices."

The Eskimo said, "You made a very bad mistake, Mr. Cole."

"Would it help to say I'm sorry?"

He said, "We know the woman is at your home and we know a man wearing a sidearm is staying with her. Mr. Duran trusted that you would do as you were told, but you didn't."

"That couldn't be helped."

"We still have what we have."

"I know that."

"Mr. Duran still wants his property. Go home now."

He hung up. No mention of a trade, no demand for an explanation. I called the house. Pike answered on the second ring.

I said, "I just heard from the Eskimo. They know Ellen's at the house and they know you're with her."

There was a pause. "Spotter. They could have found out your address, then put someone up the hill or in an empty house across the canyon."

"Better keep her away from the windows and the deck."

"No reason. Guy with the right weapon could have taken us any time he wanted. I get into that with her, we'll have to pull all the drapes and lock her in the bathroom. Be worse for her."

"The Eskimo told me to go home. He's got to have a reason for wanting me there."

Pike grunted. "Maybe pulling the drapes isn't so bad an idea after all."

"Do it without alarming her."

"Unh-huh."

"We need anything?"

"Unh-unh."

"I'm coming in."

When I got to the house, the drapes were pulled across the sliding glass doors and Pike was making dinner. Ellen was wearing her cleaned Ralph's clothes and was standing by the counter, watching him cook. She looked uncomfortable, probably because he was in the kitchen and she wasn't. I put the bag of her fresh clothes and makeup on the stairs.

"What's for dinner, girls?" Mr. Nonchalance.

Pike said, "Red beans and rice, ham hocks, cornbread." He was still wearing the sunglasses and the gun.

"He wouldn't let me help." Ellen took a sip of iced scotch from a short glass. The glass was sitting in a puddle of condensation. She'd probably been taking little sips all day. Just enough to keep things manageable.

I nodded. "He's very territorial about his kitchen."

I pushed under the drapes, opened the glass doors, then reclosed the drapes. I opened the little jalousie window off the powder room, then the kitchen window.

"Good idea," Pike said. "It was getting stuffy." It would be easier to hear with the glass open.

Ellen said, "Janet called."

"Delightful."

"She was worried."

I leaned against the powder room doorjamb. The powder room window opened on the front of the house. If anyone came, they'd have to come from the front. The downslope off the back of the house is too steep for any sort of assault.

Ellen sipped the scotch. "She wanted to put the girls on. I said no. I didn't know what to say. I don't think I could talk to them without crying."

I nodded, listening but not listening, straining to hear outside. Ellen didn't notice.

"Janet said they need me to be strong now, and I don't know if I can. I'm thirty-nine years old. I don't want to be weak. I don't want to be scared."

"Then don't be," Pike said.

Ellen and I both looked at him. He used the flat of a heavy knife to push diced onion into a small bowl. He covered the bowl with Saran Wrap.

"Don't be," she repeated.

"This Janet your friend?" Pike said.

"Of course."

Pike shook his head and put the bowl in the ice box.

The phone rang. I picked it up.

A thick voice with a heavy Mexican accent said, "The boy wants to speak with his mother."

"Who is this?"

"Put on the mother."

I motioned Ellen over, raising a finger to make her pause as I ran to pick up the living-room extension. She looked confused. When I had the phone I mouthed, "Perry."

She blurted, "Perry?" into the phone as Pike moved to stand by her, watching me.

The harsh voice said, "Listen."

There was a thump on the line, then a scuffling, whimpering sound, then a long, piercing little-boy shriek that made a clammy sweat leak out over my face and chest and back. Ellen Lang screamed. Pike jerked the phone away from her. She screamed "*No!*" and slapped at him, clawing to get the receiver back. He pulled her close, holding her tight against him. She hit and clawed and made a deep-in-the-throat gargling sound and got the edge of his hand in her mouth and bit until blood spouted down along her chin and wrist and onto Pike's shirt. He didn't pull away.

I shouted something into the phone.

The shrieking didn't stop, but the voice came back on. It said, "You won't fuck up again."

I said, "No."

"The boy is alive. You can hear him."

"Yes." I felt like I was going to choke.

"We call you again."

I looked at Pike over the dead connection.

29

Ellen thrashed and cried and finally grew still, but even then her pain was a physical presence in the room.

Pike went into the little bathroom, stayed a few minutes, then came out with gauze taped to his hand and his skin orange from Merthiolate. Ellen squeezed her eyes shut when she saw his hand.

Pike said, "Do you have any Valium or Darvon for her?"

I told him no. He slipped out the kitchen door. I poured more scotch and brought it to her. She shook her head. "I've been drinking all day."

"Sure?"

She nodded.

"Want a hug?"

She nodded again, and sighed deeply as I held her. After a while she said, "I want to wash."

She took the bag of clothes upstairs, and in a few minutes the water began to run. I turned on the evening news with Jess Marlowe and Sandy Hill, Sandy talked about Navy spies in San Diego. Not particularly relevant to Perry Lang unless Duran was smuggling state secrets to the Russkies. But in L.A., anything is possible. The water ran for a long time.

When Ellen came back downstairs she was wearing some of the clothes I'd brought and the white New Balance. Her face looked clean and blank, less vulnerable than at any time since I'd met her. She said something that surprised me. She said, "God, I could use a cigarette."

I couldn't see her having ever smoked. "When Joe gets back, I'll get you some."

She nodded slightly, then shook her head. "No." She stood next to the TV and crossed her arms. I couldn't tell if she was looking at me or past me. "I quit almost six years ago. I just stopped. Janet says she goes crazy after about a day, but when I wanted to stop, I just stopped."

"Tough to do."

She said, "What did the police say?"

I thought about lying, but couldn't think of anything good enough to explain why the cops weren't here or we weren't there, so I said, "It's a Special Operations case now."

"What does that mean?"

"It means the case was taken away from Poitras to be handled by some hotshots downtown."

"What are they doing?"

"I don't know. They shut Poitras and me out. They said they might come out to talk to you."

"When?"

"Later."

She looked at me calmly. She said, "But what are they doing about . . . all of this?" She gestured around her.

"I spoke with Joe this morning. Did he tell you anything that happened when I went to the cops?"

She shook her head, so I told her. When I was done she asked if she could have a glass of water. When I came back with it she looked just as she'd looked when I left. As if the idea that somebody on the police force could cave in to political pressure was an everyday and undisturbing event.

She said, "Sergeant Poitras goes along with this?"

"He has to. But he doesn't like it, and he's fighting it. He and his lieutenant were downtown this afternoon, trying to find out who's damming the works."

She said, "Unh-huh," and drank the water. When the glass was empty she said, "My older daughter, Cindy, she hates me. She screams that if I were a better wife, her father would be happier." She said it as if she were telling me she preferred tan shoes to cordovan.

"She's wrong."

"I tried being the best wife I could."

"I know."

"I tried."

"There's some insurance," I said. "Not a lot. But some." She didn't ask how much.

I sipped some of the scotch I'd poured for her. I said, "Look, I'll find the dope or where the dope went and who has it and we'll work something out with Duran. Then we'll bring Poitras in and put it in his lap, and this will end."

"But that man, O'Bannon, he said you were supposed to stay away."

I shrugged.

She nodded and turned away and looked at the books and the figurines and the photos and the dark steel knight's heraldry that line my shelves. A girlfriend who was a pretty good carpenter built the shelves for me from unfinished redwood. A place for me to keep my junk, she said. The TV sat at about eye level, the stereo beneath it, my books and mementos and treasures on either side. The latex Frankenstein mask was on a Styrofoam head. My junk. Out from the canyon, we could hear the first faint yelps of the coyotes, gearing up for a sing.

I drank more of the scotch but found it sour. I took the glass into the kitchen, threw out the booze, and went back into the living room with a can of pineapple juice.

"Mr. Pike says you read these same books over and over," Ellen said.

"That's true."

She touched different volumes. "I know some of these. I read the histories of King Arthur when I was in college. I worked as a teacher's aide. I read them to the children when the teachers went on break."

"I'll bet you enjoyed that."

"Yes." Ellen turned to me from the books. "Was Mr. Pike really a policeman?"

I was impressed. "He must like you. I've never known him to tell that to anyone."

"Then he was."

"For a while. Pike will never lie to you. You don't have to doubt anything he says."

"He says he's a professional soldier."

"He has gun shop in Culver City. He owns the agency with me. But sometimes he goes to places like El Salvador or Botswana or the Sudan. So I guess that makes him a part-time professional soldier."

"Was he in Vietnam with you?"

"Not with me. He was in the Marines. We didn't meet until after we'd mustered out and were back here in L.A. Pike was riding in a black-and-white. I was working with George Feider. We met on the job. When Pike and the cops parted company, I made the offer."

"He told me he wasn't a successful policeman."

"He wasn't successful, but he was outstanding. Pike and some of the cops he worked with had what we might call a grave philosophical difference. Guy like Pike, philosophy is all. He rode a black-and-white for three years and for three years he was outstanding. Even splendid. He just wasn't successful."

"He likes you quite a bit."

"That's the Marine. Marines are all fairies at heart."

"Did he get those tattoos in Vietnam?"

"Yeah."

"What for?"

"Ask him."

"I did. He said I wouldn't understand."

"Joe's got a little credo he lives by. Never back up. That's what the arrows on his shoulders are for. They point forward. They keep him from backing up."

She stared at the end of the sofa. "I understand that."

I finished the pineapple juice and crushed the can. "Don't let Joe get to you. Life is very simple to him, but it isn't always the way he'd like it to be. Part of his problem with the cops."

She nodded but didn't look any less empty.

"Think of a samurai," I said. "A warrior who requires order. That's Pike."

"The arrows."

"Yeah. The arrows allow him to impose order on chaos. A professional soldier needs that."

She thought about it. "And that's what you are?"

"Not me. I'm just a private cop. I am also the antithesis of order."

"He said you were a better soldier than he. He said you won a lot of decorations in the war."

"Ha ha, that Pike. You see what a card that guy is? A million laughs."

"He said you'd deny it."

"A scream, that guy."

"He said that everything of any real value that he's learned, he's learned from you."

"Flip it to channel 11, wouldja?" I said. "I think *Wheel of Fortune's* on."

She stared at me for a very long time. She didn't change the channel. "I can't be the person I was anymore, can I?"

I gave her gentle eyes. "No."

She nodded, but probably not to me. "All right," she said. "I can understand that, too."

30

When Joe got back he had a bottle of Dalmane and six Valiums. We put out the red beans and rice and cornbread, and ate. Ellen stared at her plate and said, "I've never eaten a ham hock before," so I slit the skin and showed her how to get out the meat.

She ate quietly and completely, finishing what Pike put on her plate. Joe and I drank beer, Ellen had milk. I pointed out a few of the more uproarious ironies of life, but neither Ellen nor Joe showed much in the way of appreciation. I was used to it from Pike.

We finished the meal, did the dishes, then went into the living room. No one said more than five words at a time. I put on a Credence Clearwater album, then went into the entry closet and came back wearing my Groucho Marx nose.

"Appropriate, as always," Pike said, then went out onto the deck. Ellen smiled once, then looked away. After a while I took off the nose and picked up *Valdez Is Coming*.

I was almost through it when Ellen made a hoarse sighing sound from her end of the couch. When I looked up, her eyes were red and tears dripped down her cheeks. I reached across and touched her leg. She took my fingers and said, "What did they do to make him scream like that?"

Pike stepped in off the deck. I slid across the couch and held Ellen for a while, until she asked for two of the Dalmane and said she would go up to bed. I went up with her and stood at the foot until the Dalmane had done its work, then I shut the light and went down.

Pike said, "I like her."

"You told her you were on the cops."

"I like her a lot."

I got two Falstaff from the box. We offed all the lights in the house, turned the stereo low, then went out onto the deck. A couple of cars moved through the canyon roads to the south and east, appearing then disappearing behind the houses that dotted the hillside. The coyotes were quiet.

Pike hung his feet off the deck. I joined him. Just like Tom and Huck.

I said, "Duran's spotter had a good deer rifle, we'd be history."

"Maybe."

We sat. Heavy clouds blocked out the moon and most of the stars. You could smell the coming rain in the air. Springsteen sang about tough kids and broken hearts on KLSX.

I said, "Remember the other day, when I said Mort had given himself up?"

"Yes."

"He didn't. She did."

"I know."

"She's over the edge right now. Mort, the kid, who she is. She doesn't have as much self-esteem as a piece of bread." Pike's beer can raised, tilted, lowered. "I want her to make it back," I said.

"Unh-huh."

I took a pull on my Falstaff. "Does it strike you odd that Duran's giving me so much time to turn over his dope?"

"It does."

"Like maybe he knows I don't have it, but he's using me to find it for him."

"Unh-huh."

"Joe, how the hell can you see at night with the sunglasses?"

"I am one with the night." Raise, tilt, lower. You never know whether he's serious. "Duran wants you to find the dope because he doesn't know how. If he tells his people to find something, all they know how to do is rack ass. That doesn't get you very far, and maybe eliminates someone with some important information."

"It would've been easier to hire me."

"Maybe."

"Only maybe I won't hire, and I turn it over to the cops."

"He probably shit himself, thinking about that one."

I nodded and sipped the beer and listened to Springsteen's courage flow into Mellencamp's raucous honesty. "Joseph, what have you learned from me?"

"Good things."

"Like what?"

He didn't answer. I finished the Falstaff, then crimped the

can square and crushed it. "A guy like Duran, worth a couple
hundred million, a hundred K can't be worth the hassle."

"He's not doing it for the money."

"That's what I don't like. Maybe we're all just running out of
time. Maybe Duran says to hell with it and smokes the kid and
the rest of us."

Pike finished his beer, set the can on the deck. Pike never
crushes cans. I guess he's man enough without that. "Maybe
you should find the dope before that happens."

A big *splat* sounded behind me, then again to my left, then
something wet hit my forehead. Joe stood up. "Good time for a
walk."

He went in through the living room and let himself out the
kitchen door, locking it behind. I picked up our cans and went
in out of the rain. My father, rest him, would've been proud.

The rain slapped at the deck and ran down along the glass.
When I was little, I would sit in my window and watch the rain
and feel easy and at peace. I didn't feel that way often
anymore, though I kept trying out windows and rainstorms
and probably always would.

I turned the stereo off, put on the lamp at the head of the
couch, stretched out, and finished *Valdez*. Much later, Pike let
himself into the kitchen, moving like a dark shadow across the
edges of the lamplight. He put muddy Nikes in the sink,
peeled out of his wet shirt and wet pants and went into the
little bathroom. "You up?" A voice in the dark.

"Yeah."

He came out of the bathroom in jockey shorts with a towel
over his shoulders. "I found the spotters. Two guys in the
yellow house ten o'clock east, just up from Nichols Canyon.
Asshole in a lawn chair on the back deck, squinting through a
pair of field glasses."

"What about the other guy?"

"Sacked out on a waterbed."

There was more. "You took them?"

"Yes."

Pike sat down on the floor beside the glass doors, his back to
the wall. He sat *sukhasen*. Yoga. A sitting pose that allows
relaxation. Did Pike do yoga before he met me? I couldn't
remember.

I said, "Your knife?"

"A house contains all sorts of useful appliances, Elvis. You
know that."

"Duran won't like it, Joe. He'll take it out on the kid."

Joe's eyes were pinpoints of light in the dark. They did not move. "He won't know what happened, Elvis. No one will. Ever. They're gone. It's like they never were."

I nodded, and felt cold.

The rain beat down, hammering noisily on the glass and the roof and Pike's Jeep parked out past the front door. I thought about the cat, holed up under a car somewhere. After a while I slept and dreamed about the Eskimo and Perry Lang and my friend Joe Pike. But what I dreamed I did not remember.

31

The sky was still gray the next morning when I drove back to
Garrett Rice's house. All down the mountain, little rivulets of
debris and mud veined the roads. Traffic moved quickly, as it
always did during the rains, with the Angelenos' innate belief
that driving in rain is the same as driving in dry, only wetter.

Maybe Barry Fein would be able to turn a lead on Garrett
Rice, but maybe he wouldn't. Maybe Garrett and the dope and
Cleon Tyner were long gone. If they were, I had to know. If
the dope was gone, I'd have to come up with another way to
deal with Domingo Duran. Maybe severe public reprimands.

I left my car on Sunset Plaza and walked up the little cul-de-
sac, gun loose in the holster and ready for the housecoated
woman and her killer Yorkie.

Everything looked just as it had yesterday, only damp. No
sign of Cleon's Trans Am or any other car. No one had moved
the letter tacked up by the cops. No lights or sounds came
from the house. I walked straight up the drive, across the little
motor court, and into the narrow alley alongside Rice's garage
as if I knew exactly where I was going and as if the gentleman
of the house expected me.

There were three large plastic garbage cans, wet from the
rain, with a heavy musty smell, and a chest-high chain-link
gate knotted with ivy and bougainvillea. A little Master combo
lock secured the latch. I looked back toward the street. Still
free from dogs and neighbors and armed response patrols. I
hopped the fence, walked the length of the garage, turned
right past a pool pump and filter, then out a redwood gate to
Garrett Rice's pool deck. The pool was a tasteful oval, small,
but still filling most of the backyard. The deck and the patio
areas were flagstone. A flagstone retaining wall followed the
curve of the pool where Rice's lot had been carved out of the
hillside, and the hill angled and rose away up behind the
house. Little piles of pebbles and silt were on the back deck
where they'd run off the hillside with the rain.

The back of the house was mostly glass, landscaped with ferns and bamboo and something that looked like a mimosa tree. There was a nice, gladelike feel to the place. Secluded. Probably just right for skinny-dipping with starlets and playing grabass.

The musty smell was stronger, the way a dark room in an old house might smell, wet and moldy and slightly sour. I kept trying to put it on the rain. Only it wasn't the rain. Cleon Tyner was face down under a giant fern at the back of Garrett Rice's house.

I slipped out my gun and went up to him, watching the windows and big glass doors. One of the big glass doors was open.

There was no pulse in his neck. His skin was cold and pliable over stiff muscles. He was lying mostly on the right side of his face, the left looking up and back toward the pool. His left eye was open but droopy, and rolled back in his head. I tried to close it but the eyelid wouldn't go down. There were no pools of blood or bullet holes in his back. I tilted him up, saw chest wounds, then lowered him. Cleon had been out here quite a while, out here while I was ringing the front door bell yesterday, out here while the rain came down and churned the ground beneath him to mud. *That Cleon, what a stick-in-the-mud.*

I went into the house. It was damp and cold and wet on the floor where the rain had driven in under the soffit and through the open door. There was a Westec Alarm box just inside the draw drapes. All the lights showed green. It had been turned off.

Garrett Rice was on the kitchen floor beside a cook island. He was naked, and even in death his flesh hung loose and crinkly and pale, his sunlamp tan ending abruptly on his upper chest. There were contusions on his face and dried blood on his mouth and nose, and a single small-caliber bullet hole above his right ear. On the back of his left thigh was an ugly spiral burn the size and shape of the largest burner on the cooktop. There was another burn like it on his stomach. He'd voided himself.

I went back out through the living room to the open glass door, sucked in wet air, then searched what used to be Garrett Rice's house for the dope. It didn't take long, mostly because I knew I wouldn't find anything. If the dope had been here, Garrett Rice would've turned it over long before his clothes were yanked off and he was pressed down onto a red-glowing stovetop.

Perry Lang!

I made an anonymous report to the cops, then tore down a shower curtain, took it outside, and covered Cleon Tyner's body. I squatted by him, trying to think of something to say, but all that came to mind were questions. *Sorry, Cleon. I'll check on Betty, time to time.* I went back to my car and drove into Westwood.

By the time I reached 11001, the clouds had broken the way they break when they're going to seal up again. I used Barry Fein's card key to get into his building through the parking garage. The cars were still in his parking slot, only they were reversed, the DeLorean on the inside now, the Porsche behind. I put the Corvette in the No Parking zone in front of the elevators, used the card key again, and rode up to 6.

Jonathan opened the door but didn't step back, playing it tough. He stood a little crooked, as if his back bothered him. I was in the right mood to make it bother him a little more. I said, "Fuck with me I'll kill you."

Barry Fein's voice came from inside. "For Christ's sake, Jonathan. Jesus Christ, in the goddamn hall."

A little smile broke crookedly on Jonathan's face. He stepped out of the door, lifting his hands to show me they were empty. We went inside; him first.

Barry Fein was fidgeting around the big room. Charles sat on the couch, leaning forward with his forearms on his knees and his hands empty. A large gauze bandage was taped along his left jawline and another smaller gauze patch spotted his left cheek. His neck and the lower half of his face were shiny, as if he were wearing suntan lotion. His eyebrows were gone.

He said, "One day."

I ignored him. "Where'd Rice move the dope, Barry?"

Barry paced. He said, "Listen, I asked everybody I could think of, right?, where Garrett might try to unload?"

Jonathan moved away from me to sit on the arm of the couch next to Charles. He rubbed Charles's shoulders, then let his hidden hand drift down behind Charles's back. I took out my gun and pointed it at Barry's furry stomach. I said, "I'll shoot him, Barry. And you, too."

Barry rubbed at his hair. "Jesus Christ, Jonathan, would you get outta there. Shit!"

Jonathan went to stand beside the bar. I suggested Charles stand with him, and when he got up you could see the butt of a piece sticking out from behind the cushion. "Jesus fuckin' Christ, I didn't know!" Barry screamed. He picked up a couch pillow and threw it at them. *You shits, you shits trying to get me killed!*

Jonathan and Charles looked sullen and mean, like a couple of fourth-grade psychopaths caught sticking pins into puppies.

I put the gun back on Barry. "You asked everyone you know," I reminded him.

He hopped around, rolling his eyes and trying to pick up the thread. Ten in the morning and he was already in another universe. "Yeah, right. Look, you gotta open your mind, see? I called around. I asked. Everybody I ask, and believe me, I know everybody Garrett Rice would know, they say Garrett ain't called. He ain't been trying to move nothing."

I shook my head. "That's not what you're supposed to tell me, Barry. You're supposed to tell me who Rice sold it to and when he made the trade." I dropped the muzzle down to his crotch, let it circle, raised it back to his eyes.

He squirmed like he had to pee. "I swear to Christ. I called. I asked. Rice ain't been trying to move *anything*."

I took short breaths, thinking. Jonathan and Charles glared. Barry hopped up and down. Jesus Christ, what if Garrett Rice hadn't had the dope after all? What if, all along, it had been an inside job, the Eskimo taking down two keys to sock away for his retirement, or one of the Italian guests Kimberly Marsh described. Or a cat burglar, just passing by. I stopped breathing altogether, then took a deep breath using my stomach, held it, then let it out slow. Focus and relax. I put my head on Perry Lang and kept it there; anyplace else and everything starts to fall apart, and maybe Perry and Ellen and the two girls with it.

I said, "You ask about two kilograms of lab-quality coke, it's going to come up if anyone else has been trying to sell some."

"Yeah. Sure."

"Tell me."

"This guy I know, he says a friend of his wants to sell some. You know, called him up, shopping price."

"What and when?"

"Key and a half. Said it was 99 percent pure. Said the guy called him three or four days ago, you know, like I said, calling around shopping price."

"Who's the seller?"

"Guy named Larson Fisk."

Great. Larson Fisk. "Who the hell is Larson Fisk?"

Barry looked impatient. "He's an actor. You probably seen his face a million times. Day player, you know. I sold him some stuff. Come here."

Barry hopped over to the bar past Jonathan and Charles. He pulled down a thick *Academy Players Directory* from a shelf beside the bar. "I got lotsa clients in here," Barry said. "Shit, I get jokes all the time how I oughta have my own star on Hollywood Boulevard. Maybe one day, eh?"

He showed me Larson Fisk. Sure, I'd seen him before. Larson Fisk was Larry, Kimberly Marsh's boyfriend.

32

The house above Universal was empty but not abandoned. The little red 914 was gone, but a rumpled shirt lay on the living room floor and a couple of Carl's Junior shake cups sat on the dining room table. Lights burned in a back bathroom. I parked my car out of sight above the house, then came back, picked the front door lock, and let myself in. I walked through the house once, gun out, to see if maybe the cocaine had been left lying out in the open. It hadn't.

I had ripped the rear bedroom apart and was starting on the little bath next to it when I heard car doors slam down below and a woman's laugh, light and lutelike.

Kimberly Marsh and Larson Fisk were climbing the steps. She was in shorts and rumpled cream safari shirt tied off beneath her breasts with the sleeves rolled up, carrying her sandals. Sexy. Fisk was in blue gym trunks, beat-up Adidas running shoes, and a black muscle shirt. He was carrying a bag of groceries in each arm and smiling. She was smiling, too.

I went back to the front of the house, took out my gun, and stepped into the little coat closet behind the front door as their key went into the lock. The front door opened. Kimberly Marsh walked in. Larson Fisk followed her. When they were past me, I shoved open the closet door, took one step, planted my left foot, and kicked Larson Fisk on the outside of his left knee as hard as I could. His left knee was the one with the scars.

There was a wet snap similar to what you hear when you joint a chicken. Larry screamed and fell, dropping the grocery bags to catch himself. Something glass shattered and the near bag turned dark and wet. Oranges and pippin apples rolled out across the floor. One made it all the way into the dining room. Kimberly Marsh gasped sharply, spun around to look at Larry, and saw me. Larry was rocking back and forth on the floor, sometimes gripping his leg, sometimes pounding the floor with his right fist. His face was purple.

He called me a sonofabitch.

I waved my gun at him. "Come on, Larry. A sonofabitch would've put one behind your ear. Besides, now you can add another scar to your collection."

He closed his eyes and rocked back, calling me a sonofabitch again, like a mantra, very softly. I shook my head. "You see," I said to Kimberly, "some people are never satisfied."

She had backed away until the plank shelves were pressing into her back. The big green fish tank with the dead fish was to her right. Why do blondes look good with green?

She didn't appear particularly frightened. She said, "What are you doing?"

"Removing Larry as an active threat. He may be stupid, but he is strong. And mean." I smiled at her.

Larry said, "It *hurts!*"

She was relaxing. Her eyes never went to Larry, but her shoulders dropped just a hair, and her hands went down, and she stopped clenching her teeth. I imagined a window in her forehead, behind it little watchwork wheels and gears, spinning and rocking and making ticking sounds. I smiled wider.

She smiled back. "Did you find out what happened to Mort?"

"Unh-huh."

"Thank God. Can I move back to my apartment now?"

"Nah. Not right now. Now, I want you to give me the cocaine."

Her eyes got a little bigger, and that was it. She just stood there. The gears spun faster. The ticking got louder. I think of the damnedest things.

I wiggled the gun. I stopped smiling. "Dom wants his dope back, Kimberly."

Her eyes flicked to Larry, then back. "I don't know what you're talking about."

I cocked the gun and I pointed it at Larry. "She doesn't know, Larry." Larry was watching the gun and clutching the knee. I said, "She sees the stuff just sitting around over at Duran's, right? And thinks, boy, wouldn't that be great to have. Only she's got no way to get it out of the house. So she finds a phone and gives you a call and gets you involved. She throws it out the window and tells you where and you sneak over and pick it up. Risky, Larry. That took balls, with all the goons Duran keeps around. You do all that, and here I am pointing a gun at you, and now she doesn't know what I'm talking about."

She flipped her head to get the blonde hair out of her eyes and smiled at me as if I'd just told her I thought she had sexy toenails. "That's silly." She stepped away from the shelves and cocked her head at me, lifting her ribs to pull her abdomen tight and pushing out her hips to the side. Moving on me. Like she'd seen gun molls do in a thousand movies.

I said, "How about you tell me, Larry? Before I do your other knee."

Neither of them said anything, but you could hear the breathing.

I said, "Right now you guys are in a survivable position. If the cops walked in, all they could hang on you is possession with intent to distribute and obstruction of justice. They might push for an accessory to murder charge because of Mort but they wouldn't get it. You give me the dope, then you're no longer possessing. You give me the dope, and even though you're a couple of scumbags, I'll put in a word with the cops."

Neither of them said anything, but the breathing was louder.

"Okay," I said, "let's go back to basics." I pointed the gun at Larry's good knee. "It'll be a bone shot, Larry. You'll limp."

Larry nodded. "Okay." His voice cracked.

"Don't tell him." Kimberly was calm.

"Sure," I said. "It's not your knee."

Kimberly Marsh's eyes got dark. "This stuff is worth a lot of money," she said. "We could share. We could share a lot."

"What about the boy?"

"What about him?"

Something hot throbbed in my head and I felt my face grow tight. "No wonder Mort went for you, Kimmie. You're all class." I toed Larry's bad knee. He went purple again. "The dope."

Kimberly yelled, "No!" then snatched something from the shelves, threw it at me, and plunged her hands into the slimy aquarium. As she did, Larry grabbed my legs. I hit him with the butt of the pistol, but he hung on, digging at my crotch. I hit him again, harder. His forehead split and blood spilled down over his nose and brow. Kimberly pulled what looked like a large brick from the algae and seaweed, and ran back toward the kitchen. Her arms were green from the slime, and the stink of fish was strong. Larry gasped, still trying to pull me down, but his grip was weaker. I hit him twice more, this time over his ear, and he let go.

I stumbled away from him and ran toward the back of the house, around through the dining room, and into the kitchen. Kimberly Marsh was clawing at the back door when I caught her and slapped her as hard as I could. She made an *unh!* sound and dropped the brick. It was about the size of a five-pound sack of Gold Medal flour. Bits of scum and seaweed still clung to it.

She scrambled after it, kicking at me and making grunting noises. There were flecks of saliva on her chin. I lifted her by the arm and hit her again. It was hot in the kitchen. I shook her and hit her once more, hard enough to knock her down. It hadn't been necessary, but then, most things aren't.

On the floor, she started to cry.

I picked up the dope and went back through the house. Larry was where he had fallen, lying on his back, staring at the ceiling. He looked the way pro wrestlers look when they've popped blood capsules all over their faces, only he hurt. He hurt bad.

"She went all the way for you, Lar," I said slowly. "Just like she did for Mort."

Larry's eyes began to leak.

I went out the door and down the steps. He was crying. She was crying. But they weren't crying for the same thing.

33

I drove to my office, called a woman I know at the phone company, and gave her Domingo Duran's address in Los Feliz. She told me four phone numbers registered to Duran's address. The first one gave me a tentative female voice with a heavy accent. When I asked to speak with Mr. Duran, she didn't seem to understand, then there was a long pause and she hung up. Probably kitchen help.

On the second number a man with a very light accent said, "Mr. Duran's residence."

I said, "This is Elvis Cole, calling for Mr. Duran."

The voice said pleasantly, "Mr. Duran is not available at present."

"He'll talk to me."

"I'm afraid that's not possible. Mr. Duran is entertaining guests, you see."

"Tell him it's Cole. Tell him I want to talk about the dope."

The line went dead. I hung up. Pinocchio's eyes tocked back and forth, the second hand swept his face. I picked up one of the Jiminy Crickets, inspected it, and blew off dust. I should dust more often. What had Jiminy Cricket said? "*Hey, enough's enough!*" The phone rang.

"Cole."

The Eskimo said, "You do not help yourself."

"It's been that kind of day. Let's talk trade. I got the dope."

"Be at the curb in front of your building in twenty minutes."

"What if I don't want to?"

He didn't say anything.

"Just a joke," I said.

Fifteen minutes later the limo pulled up and the rear door opened. I got in, and we pulled into the alley beside the building. Kato wasn't driving. This was another guy, probably a machete killer specially imported from Brazil. The Eskimo said, "Where is it?"

"Are we going to fool around or are we going to do business?"

He looked at me without moving. I think he was chewing a piece of Dentyne. He nodded. "All right."

"We pick a time and a place for the trade. I come alone, so do you. I give you the dope, you give me the boy."

"All right."

"Griffith Park," I said. "Noon tomorrow, back by the tunnel. You drive up, I drive up. I bring out the dope, you bring out the kid. We swap, go back to our cars, that's it."

The driver was staring at me through the rearview. Maybe he had a gun in his lap. Maybe the Eskimo would suddenly yell *Kill him!* and the driver would open up through the seat. There are so many maybes in my life that they begin to lose all meaning. Maybe I should retire.

The Eskimo said, "There could be many people in the park."

I made my eyes wide. "Garsh, I never thoughta that." I do a pretty good Goofy.

He stared at me, nodded. "Bring the boy's mother."

"No."

"I do not want to meet you for the exchange. Send the mother out with the cocaine. I'll send the boy alone. She can leave the dope on the ground and bring her son back to you before I move forward for the dope."

"No."

"The boy's hand is injured. He is frightened. Knowing the mother is there will calm him. If the child isn't calm, it will not go well."

"No."

The Eskimo spread his hands. "Then we still have a problem. Perhaps you should keep the cocaine and we should keep the boy. Or perhaps we will simply come take the cocaine."

"You'll never find it."

He was pressing hard for the mother. Maybe he wanted a family snapshot for his memory book. He spread his hands again and looked at me.

"All right," I said. "Tomorrow noon. I send the mother. You send the kid. Back by the tunnel. You're alone. I'm alone."

"Yes."

I got out of the limo, watched them pull away into traffic, then went in and down to my car.

Pike and Ellen were standing on the east side of my house when I pulled up. I got out of the car with the foil brick and walked around the front of the house toward them. Pike was saying, "You're holding it too hard. Hold it firmly, but don't clutch it. It won't fly away from you."

They were standing in the grass on the part of the hillside that tabled out and was flat before falling away. Ellen Lang was aiming a blued Ruger .25 automatic at one of the two young gum trees that I'd planted there last year. Pike was standing to her right, adjusting her form with a touch here, a touch there. Her right arm held the gun out straight, her left bent slightly at the elbow so she could use her left hand to cup and brace her right. "Okay," Pike said.

She exhaled, steadied, then there was a loud *snap!* Dry firing. Pike looked at me. "She's pretty good. Her body's quiet."

"What does that mean?" Ellen said. When she wasn't aiming the gun she cradled it in both hands against her stomach.

"It means your body damps your pulse and your muscles don't quiver when you try to hold still. That's natural. You can't learn it." Pike nodded his head at the foil brick. "Who had the dope?"

Ellen's eyes went to the brick as if Pike had just said, *"Who's the Martian?"* She said, "Mort didn't steal that?"

"No. Kimberly Marsh and her boyfriend stole it."

"That woman had a boyfriend?"

"Yeah."

"Someone besides Mort?"

"Yes."

"Behind Mort's back?"

I nodded.

Ellen pulled back the slide to cock the .25, then aimed at the gum tree again. *Snap!*

Pike said, "You set it up with Duran?"

"The Eskimo. Noon tomorrow back by the tunnel at Griffith Park. Ellen brings the dope to the tunnel, puts it on the ground, then they send out Perry. She brings Perry back to me, the Eskimo goes out for the dope. End of deal."

Ellen looked at me. Pike was looking at me, too. His mouth twitched. "So. They're going to let you and Ellen and the kid walk away and expect everybody to keep their mouths shut."

Ellen looked at him.

"No," I said. "What happens is something like this: they set up some soldiers early, and when we're all together they eliminate us, recover the dope, and an hour later the Eskimo and the soldiers are on Duran's private jet, heading for Acapulco and a long, expenses-paid vacation."

"Ah," Joe said, "reality raises its ugly head."

Ellen said, "Shouldn't you call Sergeant Poitras?"

"Not if Duran owns somebody downtown. If all we can get is a couple of soldiers, you've still got a problem."

"Then what are we going to do?"

"We get there earlier than they do. We watch them set up. we see if I'm right about their intentions. If I am, we figure a way to get Perry away from them. If I'm not, we go through with the trade and worry about Duran after you and the boy and the girls are away from here and safe."

"What if they don't wait?" Ellen said. "If they want these drugs and they know you have them, won't they just come here instead?"

Pike's mouth twitched again. For Pike, that's a laughing fit. "It'll cost too much," he said. "Here, we're dug in. Here, a cop car could roll by, there's neighbors, bad access. In Griffith, they're hoping we'll be exposed. They can set up a free fire zone, snipers, ambushes, roadblocks, you name it." You could tell he was pleased.

I cleared my throat. Loudly. "They want the dope," I said, rationally. "I told the Eskimo it was hidden somewhere and that I'd have to get it. That's why they won't come." I glared hard at Pike. "*Right?*"

Pike said, "Gonna get a guitar. Back later." He disappeared around the front of the house. Purring.

Ellen said, "Does he play?"

I just looked at her, then went into the house and opened two Evian water. Ellen had come in and had just thanked me for the water when the phone rang. She went as white as a sheet of clean new paper.

I answered. Janet Simon said, "Elvis? It's Janet Simon."

I covered the mouthpiece and told Ellen it was Janet. She was relieved, but she wasn't thrilled. She made that funny mouth gesture where she keeps the front of her lips together and blows out the sides.

"I was beginning to think you never wanted to speak to me again," I said into the phone. Mr. Charm.

"Yes. Well." Janet's voice was low and measured and

sounded like she never wanted to speak to me again, only now she had to. It's a sound I've heard before.

"How is Ellen?" she said.

"Sitting on a rainbow."

"Is it almost over?"

"Yep."

"Is she keeping it together?"

"She's doing okay."

"I could come over."

"Not a great idea."

"She might need me to do something."

I didn't say anything. Ellen looked suspicious and uneasy and not anxious to talk. But that could have been my imagination.

Janet said, "Maybe there's something I could do. She might have dry cleaning. She might have a prescription. She forgets things."

I held out the phone to Ellen Lang. "For you."

Ellen made the blowing gesture again and took the phone. She cradled the receiver into her neck beneath her jaw and said, "Hello?" She listened a while, then said, "Actually, I'm fine. How're the girls?" Not thrilled. Definitely not thrilled.

She said, "I don't know that yet. I don't know if he's dead or alive or what."

She did not look faded or uneasy or intimidated.

"I should go now."

She looked angry and bored.

"No, I'll call you."

She hung up. She did not do so lightly.

I took the two Evians out onto the deck. After a while, Ellen joined me. She said, "Janet," as if she were going to follow it with a lot more, but then she fell silent.

An hour and forty minutes later Pike was back. Ellen and I were sitting on the edge of the deck, listening to a Lakers game and not talking about Janet Simon. The Lakers were out at Washington playing the Bullets. It sounded like a physical game. The Evian water was warm.

Pike unloaded a large green duffel bag and two olive-green guitar cases from his Jeep and carried them toward the house. Ellen went over to the side rail to watch him.

"Do you know Segovia?" she asked.

"Rock 'n roll," he said.

He brought his things into the living room through the front door. Ellen went in, then came out a few minutes later, looking distant.

"Those aren't guitars."

"Nope."

"He has guns."

I nodded. The Lakers were down by four but Kareem had just scored six straight from inside.

She said, "You seem so calm."

"I'm working at it."

"I know this is what we have to do, but it seems so unreal."

"Unh-hunh." Fantasy in fantasyland.

She said, "It's like a war, right here in Los Angeles."

I nodded some more.

After a very long time, she said, "I hope we kick their asses."

I looked at her. I drank the warm Evian water. Kareem made it eight in a row.

34

It began to rain again just after four the next morning, a slow leaking drizzle that fell out of silver clouds, lit from beneath by cityglow. Pike sat at the dining table in the dark, sipping at a finger of bourbon in a tall glass. He said, "It's about time you were up."

I went into the little bathroom without saying anything and dressed. Levi's, gray Beverly Hills Gun Club tee shirt, CJ Bass desert boots. A client had given me the Gun Club tee shirt, but I'd never worn it. When I went out to the kitchen Pike looked at the shirt and shook his head.

There was coffee in the pot and a plate of dry toast, and Pike's big Coleman thermos, also filled with coffee. I got out a loaf of white and a half loaf of whole wheat and laid out bread for nine sandwiches. There were two packs of pressed ham, most of a pack of processed chicken, and two ham hocks left in the refrigerator. Enough for nine. I wrapped sweet gherkins and jalapeño-stuffed olives in foil, put them in a Gelson's bag with napkins, then put the sandwiches on top. In another sack I put two six-packs of RC 100, a plastic bottle of water, cups, and some Handi Wipes.

When the food was ready, Pike took the bags out through the kitchen door and put them in his Jeep. Cold air came in through the open door. While he was out, Ellen Lang, dressed in her jeans and one of my sweatshirts, came down and sat quietly on the stairs, elbows on knees.

"How ya doing?" I said.

She nodded.

"Want some coffee?" I poured half a cup and brought that and a slice of the dry toast to her. "It's good to have something in your stomach."

"I don't think I can."

"Nibble."

From the entry closet I took out a slicker for Ellen and a nylon rain shell for me. I put Pike's duffel bag and the two guitar cases by the couch. The duffel bag weighed a ton. I shrugged into my shoulder holster, checked the load in the Dan Wesson, and snapped the catch. I went upstairs, found my clip-on holster, and took a 9mm Beretta automatic from the drawer beside my bed and two extra clips. Each clip held fourteen hollow-point hot loads. Pike had made them for me a long time ago. Illegal. But what's that to a tough guy like me? With the rain shell on, you couldn't see either gun. It wouldn't be easy to get to the Dan Wesson, but I didn't expect to have to quick-draw walking out to the Jeep.

When Pike came back, he was wearing the cammie field jacket. He opened the first guitar case and took out a Weatherby Mark V .30–06 deer buster with an 8-power Bushnell scope and a box of cartridges. He fed four into the gun, locked the bolt, then stood the gun against the arm of the couch. When he opened the second case, Ellen Lang leaned forward. She said, "What's that?"

"Heckler and Koch .308 assault rifle," Pike said.

"Pike shows it to people to scare them," I said. "It doesn't really shoot."

Pike's mouth twitched. The HK was entirely black. With its Fiberglas stock, pistol grip, carry handle, and flash suppressor, it was an ugly, mean gun. Pike snapped the bolt, then took a sixty-shot banana clip from the duffel bag and seated it. He sprayed the external metal parts of each rifle with a mist of WD40, then wiped each lightly with a greasy cloth. His hands worked with a precise economy. Finished, he stood up, said, "Whenever," and brought the big guns and the duffel out to the Cherokee.

I gave the slicker to Ellen. "Put this on."

She put it on.

I put the foil brick into a third shopping bag and gave it to her. "Are you scared?" I said.

She nodded.

I said, "Try to be like me. I'm never scared."

She carried the dope out to the Cherokee. I watched her climb into the backseat from the kitchen, then stood around, wondering if I'd forgotten anything.

The cat walked in and looked at me. I fed him, poured out a saucer of beer, then locked the door. We drove to Griffith Park in a rain so light it was very much like falling dew.

35

At ten minutes before six, the park was dark and empty and cold, with only light traffic passing the entrance off Los Feliz Boulevard. We turned in and cruised to the back of the park toward the tunnel, past the picnic tables and green lawns and public rest rooms that are habitat for bums, muggers, and homosexual mashers. An old Volkswagen microbus and a Norton motorcycle were parked in the spaces past the rest rooms, but there was no sign of life.

Pike had the radio tuned to the farm reports. To the best of my knowledge, Joe Pike has never been on a farm in his life. Ellen sat in the backseat, the dope on her lap, her eyes luminous in the glow from reflected streetlights.

At the tunnel the road split, one fork disappearing into the tunnel, the other taking a hard right to climb into the mountains up to the observatory. A steel pipe gate blocked the fork that went up. I said, "There's a fire road about a half mile ahead that's good for us."

Pike nodded.

I got out, picked the Yale on the pipe gate, let Pike through, then swung the gate back across and relocked it. It was colder here in Griffith than in my own canyon, with clouds pushing down out of the sky to touch the mountains above us, and my breath fogging the air as I worked against the gate.

The sky along the ridgeline to the east was just beginning to turn violet when Pike engaged the four-wheel-drive and turned off onto the fire road. We went out along the ridge between scrub oak and tumbleweed and yucca trees for about a hundred yards until we came to a small grove of scrub oak. Below, the flat of the park spread in an irregular green triangle, from its apex at the tunnel widening all the way out to the park's entrance off Los Feliz. We could see everything we would need to.

Pike nodded approvingly. "Nice view."

"Glad you like it."

He killed the engine but left the radio on.

We waited.

At ten minutes to seven a Park Service Bronco came out of the tunnel and turned up toward the pipe gate. A woman in a brown Park Service uniform unlocked the gate, swung it out of the road, then climbed back into her Bronco and disappeared through the tunnel. I ate a processed chicken on white and drank coffee. Ellen didn't have anything. Neither did Pike.

The world brightened even though the sky remained dark gray. The clouds pushed lower, now sitting halfway down the mountains, slowly bleeding moisture. Traffic grew heavy down on the boulevard, and people began to gather at the bus stop, mostly short, stocky Chicano women carrying large purses. Some of them had umbrellas, but some didn't, and not everybody looked willing to share.

In the back, Ellen pulled her feet up, leaned against the cab wall, and slept. Or pretended to. Pike slouched down behind the wheel, his eyes closed to little slits. That Ellen, that Pike, what a couple of wet blankets. Just when I was going to suggest charades.

At seven-thirty, a white Cadillac turned in off Los Feliz and rolled down past the picnic tables to park across from the rest rooms. Ten minutes later, a cruising police prowl car stopped beside the Volkswagen microbus. Two cops in black slickers got out. One of them rapped on the bus' side door with his nightstick while the other stayed by their black-and-white with his hand on the butt of his Smith. A young guy in jeans and no shirt climbed out of the bus and talked to the cops for a while and did a lot of nodding and a lot of shivering. Then the cops got back in their car and the kid went back into his bus and the cops drove away. I drank more coffee and ate a sweet gherkin and watched. Two lean women in racing tights pedaled fancy bicycles up through the park from out of the Hollywood traffic and zinged back through the tunnel, their bikes throwing up sprays of water, their fine legs churning. An occasional car took the same path but turned up the mountain instead, passing us moments later. Probably people who worked at the observatory. A tall Hispanic man in tight black pants, plaid shirt, and down vest came up from Hollywood under a pale pink umbrella. He stopped under the restroom awning, shook out his umbrella, then went inside. After a minute, the Caddie opened and a middle-aged white man in designer jeans, tweed sport coat, and glasses hustled across, hands over his head against the rain, and also went into the restroom. More cars passed, more cyclists, some runners. The kid came out of his bus, this time wearing a shirt and shoes and rain jacket, wiped off the Norton's seat with a piece of newspaper, fired it up, and took off. The middle-aged guy came out of the restroom, hustled back to his Caddie, and drove away. Then the tall man came out, looked at the sky as if expecting it might have cleared, opened his umbrella, and headed back to Hollywood. I ate four jalapeño olives and drank more coffee. Life is drama.

Just after nine, the clouds let go. Rain banged down in big heavy drops that sounded like hail against the Jeep. Pike took a sandwich from the bag and ate it without saying anything. Ellen stirred and sat up but neither ate nor drank.

Just before ten, a Mercury Montego turned into the park and stopped by the picnic tables. There were three men inside, two in the front, one in the back. I said, "Joe."

"Got'm."

Ellen Lang leaned forward.

Five minutes later two more sedans pulled up next to the Montego, and five minutes after that, two more cars came. The second-to-last car was the blue Nova.

"He's fielding a goddamned army for this," Pike said.

"Sure. He's heard of us."

"I don't see Perry," Ellen said.

"There's still time," I said.

Pike frowned and looked back out the window.

The Tattooed Man got out of the third car and walked up to the Montego. You couldn't see his tattoos because of the rain jacket he wore, but Ellen said softly, "He's one of them." I nodded and finished the jalapeño olives. No one else had had any. Pity.

The Tattooed Man leaned into the Montego, spoke briefly to its driver, then it pulled away, heading toward us. It slowed at the mouth of the tunnel, then swung onto the gated road and came up. The rain had slacked to a dull gray drizzle again. The Montego climbed past us, probably all the way to the observatory, then came back down and pulled up by the other cars. The Tattooed Man got out of his car again, spoke with the Montego, then gestured at the other cars. Men stepped out into the rain. The Tattooed Man pointed to different spots along the parking perimeter, then to different spots along the hills surrounding the tunnel, then at the kid's microbus. A chunky guy with slicked-back hair put his right hand in his coat pocket and went over to the bus. He knocked, then went around to peer in the windshield. He said something to the Tattooed Man and shook his head, then joined the others. Close for the kid on the Norton. Very close. Pike took field glasses out of the glove box and watched them. Some of the men took long guns out of their cars and walked into the woods holding the guns close to their bodies. When everyone was out and armed, the drivers spread their cars, parking two by the restrooms, two more by the picnic tables, another at the mouth of the park by the entrance. The Tattooed Man spoke to Sanchez, who nodded and trotted off to an olive grove in the low hills behind the restrooms. Then the Tattooed Man got back in his own car. After a while you could see him sipping something. Rank hath its privileges.

At twenty-two minutes before noon, a black stretch limo turned in off Los Feliz Boulevard, cruised the length of the park road, and parked under an elm tree by the mouth of the tunnel. Kato was driving. Ellen Lang dug her fingers into my shoulder like pliers' jaws and made a noise in her throat.

Pike sighted down through the Weatherby's scope, then lowered the gun and shook his head. "Can't see. Back in ten."

Pike left the Cherokee with the Weatherby, easing the door shut with a soft *click*, then disappeared down the hill. Ellen said, "Where's he going?"

"To see if Perry's in the limo."

She edged sideways in the seat. "Of course he's down there. He has to be, doesn't he? They want to trade for the drugs, don't they?"

I didn't say anything. With the artillery they'd deployed it was clear that Duran's plan was what I thought it would be: let us in, but not out. The only question was whether they would do the boy here, with us, or later, after we were gone. If the boy wasn't here we'd have to find him.

I ate a ham hock sandwich. I ate more sweet gherkins. I drank most of an RC 100. Halfway through the RC, Pike opened the door and climbed in, wet and muddy. He got a Kleenex from the glove box, took off his sunglasses, and cleaned them. It was the first time in weeks that I had seen Pike's eyes, and I'd forgotten how blue they were, so clear and rich and deep that they looked artificial. When the glasses were clean and dry again, he refitted them. "No kid," he said. "Gook behind the wheel, a couple of bruisers in back. One looks like he could be your Eskimo."

Ellen began to shake. Her face tightened and turned red and her lips came away from her teeth and her eyes filled. Not pain this time. Anger. I squeezed her arm hard and said, "He's alive. They have to keep him alive in case this fails. If he were dead and they blew this, they'd have nothing. So they'll keep him alive. See?"

She nodded, neck rigid.

Pike said, "Any ideas?"

I said, "Yeah. The guy who owns the blue Nova, Sanchez, he's in the trees behind the john."

Pike nodded. "I'm better in the bush than you. I'm also better at getting people to talk."

"Woods, Joe. Here in America it's called the woods, not the bush."

Pike put the Weatherby back by the HK, then left the car again. I dug up under my rain shell, took out the Dan Wesson, and gave it to Ellen. "We're not going to be long," I said. "If we're not back in twenty minutes or if you see something bad happen, drive out of here, back the way we came. Use the gun if you have to. Go to the North Hollywood P.D. and see Poitras."

She stared at the gun in her hands.

"Are you all right?"

She nodded, then said, "Yes. Yes, I'm all right."

The rain had eroded deep grooves into the hillside and made the earth slick and the footing treacherous. I slipped more than Pike, but the rain splattering on leaves and grass and rocks and road masked our sounds. Dry leaves were wet and spongy and no longer crackled. Whip grass gave way easily, heavy with water. Twigs bent without breaking. We moved down off of our ridge onto a low rise that bottomed out behind the picnic tables and the restrooms, staying low under scrub oak and olive and the occasional elm, Pike moving like something from another age, like part of a medieval mist, slewing down over the ground and between the trees with no apparent effort and without apparent effect. The jabberwock. When we were most of the way down the prowl car came back, driving smoothly back toward the tunnel, oblivious, then turning up the mountain to cruise the observatory.

When we saw Sanchez, sitting on a paper bag beside an olive tree sixty yards down the slope, he was not alone. Pike, out front, held up a hand, pointed at them. I nodded. The man with Sanchez was short and squat with a beaked nose and a pockmarked face. He was picking a Styrofoam cup to pieces and murmuring to Sanchez, who grunted every once in a while. There was a 12-gauge Ithaca pump gun across the squat man's legs.

I caught Pike's eye and made a fist. He nodded. We waited. After a few minutes, the prowl car came back down off the mountain, continued on through the park and back out into the Hollywood traffic. Pike looked at me. I eased out the 9mm, then nodded.

We separated and worked our way through the trees until we were on opposite sides of them. Then I stood up, walked out from behind a tree that was to their left, and showed them the gun.

Sanchez gasped, eyes bulging, but stayed where he was. The other guy rolled sideways, scrambling to come up with the Ithaca and saying "¡Hueta!" quite loud. Pike grabbed his face from behind, twisted it hard to the side, and jammed his Marine Corps knife into the base of his skull, angling up and twisting. It sounded like empty peanut shells when you step on them at the ball park. The man collapsed, his body jerking and trembling, but no longer trying to yell or trying to shoot us. Pike eased the body down, and put a knee on its back to keep the jerking from getting too wild. His bowels and his bladder went at the same time. On TV, a guy gets knifed or shot and he's dead. In the world, dying takes a while and it smells bad. Sanchez stared at his friend. Pike stared at Sanchez, the reflective lenses blank. I touched Sanchez with the pistol, and when he looked at me, put a finger to my lips. His face was the color of wheat. He nodded.

When Pike pulled out the knife it made a wet sound.

I said, "If you lie to me, he'll do that to you. Do you speak English?"

Sanchez answered without taking his eyes off Pike. "Sí. Yes."

"Is Duran sending the boy here for the trade?"

Sanchez shook his head, watching Pike wipe his knife on the dead man's shirt.

"Where do they have the boy?"

"I don't know."

I put the barrel of the 9mm under his eye. He jerked, then looked away from Pike to me. "I don't know. They been keeping him at a place in Silverlake but they moved him this morning. I don't know where."

Pike gestured at the surrounding area. "Would any of these guys know?"

"If one of them drove. If one of them heard. I don't know."

"The Eskimo would know," I said.

Sanchez nodded. "Luca," he said.

"Yeah, Luca."

Pike said, "He in the limo?"

Sanchez nodded again. Pike looked at me. "You want Luca, it's going to be loud and messy. We're going to have to go through a few of these guys."

"Duran would know," I said.

Pike's mouth twitched.

I touched Sanchez gently with the gun barrel. "Is Duran at home?"

He nodded.

I looked back at Pike. "All his soldiers are here."

Pike squinted out through the misted trees. "It's ten of, now. Pretty soon these clucks are going to figure out they've been stood up. Then they're going to go back home. Not much time."

I slid the muzzle of the 9mm down the length of Sanchez's nose and rested it at the tip. "How many are left at the house?"

Sanchez shook his head. "The *patrón* has guests. Important people." Sweat on his forehead mixed with the drizzle.

"If he's got guests," I said, "he won't want a bunch of pugs standing around his living room. There's twelve here. How many soldiers can he have?"

Pike's mouth twitched again. "Didn't somebody say that about the Viet Cong?"

The three of us started back up the hill. By the time we made the Jeep, the drizzle had evolved back into rain—heavy, gravid drops that beat at you, and thudded into your head with a sound I imagined to be like that of the hooves of bulls, pounding damp earth, earth damp with blood.

36

The Cherokee was thick with the smell of wet clothes and mud and sweat and fear. We eased down off the mountain under the canopy of rain, Ellen under the dash up front, me and Sanchez squeezed onto the rear floorboard, Pike driving. I'd wrapped Sanchez's wrists behind his back with duct tape. I'd once kept a car running for years, held together by duct tape. There's nothing like it. I put the 9mm between Sanchez's legs and told him if he made a sound he could kiss them good-bye.

When the road finally leveled out down by the tunnel, Pike said, "Uh-oh, the Eskimo just jumped out and is waving at us." I shoved the gun harder into Sanchez's crotch and felt the drop-stick feeling you get from adrenaline rush. Then Pike said, "Ha ha. Just kidding."

That Pike.

The Cherokee moved steadily forward for several minutes, then slowed and Pike said, "We're out of the park. You can get up."

"Is this another joke?"

"Trust me."

We turned left into the heavy lunch-hour traffic on Los Feliz. When we were up in the seats, I stripped the tape from Sanchez's wrists and rebound them, taking time to make sure the job was done right. Ellen watched Sanchez as I did it, her face empty. Maybe she was studying to be like Pike.

She said, "What did you do to my son to make him scream like that?"

Sanchez looked at me. He'd probably never seen her face. Just a woman with a bag for a head.

"She's the boy's mother," I said.

Sanchez shook his head.

Ellen continued to stare at him as we eased to a stop at a traffic light. The pounding rain had slacked to a misty drizzle. A black kid in a big yellow Ryder truck pulled up next to us with his radio blasting out Mozart's *Piano Concerto in D*

Minor. Probably trying to found a new stereotype. Pike took a sandwich out of the bag under Ellen Lang's seat, ham and white bread, and ate.

Ellen lifted the Dan Wesson and pointed it at Sanchez's face. "Are you the one who murdered my husband?"

Sanchez straightened. I didn't move. Pike took another bite of sandwich, chewed, swallowed. His lenses were blank in the rearview mirror. Sanchez said, "I swear to God I know nothing."

Ellen looked at me. "I could kill him." Her voice was calm and steady.

"I know."

The .38's muzzle didn't waver. Pike was right. She had a quiet body. She said, "But we might need him to get Perry."

"Unh-huh."

She lowered the .38. Something like a smile pinched the corners of her mouth. She turned around and sat forward, resting the gun in her lap. Joe reached across and patted her leg.

I said, "We should drop these two off somewhere."

Pike said, "Where? Your Eskimo's probably tapping his watch right now. Maybe they've already found the body."

"This isn't going to be easy," I said. "It might go wrong."

Pike shrugged. "She can handle it. Can't you?"

"Yes," Ellen said. "Let's get Perry."

Five minutes later, we came to the massive mortared wall, followed it up past the gate, turned around at the side street, then drove back down. We parked the Cherokee off the road about a block from the corner of Duran's estate. Pike got out, said, 'C'mere, you," and pulled Sanchez out into the street. Pike turned him around, then hit him behind the right ear with the flat of his pistol. Sanchez smacked against the Cherokee and collasped. Pike hoisted him into the rear seat again, then dug out the duct tape and put strips over his mouth and eyes, and bound his ankles.

I helped Ellen into the driver's seat, then closed the door and spoke to her through the open window. "If anyone comes, get out of here and go for the cops. If they stand in front of the car, run over them. If you hear shots, go for the cops. If Sanchez tries to make trouble, shoot him. When you see us coming, start up and be ready to go."

"All right."

Pike slammed the rear door, then came around and looked

at Ellen. He looked at her the way you examine something that you don't want to make a mistake about. "There's going to be killing," he said.

She nodded. "I know."

"You might have to do some."

Another nod.

"You got a lipstick, something?"

She shook her head.

"Look in the glove box."

Ellen bent across the seat. Sanchez moaned and shifted in the back of the Jeep. "Joe," I said.

Ellen leaned back into the window. She had a brown plastic tube. Estée Lauder Scarlet Haze. Pike ran the color out, then drew a bright red line down his forehead and along the bridge of his nose and two parallel lines across each cheek under his eyes.

"You're getting crazy on me, Joe," I said.

She watched him without a word, and she held steady when he did the same with her. "Not crazy," he said. "She's going to want to forget, so reality ends now. It's easy to forget the unreal. In a year, in five, she thinks of this, it's all the more absurd."

"You two look silly," I said.

Ellen Lang twisted the sideview mirror so she could see herself, first one side, then the other. No smile, now. Just consideration.

Nobody said good-bye or I'll be seeing you or keep a stiff upper lip. When Sanchez was secure and the doors were closed and locked, Pike and I trotted back up the hill toward Duran's, me carrying the 9mm loosely in my hand, Pike the HK.

When we came to the estate, we turned onto the side street and followed the wall until we came to an ancient olive tree, grown gnarled and crooked with huge limbs twisting up and over. Pike said, "You remember what I said about the layout?"

"You look dumb with that lipstick on."

"You don't remember, do you?"

"Just past the front knoll is the motor court. Main house with two levels. Guest house in the rear. Pool and poolhouse. Tennis court to the northeast of the pool."

He nodded. Pike went up first. I handed up the HK, stuck the 9mm in my belt and followed. Water from the rain-heavy leaves showered down on us every time the tree shook. When we dropped down, I thought we were behind the Mexico City Hilton, but Pike said no, it was only the guest house, the main residence was larger. We followed the perimeter of the guest house toward the rear of the estate and came out by a small stand of newly planted magnolia trees. Three women and four men were standing around a sheltered brick barbeque off the poolhouse, cooking hamburgers. They were wearing sweaters and long pants and one of the men wore a hat. It never rains in Southern California. They looked comfortable and at ease and more than a little drunk. None of the men was Domingo Duran. The man with the hat laughed loudly, then grabbed the breast of the nearest woman. She swatted him away and he laughed louder. He had a flat, round face and a nose with jagged scars from the time someone had tried to bite it off, and he dressed like a hick from back east: black lace-up shoes, Sears pants, and a lime green golfing sweater over a white Arrow shirt, all of which went beautifully with his crushed gray felt hat. I looked at him and smiled and said, "Well, well."

"What?" Pike said.

"You see the gentleman in the hat?"

"Yeah."

"Rudy Gambino."

"What's a Rudy Gambino?" Pike refused to keep himself current on underworld figures.

"Mobster from Arizona. From Newark originally, until his own people sent him out west because they couldn't control him. Duran's connected with him. Buddies."

Pike said, "I like his nose."

Inside the poolhouse, two young thick-necked Chicano kids in black suits leaned against a pinball machine and smoked. Muscle to keep Uncle Rudy safe.

We went back past the guest house, slipped along a narrow shrub-lined walk, and edged up against the side of a fountain behind pale red oleander. The drizzle had stopped altogether now, but the clouds were still dark. We had a clear view of the front of the guest house, as well as the pool and the poolhouse and the back side of the main house. As big as the guest house was, the main house was larger. An enormous white Spanish Mediterranean, heavy-walled, with quarry-tiled patios and red-tiled roofs and oversized beams. The patios were covered and partially hidden behind lush landscaping. A man in a trench coat sat at a small glass table, well out of the rain. He was holding a paperback copy of Stephen King's *The Dead*

Zone but he wasn't reading. A Remington over/under shotgun rested on the table. Arizona muscle.

A guest house had three separate facing doors, like a triplex. The door farthest away from us opened and two thugs came out with Perry Lang between them. The boy was blindfolded and his left hand was heavily bandaged. He walked the way you walk when you haven't slept well in a while. I felt Pike shift next to me. Good luck, and bad. Good luck, that the boy had been brought here. We wouldn't have to force his whereabouts out of anyone. It wasn't smart for them to have him here, but Sanchez said they'd moved the boy this morning. They'd probably been keeping him in a safe house, but decided to bring him closer in case something went wrong with the ambush and they needed a little extra leverage. Maybe I should call Poitras. I could tell him the kid was here and he would act on it. But maybe by the time I got to a phone and called the cops and the cops got here, the Eskimo would've come and gone and taken the boy with him, maybe not quite as alive as last reported.

Bad luck because of Gambino. How many Arizona soldiers did he have hanging around the guest house and the main house and the garage? What would Gambino do when Pike and I made our move? Normal business practice would be noninterference. But he was a guest in Duran's home. They were friends. Besides that, he wouldn't know for sure if we weren't coming for him. Shit.

Gambino left the barbeque and sloshed across to the main house. He carried a Coors and belched so loudly we could hear him sixty yards away. Classy. He didn't bother with the walkways. Guess he didn't give a shit if he tracked messy into his good friend Domingo Duran's home. Maybe he figured Mexicans didn't mind.

The two guys holding Perry stopped outside of the guest-house, talking, then one of them continued on with the kid across to the main house. The second one came our way, toward the garage. We dropped along the row of oleander until we were out of sight of the rear yard, then came out onto the walk.

"If we're going into the main house," Pike said, "we're not going to do it through the back. Too many people."

We were zipping along, backpedaling along the walk toward the garage. "Did you see a way in through the front?" I said.

"Sure. Windows. Doors."

Smartass. "You always carry lipstick in your truck?"

"You wouldn't believe what I got in there."

The walk ended at a door off the rear of the garage in a nice circular spot strewn with pretty white rocks. There was a heavy adobe wall to the right, as thick as but lower than the main wall, extending from the garage to the main house. To the left the grounds sloped away to an open rolling lawn. It was through the door or across the lawn. On the lawn, we could be seen. The door was locked.

We stepped back off the walk into the shrubs and waited. There were footsteps, then the second thug came along, hissing air through his teeth and digging in his pocket. When he stopped at the door and took out a silver key, I stepped out and hit him once in the ear, hard. He sat down and I hit him again. Pike picked up the key. "Not bad."

I waffled my hand from side to side. "Eh."

Pike put the key in the lock and opened the door. A short Mexican with a broad face and a gray zoot suit took one step out, pushed a gold Llama automatic into Pike's chest, and pulled the trigger. There was a deep muffled *POP*, then Pike came up and around with his right foot faster than I could see. There was a louder sound, what you might hear if you drop an overripe casaba melon onto a tile floor. The Mexican collapsed, his neck limp. Pike looked down at himself, put one hand over a growing spot high and to the right of his chest, then sat down. "Keep going," he said. "Get the kid."

I felt like I might scream. I looked at him, nodded, then pushed through the door. Forward. Never back up.

There were three Cadillac limos, two Rolls-Royces, and a bright yellow Ferrari Boxer in the garage, but no more thugs. I went out to the edge of the motor court and looked at the front of the house. Another limo was there. A service drive branched off the motor court and ran around to the side of the house, then looped back around to the garage. That would be the kitchen. I walked out across the motor court to the service and followed it around to the side of the mansion. Maybe the way to get the kid was to walk up to things and shoot them and when I ran out of things to shoot I'd either have the kid or be dead.

The service drive led to a carport attached to the house. There was a single door there, and a little metal buzzer. When I pushed the buzzer a tiny woman, as nicely browned as good leather, opened the door. She looked disgusted. "¡No más comer!" she said.

"Do you speak English?"

"No, no." She shook her head and tried to push me out of the door. Probably thought I was one of Gambino's goons.

I showed her the gun and jerked my head out toward the front gate. "Vamoose!" Then I went into the kitchen.

Manolo was eating a sandwich at a chopping block table. His jacket was off and he was wearing a shoulder holster over a blue shirt with white collar and cuffs. When he saw me, he clawed at his gun. I shot him twice. The hollow-points picked him up and kicked him back off the stool. The 9mm high-velocity loads echoed like a cannon in the tile kitchen.

I went out through a serving hall and into a living room that made Barry Fein's place look like a phone booth. Gambino's hood was coming in off the balcony with his shotgun. When he saw me he said, "What the hell was that?"

I said, "This," and clubbed him in the side of the face with the gun. He stumbled and dropped the shotgun but didn't pass out. I pulled him up to his feet and shook him and pressed the muzzle up under his jaw. "They just brought a kid in here. Where?"

"I swear to God I don't know. I swear."

I hit him in the mouth with the butt of the gun. His teeth went and blood sprayed out along my arm and he went down to his knees. "Where?"

"Shwear to Chri I dunno." Hard to talk with a ruined mouth.

"Where's Duran?"

"Offishe. Upshtairs."

"Show me."

I could see out the elegant French doors, across the patio and the lawn to the poolhouse. If they'd heard the shots, no one showed it. Burgers still sizzled, music still played, men and women still laughed. I was vaguely aware that Ellen Lang, sitting out in Pike's Cherokee without benefit of laughter or music or gaiety, might have heard the shots. And having heard them, might be on her way to call the cops.

I pulled him up again and we went out the living room, up a monstrous semicircular stairway to the second floor. Voices and the sound of closing doors came from the back of the house. On the upper landing, I said, "Where are you taking me?"

"Offishe." He looked to the left down a curving hall. "Door, wish a couple guysh. Go shrough into she offishe."

"Just a couple of guys, huh?"

"Yesh."

"There another way in or out?"

He looked confused, then shook his head. It hurt him to do that. "I don't live here, man. It'sh tight. Shoundproo."

Shoundproo. Perfect.

"Why are you people here?"

His eyes flagged and he started to crumple. I hoisted him up, gave him a shake, asked him again.

"Bushnesh," he said.

"Business. Dope deal?"

He nodded.

The hall was long and paneled with a very rich grade of walnut. Impressive. The St. Francis Hotel in San Francisco has walls like that. I stopped us before we got to the door, held up the Beretta, and touched my lips.

He said, "I beliee you."

A slim, well-manicured Mexican sat at a bank president's desk and spoke into a phone. A tall, blocky blond guy had half his ass on the edge of the desk, listening in with his arms crossed. Across the room there was a handsome copper-façaded door that would lead to Duran's sanctum sanctorum. The blond guy was in a pale yellow sport coat. The Mexican wore a charcoal gray Brooks Brothers three-piece and looked better than the blond guy. Executive secretary, no doubt. He was speaking English, asking about the noises he'd just heard. I shoved Mr. Teeth in through the doorway, walked in after him and shot the Mexican and the blond once each. The hollow-points flipped the Mexican over backward out of his chair and knocked the blond guy off the desk.

I looked at the door. It was thick and heavy and I didn't know how I was going to get in there. No knob. *Knock, knock, knock, Chicken Delight!* There would probably be a buzzer somewhere around the secretary's desk that would make little metal gears push little metal rods to swing open the door. They would have to be strong rods. It was a big door.

Mr. Teeth and I were halfway across the outer office when the copper door opened and Rudy Gambino stepped out, saying, "The fuck's goin' on out —"

He had a Smith Police Special in his left hand. He dropped it when he saw me.

"Back up, fat man," I said.

He backed. And in we went.

37

Perry Lang was not in the room.

Domingo Garcia Duran was sitting on a maroon leather couch under a wall of black-and-white photographs. Most of the shots were of bullrings and bulls and Duran, I supposed, in his Suit of Lights. Still others showed Duran with other matadors and Duran with various political personalities and Duran with assorted celebrities. Everyone smiled. Everyone was friends. *Hooray for Hol-ley-wood!* There were trophies and black horns mounted to teak plaques and tattered black ears mounted to still other teak plaques. Gray-black hooves stood hoof up off little wooden pedestals like demented ashtrays. You could smell death in the room like mildewed satin. A cape was hanging off a tall leather pedestal near the window, and crossed swords like the ones on the front gate, only real-size, were fixed on the wall above it. The walls were hung with oil paintings of bulls and an enormous life-size rendering of Duran poised for the kill. Still more statues of bulls and matadors and men on horses with long lances lined the bookcases.

"Really, Dom," I said. "A bit much, don't you think?"

Rudy Gambino said, "Your ass is shit, bubba."

I said, "I got the gun, Rudy."

There was a marble coffee table in front of Duran with an open briefcase on top of it. The briefcase was filled with neat stacks of thousand-dollar bills. Duran's well-worn bent sword was on top of it. Duran leaned forward, picked up the sword, and closed the case. *Estoque*, Pike had said. The sword used for the kill.

I pushed Mr. Teeth down onto the floor and told him to stay there, then pointed the gun at Duran. "I want the boy *now*, Dom." I could see Pike bleeding to death out in the yard. I could see Sanchez getting loose, getting Ellen's gun. . . .

Rudy said, "The fuck is this, Dom? He knows who I am."

I fired a round into the couch next to Duran. The leather

dimpled a foot from his shoulder as the bullet yanked through the cushion. The high-velocity load was so loud my ears rang. Rudy jumped but Duran didn't, and he never took his eyes off me. Balls, all right. He said, "We will trade."

I shook my head. "Get me the kid."

Rudy moved forward, swinging his right arm in a broad gesture and talking to me like we were used to this. Maybe he was. "How the hell you know who I am?"

"I stayed at the same hotel as you once. In Houston. I saw you walk through the lobby."

"Bullshit." He shook his finger at Duran. "No one's supposed to know I'm here, goddamnit. Carlos and Lenny find out I'm here right now instead of in Colombia I'll have to go through all kindsa shit."

"Shut up, Rudy," I said. "You cutting out your partners is the least of your worries." I didn't know who the hell Carlos and Lenny were. But there was a briefcase of money on the table. Carlos and Lenny thought Rudy Gambino was in Colombia. There was a known dope connection between Gambino and Duran, as well as a history of investment partnerships. It looked good that Gambino was moving dope through Duran to cut out the middleman.

Gambino screamed, "I ain't cutting out nobody, goddamnit!"

I fired another round, this one slamming through a picture into the wall beside Duran. Four inches from his ear. He didn't flinch. I wouldn't be that good. "I take the kid, and I go for the police," I said. "If you're good, you can make an airport."

He didn't say anything.

This wasn't working. I was making a lot of noise and taking a lot of time and not getting any closer to Perry Lang. Sooner or later someone would come. When enough someones came, that would be it.

"Okay, motherfucker," I said, "bring me to the kid or eat one." I aimed the Beretta between Duran's eyes. I meant it.

He shook his head. "No. I do not have to."

Something hard pressed against my neck and the Eskimo said, "That's enough."

Rudy Gambino hopped over, jerked my gun away, then hit me in the face twice with his right hand. His punches split my lip but didn't put me down. "Now what you got?" he shouted. "You got dick is what you got!"

Gambino went over to Mr. Teeth and kicked him. "Eddie?" Eddie was passed out.

Duran leaned forward again and tapped the marble table with the sword. He said, "Here is how I will deal with you. I will kill you, and I will kill the boy, and I will kill the mother, and then it will be done." He looked serenely calm as he said it, almost in repose, and I knew this must be the way he used to look when he faced the bulls. Assured and in absolute control of the pageant. The Bringer of Death.

"But you won't have your property."

He shrugged. "The property was never what was important."

"Sure." The Eskimo was an enormous presence behind me, something dark and gargantuan and primordial. I could feel the gun there, hovering. I took deep breaths through my nose, filling my lungs with air, trying to will my body to relax, to calm. *Pranayama*. Start with the feet. Prepare yourself. Focus *ki*. If Gambino or Duran moved close enough, if I could move fast enough . . . If I couldn't, it wouldn't make much difference.

Rudy Gambino leveled the 9mm at me and said, "This kinda shit ain't supposed to happen when I'm here, Dom." When he said "Dom" there was a sharp *pow* out in the secretary's office. A red spot grew low on Gambino's abdomen. As he looked down at himself there was another *pow*, this one closer, in the doorway, and his right leg kicked back and he fell.

Ellen Lang stood in the doorway with my .38, right arm out straight, left bent at the elbow and cupping the right, just the way Pike taught her. The lipstick didn't look silly anymore. She was dark and alien and threatening, the way guys in the Nam who wore paint had looked. Duran saw the lipstick and smiled.

When the Eskimo's gun moved I went into him, grabbing his gun hand with both of mine and forcing it in toward the elbow and away from his body. The gun kicked free and the Eskimo hit me on top of my right shoulder with an MX missile. My whole side went numb. I stayed inside, wrapping his hips and lifting and driving him away from the gun. His hands came down on my back, he pushed backward, and I let go. He landed on the floor sideways and went over on his hands and knees. I drove straight in with a power kick to the ribs and followed it with two punches, one to the same spot on the ribs, the other behind his left ear. The head punch broke one of my knuckles. Head punches will do that. I hit him a third time, this one beneath the ear where it was softer. The Eskimo grunted and heaved himself up. He didn't look too much the worse for wear. You couldn't say that about me.

Ellen was still in the door. Duran was on his feet now, saying something to her, but I couldn't hear what. I said, "Only pussies kill seals and polar bears."

The Eskimo smiled.

I threw an ashtray at him. It bounced off his arm.

He smiled some more.

I threw a Waterford lamp at him. He batted it aside.

There are any number of innovative ways to best an opponent. I simply had to think of one.

The Eskimo came for me. I faked to the outside, planted my left foot, and roundhouse kicked him in the face. His head snapped back and his nose burst into a red mist. He looked down at himself, then charged again. I dropped, spun, and kicked the outside of his knee. His leg buckled and he went down. I went in close, hitting his smashed nose with the heel of my hand and driving in behind it hard with my knees. His head rocked back and his eyes looked funny. I hit him with my left hand and lost a second knuckle. Bruce Lee could fight a thousand guys and not even split a fingernail. Karma. I saw Duran moving toward Ellen, walking across the room, the little sword in front of him.

"Ellen," I said.

The Eskimo came up from underneath, locked his arms around my chest, and squeezed. It felt the way they describe a massive coronary: your lungs stop working, an elephant sits on your chest, and you know with absolute certainty that you are going to die.

Ellen stepped toward Duran and there was a loud *BANG*, louder than before because she was in the room now. Duran missed a step, then kept going, holding the sword straight out now and picking up speed.

I hammered down into the Eskimo's face, hitting him on the top of the head and in the temples and in the eyes. He squeezed his eyes tight and hugged me closer. I felt something snap in my lower back. Short rib. What the hell, don't need'm anyhow.

Ellen's gun went off again. *BANG*.

I wanted to yell for her to get out of here, but knew if I gave up what breath I had I wouldn't get any more. I stopped punching and tried to dig my thumbs into the Eskimo's eyes, but he pressed his face into my chest. Everything in my peripheral vision began to grow fuzz. From out of another solar system I heard a gutty *choonk-choonk-choonk, choonk-choonk*. The HK. Pike. Not lucky for them, finding Pike. Ruin their whole day.

I reached above my head and brought my elbow down on the crown of the Eskimo's head. A sharp pain lanced up my arm and another rib went, this one higher in my back.

Ellen's gun sounded again. *BANG*. Duran stopped and staggered sideways a step. Then he went on.

I brought my elbow down again, and this time the Eskimo sobbed. I did it again and his arms loosened. Whenever I hit him, something hot flashed in my elbow, letting me know the bone was broken. That didn't seem to matter much. Not much mattered at all. Life's priorities tend to shift when you're in the process of dying.

I was seeing mostly gray shadows and squiggly bright things. I heard another *BANG*. That would be six. Ellen wouldn't have any more. I hit the Eskimo again, and this time his arms released. I backed away, sucking air, each breath sending razors through my chest. The Eskimo tried to stand, pushing himself up onto one leg, then the other. He looked at me, swayed, and fell. Some tough sonofabitch.

Domingo Duran was on the floor at Ellen's feet. She lowered the gun. Then she spit on him. She hadn't moved, or flinched, or cowered. She hadn't backed up.

I walked over to her, but it took a while. Not much was working right. I seemed to go sideways when I wanted to go straight, and I very badly wanted to throw up.

"Perry," I said. "Perry."

Then there was a lot of noise in the hall, and I dropped down to the rug, trying to find my pistol. I couldn't and I started to cry. It had to be there somewhere. I had to find it because the game wasn't over. It couldn't be over until we had the boy, only the goons were coming and there didn't seem to be anything I could do to stop them.

Men with blue rain shells that said FBI or POLICE on the back came in with M-16s. O'Bannon was with them. He saw Ellen Lang, and then he saw me, and he said, "You sonofabitch."

I remember smiling. Then I passed out.

38

For one of the few times in my life, I thought wouldn't it be grand if I smoked. I was in the Hollywood Presbyterian Emergency Room watching the nurses, one nurse in particular, and waiting for my elbow cast to dry. They had the cast held away from my body by a little metal and plastic brace. A kid waiting to get his lip stitched asked me how I'd busted it, and I said fighting spies loud enough for my nurse to hear. All I needed now was a London Fog slung casually over my shoulders and a cigarette dangling from my lip, and she'd probably rape me.

Poitras came though a set of swinging doors, with O'Bannon playing shadow. Poitras was big and blank and carrying two Styrofoam cups of coffee. They looked like thimbles in his hands. O'Bannon looked like he'd bitten into a Quarterpounder and found an ear. Everyone in the waiting room stared at Poitras. Even the doctors. What a specimen.

"My," I said. "What a delightful surprise."

Poitras held out one of the coffees. "Black, right?"

"Black."

The doctor had put three layers of tape around my ribs, splinted my hand, and given me an analgesic, but it still hurt to reach for the coffee. Driving would be an adventure.

"How's the kid?" I said.

They'd found him hidden away in a closet on the first floor. He was still blindfolded and didn't know what was happening. "Okay," Lou said. "Cleaned up his hand, gave him some shots. You know. His mom took him down to the cafeteria. He wanted a hamburger."

One of Duran's thugs had put an ice pick through the boy's hand to make him scream. I didn't know who. With any luck I'd killed him. "You talk to him yet?"

"Mm-hmm." Lou said, "You left a lot of bodies back there, Ace. Sorta like Rambo Goes To Hollywood."

I nodded.

"Between you and Pike and Mrs. Lang, if we include the one in Griffith park, looks to be eleven stiffs."

"Me and Pike. Mrs. Lang had nothing to do with it."

"Yeah."

O'Bannon leaned toward me. His face was very tight and getting tighter. If it got much tighter his brain would probably pop out. He said, "Goddamn you, you ruined four months of undercover work, do you know that? We knew Gambino was setting up a move with Duran. We had his phone bugged, his bed bugged, his goddamned jock strap bugged. We ate, slept, and shit with that sonofabitch."

"I can tell," I said. "Try Lavoris."

Poitras said, "They had the house across the street. You had two Feds watch you and Pike hop the fence, wondering what the hell was going on. They like to shit, you and Pike jogging down the road like a couple of National Guardsmen, Pike with that howitzer of his, paint all over his face." Poitras looked at O'Bannon and made a hard, nasty grin. "Only no one could make a decision until the big boss got there. No one knew jack shit who was doing what since no one had been told anything." O'Bannon chewed at his lip. Poitras finished, "They thought you guys might be cops, so they just sat on things until Mrs. Lang went in through the front gate. Then they hoofed it across the street."

I nodded. Figured it had to be something like that. If Ellen had called the cops, blue suits and prowl cars would've come.

O'Bannon said, "We ran an efficient, tight, *secure* operation."

"Swinging," I said. The coffee felt gritty in my mouth, like it was mostly sediment. Maybe I should ask the nurse to have a look-see.

"Goddamnit," O'Bannon said, "do you know how much this has cost the taxpayers?"

Poitras said, "Shit."

O'Bannon's Stanford Law/three-sets-before-breakfast tan was a nice mottled color. He said, "We were finally going to nail Gambino and Duran both. They were making a major cocaine buy together. We *had* them, and you fucked it up, Cole. You were ordered to stay away from this and you didn't. Your goddamned license is *mine*."

I stared at him. There was a petulance to his face that one does not often see in law-enforcement personnel. I wanted very much to pat his head, tell him everything would be okay, and send him to his room. Instead, I carefully set the cup down on the seat next to me and stood up. It hurt to stand.

"Screw you, O'Bannon," I said. "You were ready to trade the kid for that bust."

He stood, breathing very hard, his hands balled into fists at his sides. "We would have moved when the time was right to maximize our results."

The nurse behind the station was looking at us. I wondered if she'd ever seen someone split a brand-new cast over a Spec Op before. "Right," I said.

Poitras edged between O'Bannon and me, dwarfing us both. "Go back to Special Operations, O'Bannon," he said. "Tell them the results have been maximized. Tell them that they won't have to waste any more of the taxpayers' dollars on Domingo Duran or Rudy Gambino."

O'Bannon pointed his finger at me. "Your ass is mine."

I said, "Get out of here before I beat you to death."

O'Bannon gave Poitras another attempt at a bad look, then walked away. It was sort of a cross between a wince and a squint. I guess it really wilted them in court.

Poitras said, "The kid doesn't know about his father. We're going to let the mother tell him."

I was still staring after O'Bannon. Then I looked over at the nurse. She smiled. It was a nice smile.

"We did a little talking," Lou said. "Mort and the kid weren't kidnapped on their way home from school. Mort didn't even get to pick the kid up. One of Duran's people snatched him when he was walking out to his father's car."

I stared at him.

"I talked to Lancaster," he said. "They didn't find a .32 in Lang's Caddie."

"No?"

"So I had the ME run a paraffin. Came back positive."

I nodded, thinking about Ellen Lang, thinking about Mort and his .32, thinking about a positive paraffin test.

Poitras said, "Hound Dog?"

"Yeah?"

"When you knew for certain, you shoulda come to me. O'Bannon or no O'Bannon, downtown or not, I woulda moved on it. It's my job. I woulda done it."

"I know."

"I don't like any goddamned cowboys thinking they can go

off half-cocked, goddamned Pike running down the street with a goddamned HK-91."

I felt very tired, the sort of deep, bled-to-the-bone tired you feel when you've tried very hard to keep something dear to you only to lose it. I said, "Are we going to be charged with anything?"

"Baishe has already been with the D.A. O'Bannon got there first, but Baishe thinks we might be able to square it. I don't know about Pike. He gets picked up, they say what's your occupation, he says mercenary, goddamned paint all over his face like he's still in the jungle. Nobody likes that. Nobody on the department likes Pike anyway."

"If the department kept more guys like Pike, they'd have less guys like O'Bannon."

Poitras didn't say anything.

"If you charge Joe, you charge me."

Poitras took a deep breath, sighed. He needed a shave. "I want you to come in. We gotta get a statement."

"Can you wait?"

He stared at me for a while, then nodded. "No later than noon tomorrow."

We shook hands. "Tell Baishe thanks," I said.

Poitras nodded again.

I took off the little brace and started for the door. The nurse had left her station with a tall black orderly who looked like Julius Erving. Good looking. Neat moustache. He'd said something funny and she'd laughed. Screw him.

Poitras said, "Hound Dog?"

I stopped.

"At least it wasn't a buy-off. That's something."

"Sure."

39

I found Ellen and Perry Lang sitting alone at a big table in the back of the cafeteria. I went up behind them, put my good hand on Ellen's shoulder, and said, "Come on. It's time to go home."

She looked back at me silently for a moment, then nodded. She had cleaned the lipstick off, leaving her face pink and fresh from the scrubbing. "I should get the things I left at your house."

We picked up Pike's Cherokee from a cop out front and took the drive west to Fairfax, then north up Laurel and into the hills. It was almost six when we got there. The cloud cover had broken, and the air had a fresh, scrubbed smell. Nice. A red-winged hawk rode the wind pushing up the canyon above my house. I could see his head turn, looking for mice.

When Ellen got out, Perry got out with her. He had made her sit in the backseat with him, and he wasn't about to let her get out of reach now.

The cat was sitting in the middle of the floor, waiting, when we walked in. He hissed when he saw Perry and crept under the couch, ears down. Ever the gracious host.

While Ellen and Perry were upstairs, I went into the kitchen, drank two glasses of water, then called the hospital and asked after Pike. A woman with a very direct voice told me he was out of surgery now, in serious but stable condition, with a good prognosis. He would be fine. I thanked her and hung up.

When Ellen and Perry came back, she was carrying the Ralph's bag I'd brought from her house. She had taken off my sweat shirt and the dirty jeans and replaced them with a pretty pink top and cotton pants. Pike was right. A year from now, she would not remember the smell of gunpowder or ferocious red marks on her face. At the bottom of the stairs, Perry Lang asked her about his father.

She went white and looked at me, but I did not help her

with the decision. She had to do what she thought she could do. After a while, she took Perry into the living room, sat him on the couch, and told him that his father was dead.

They sat together a very long time. Perry cried, then grew quiet, then cried again until he fell asleep in her lap. At ten minutes before eight, she said, "We can go now," and stood up with her nine-year-old son cradled in her arms like a baby.

We put him, groggy and whimpering, into the back of the Cherokee, then took the long drive to Encino. Coming down off the mountain into the valley, the lights were like brilliant crystal jewels in the rain-washed air. Better than that. It was as if the stars had fallen from the sky and lay stewn along the desert.

"I can do this," she said.

"Yep."

"I can pull us together, and keep us together, and go back to school maybe, and go forward."

"Never any doubt."

She looked at me. "I won't back up."

I nodded.

"Not ever," she said.

I exited the freeway and rolled down the cool silent Encino streets to Janet Simon's house. It was brightly lit, inside and out. The older daughter, Cindy, passed by the front window as we pulled into the drive. "Would you like me to be there when you tell them?" I said.

She sat silently, chewing her lip, staring at the house. "No. If I need help there, let it come from Perry."

I nodded. A car passed, washing her with light and revealing something ageless in her face. A sort of maturity and life that hadn't been there before, and that you never see in most people. The look of someone who has assumed responsibility.

We got out. I liked it that she didn't expect me to open the door for her.

"You didn't throw away your life with Mort," I said.

She stared up at me.

"Mort wasn't kidnapped and Mort wasn't dealing with these people. Duran's goons took the boy and Mort went after them. That's where the .32 was. Maybe Mort wasn't there for you anymore, but he tried to be there for Perry. He died trying to save his boy."

Her eyes looked deep in the night. "How do you know?"

"Poitras ran a paraffin test. The test says Mort fired a gun.

He wouldn't have had to do any shooting unless he was trying to get his son back."

She took a very deep breath, let it out, and stared down the street. Then she nodded, raised up on her toes, and kissed me. "Thank you."

The front door opened and Janet Simon appeared in the light. We didn't move toward her and she didn't move out toward us.

"There's more to bring away from this than firing a pistol," I said.

"I know."

"You're different now."

She looked at Janet Simon. "They'll have to get used to that, won't they?"

I helped her lift Perry out. His face was puffy and pale and he clung to her even in sleep. She said, "Would you like to come in?"

I shook my head. "Not if you don't need me. If you need me, I'll stay. If you don't, I'll go sit with Joe."

She smiled and told me she'd come see Joe tomorrow, then she kissed my cheek once more and walked up to the house. Janet Simon stepped aside to let them in, then shut the door.

Perhaps Janet hadn't seen me.

I stood there, breathing deep, and looked at Pike's Jeep. Even in the dark, I could see it was a mess, muddy and streaked and dusty. I found a self-wash on Ventura Boulevard that was still open, and worked there until the Cherokee sparkled. Then I rolled down the windows and drove slowly in the cool fresh air, drove back to the hospital to wait for Joe Pike.